The Hottest Place

'I prefer a woman who makes noise,' Trent said. 'Oh, God, I love those sounds women make when they're having a good time, when they're really up for it.' He then made a crude imitation of a woman coming. I was scared the people on the next table would hear.

'What noises do you make?' he asked.

'The usual, I guess,' I said quickly.

'Come on, be specific.'

'It depends on the situation.'

'Let's say he has pulled your knickers down and is staring at your lovely bush. And he's slipping his hand in, stealing a feel, and you're all wet; it's like, who put the tap on, baby? And he's undoing his jeans, and he's harder than –'

'I think that's enough,' I said, blushing scarlet. I had started talking to Trent with the confidence of knowing we were *not* going to have sex. Now I wasn't so sure.

Other books by the author

TONGUE IN CHEEK

The Hottest Place

TABITHA FLYTE

BLACK
lace

Black Lace novels contain sexual fantasies.
In real life, make sure you practise safe sex.

First published in 2000 by
Black Lace
Thames Wharf Studios,
Rainville Road, London W6 9HA

Typeset by SetSystems Ltd, Saffron Walden, Essex
Printed and bound by Mackays of Chatham PLC

ISBN 0 352 33536 X

Chapter One

I'm on the luggage conveyor belt. We all are. All the lovely ladies from the flight are sprawled on the moving belt. The male passengers surround us. They're all anxious to pick out the right woman, all leaning forwards as we rotate.

Perhaps I'm the most unwilling. I'm trying to cover my lacy bra and stop the men from peeking at my knickers. But we're revolving at speed, and I can't get up. Every time I make to get off, I'm thrown back, dishevelled, legs akimbo, luggage labels hanging round my neck. The other women are laughing. I see their big teeth stained with lipstick and hilarity. Some of them have even started masturbating for show. I'm wearing black shiny high heels and they weigh me down. I get up and crawl, but every time I nearly escape, the belt turns unforgivingly faster. My entire world is spinning.

Around me, men have started picking up scantily clad women. They pull them off the conveyor belt, as easily as you pick up plates of raw fish from a revolving sushi bar. Once selected, the men kiss their catches deeply, pushing them up against luggage trolleys, all fumbling hands. Sometimes, however, the men just throw themselves down onto the belt and start fucking there and

1

then. I see one couple rutting; the man's trousers are still on, only his prick is free and his bottom is going up and down. They're shagging like rabbits. Legs gripping each other closer, hands clawing at buttocks, bringing his cock nearer to her swollen pussy: passports to frenzy. The conveyor belt grows sticky with arousal and spent spunk.

The airport is ringing with desire. There are screaming commands for more, more. Even the guards are ripping off their uniforms and joining in. But still I go round and round alone, clutching my things about me, rotating like a fairy in a jewellery box. I'm afraid of not being picked. I'm unclaimed baggage. I'm the person no one wants. I'm desperate for the machine to stop. My bra strap catches on the side, and my bra peels off. I collapse, unsuccessfully trying to shield my rigid nipples from the world. I burn with shame: wanting, not wanting; desiring, not desiring.

Someone hauls me off. He isn't the one I'd have liked. I'd set my eyes on a louche blond gentleman, watching the proceedings with a grin of approval. The man who picks me up, though, is dark, heavy-set with a large face; a large everything. He yanks me up and plants me down on a mountain of suitcases, rucksacks and golf bags. I struggle, trying to escape, but he pushes me back down. His hands leave little red marks on my arms. I kick out and he calls me a wildcat, says that I look so hot, so horny, that he can't believe his luck. He says I've been one of the last selected because I'm too gorgeous. The other men are afraid of that, he says, but he isn't. No, siree.

I'm still wearing stockings, although the suspender is long gone, and he rolls them down my thighs. He rolls them like cigars and his movements, his confidence, his self-assurance, fill me with arousal. I like my stockings, but I adore having them taken off. I love feeling how tightly they grip and contain my legs. I want to remove them completely, but he insists I keep them on. Then, before I can move, he undoes his trousers. I note approv-

2

ingly the button fly, and his nimble fingers pulling at his pants. His cock springs out impatiently, and I lean forward to get an eyeful. It's enormous, a real collectors' item, but he mistakes my admiration for hunger. He aims for my mouth but I clamp my lips shut. You could do a lot of damage with that. Then he simply belly flops over me. He weighs so much that my legs open involuntarily around him to support us. Seconds later, the stranger fingers aside my lacy knickers and enters me with a fat thumb. Slick and warm, it's his heat I understand first, and then the sound: a deep groan that's coming from my throat. I feel my clit engorge and my sex respond as though it's been waiting for this all its life.

My hot sex is clamped around his thumb. I rub up and down on him, going like the clappers. He's amazed, telling me to slow down, 'wait a sec'; he wants to put his cock up me. He pulls out his thumb and, for a second, I'm wild with fury, but then along comes something a lot better – thicker than three thumbs, longer than a hand. He parts my lips, massaging my clit, and then, wham, in comes his cock. It fits me tightly. I'm overflowing with him. I press against him, creating friction between his cock and my clit. Before long I'm screaming my pleasure. The rest of the passengers hear my howling excitement, and rush over to view the fun.

When I woke up, a grey blanket was covering me, like a settle of fungus over bruised fruit. My glasses were in luggage high over the seats and I couldn't work out how long I'd been dreaming. I stayed scrunched up in economy-class seats, watching the stewardesses stride up and down the aisles as though they were catwalk models. One of them banged hard against my elbow. I wished I'd claimed a window seat but Roger had insisted I took the aisle.

Roger. He wouldn't believe I was going at first. In fact, I don't think he realised until yesterday. But I knew if I didn't take my chance to go then I never would. And

3

sometimes, events just take care of themselves. I'd given up my job and my flat, and spent the money on the tickets. I had the visas, the suitcases and the skin protection factors 10–50. Momentum carried me off full-steam.

Roger insisted that he needed me, but that was only half-true and we both knew it. All the same, I wanted him so much it made my heart ache. I know this sounds mad, but when I thought of him, my heart thudded so much it seemed as though it would stop beating.

The night before, at the airport hotel, Roger made love to me more tenderly, more thoroughly, than he had in ages. And this morning, at the airport, waiting over the trolleys, he promised me, wringing his hands, swearing on his mother's life that, as soon as he could, he would join me in Thailand, and then we would travel around the world together. I believed him, of course. What else is there without trust?

The woman next to me, in the middle seat, was also just waking up. I noticed her nails first – severe red files – and then her delicate pink fingers like rose petals. From her clothes, I could tell she was an urbane thirty-something. She looked relaxed, the kind of person who had been all over the world and is used to flying. She had been knocking back the alcohol, whereas sensible me was drinking only water. She stretched out languidly, catlike, and then turned to the man in the window seat. He had a well-shaped nose and a shadow of stubble on a square cowboy's jaw. His chestnut hair was scraped back into a ponytail and he was wearing grubby jeans and a T-shirt. I wouldn't have put the two of them together – she the professional sophisticate; he the street-wise Casanova – but they were talking companionably, though I couldn't quite make out their conversation.

The lights were switched off and a video began. The young boy in the seat behind intermittently kicked at the back of my seat, but every time I turned to tell him to stop, he snuggled up, playing the innocent to a formidable-looking grandfather.

4

My pretty neighbour leaned towards the man and planted a kiss on the side of his mouth. He looked surprised, and then kissed her full on the lips. They gave each other pursed kisses and then firmer, deeper ones. They were squeezing their lips on each other, pressing their softness closer. He cupped her chin and pulled her face forwards. Her hand crept around to touch the back of his head, and to drag him into her. Their lips joined and opened wide. I could see the healthy pink of his tongue as it peeped forwards into her welcoming mouth.

I tried not to look, but they were really going for it. Then his eyes clicked open and he stared straight at me as his lips wrapped around the fullness of her mouth. She must have sensed his wandering eyes, or felt a change in his rhythm, because she stopped kissing him and they started whispering heatedly. She giggled, then leaned over to me.

'You are cute.'

'Thank you,' I replied severely. I try not to be flattered when people say that kind of thing, but I eat up attraction as delightedly as birds given crumbs in a frozen winter garden.

They were kissing again: heavy, lids-closed kissing. His hand made a slow crawl across her thin silk shirt, moving stealthily before arriving at the alluring roundness of her breast.

I held my breath. I could almost feel his touch. My body grew damp and eager. I could sense their mouths working more earnestly now, and I heard her let out small but desperate groans of arousal. I clutched myself tightly about the arms. I felt shamefully voyeuristic. But it wasn't my fault, was it?

His hands were fondling and feeling her. I wished I had my glasses but, even without them, I could see her nipples harden through the soft silk of her shirt. I realised disgracefully that my nipples, echoing hers, were becoming stiff too. I remembered the night before: the way Roger had pulled at my shirt and clutched me towards

5

him; the way he'd fondled me before nursing at my breasts, my fingers in his hair. My pussy was fluttering.

She pulled him closer. I saw that she was running her fingers up and down his shirt before grasping at the gap. Tickling at the buttons, she pulled his shirt apart and succeeded in sliding her fingers inside. She was touching his nipples. I wondered what they felt like. I remembered sucking Roger's nipples the previous evening. I'd stabbed them with my tongue, and watched how they'd hardened in response. I'd teased my tongue around the tender pinkies but when he actually penetrated me I had to leave them, fearing I would bite them off in my frenzy. Instead I rested, open-mouthed and drooling, around his neck, sucking the loose skin there. He wouldn't let me bite him, not ever. I knew it was forbidden but I still tried.

The couple were clutching each other and when they weren't kissing each other's lips they were kissing each other's faces, noses, and eyes. He sucked her eyebrows respectfully, sensuously. I remembered then how Roger had licked me between my legs, tending to my clit, his face wet with my juices, feeding off the small ball of pleasure. He loved it when I moaned his name.

The man's other hand was working too. No rest for the wicked. He was stroking her knees. I watched the progress of his fingers. I dare say I was mentally egging him on. I wanted to see how far they would go, how far they would dare. He raised her skirt. She had shapely brown thighs; smooth, with crisp golden hairs. His hand roamed higher to reveal her tiny white knickers – bikini briefs, I think. There was really nothing of them, just a gate of white cotton. Only the truly beautiful, as she was, could wear them with aplomb. He edged them down, and I couldn't help feeling that he was doing it partly for me to see.

I busied myself with my guidebook. I pretended that the article about the Thai royal family was engrossing. But I still wanted to hear what would happen next. I could hear the sound of her wetness. The squelching made my stomach turn. But then I couldn't help wishing that Roger were with me, doing that to me.

There were more groans and then the sigh of a zip being undone. I couldn't resist looking. She was lying back, her black hair straggling bohemian over the staid airline seat. She looked like an artist's model from the nineteenth century – all bow lips, cherubic pink cheeks and fluttering black lashes. She was small and wiry; her belly was flat and brown.

Look away, Abigail, look away.

OK, I told myself, maybe he was fresh out of jail. Hadn't had sex for years. I've always liked that idea. He was wrongly convicted for something, some lovely juicy crime, and there's me waiting outside in the convertible. No, too old-fashioned. Maybe she's been in jail. For? Yes, a love crime, and he took her away. Or perhaps he'd been exiled from his country since they were childhood sweethearts and only now could they meet again. Possibly, they hadn't been together for ten years or something while he struggled to restore his country to democracy. Or maybe this is simply how people start their honeymoons.

He held her face and looked at her in amazement, then kissed her deeply, passionately. Their soft and probing fingers produced sighs of pleasure wherever they roamed.

I'd never felt like that. I'd never let my passion sweep me away like that. Not even in private, with the doors closed and curtains pulled. Not even with Roger.

His finger was exploring her pubic lawn and I couldn't stop looking. She sat back complacently in the seat, widening her legs, opening up. It looked fantastic; a prize-winning pussy. I wanted to put my finger there, too. I didn't want to do anything with it, I just wanted to feel the smooth slimy surface; to know what it was like.

And then she was tearing at his flies, her little fingers working on his zip like a hundred tiny insects. She yanked down his jeans, and he had on just a small pair of pants and then they came down too.

I was surprised he had managed to bring his cock on the plane without declaring it: it was a hard bullet shape. She tugged at the shaft and with her other hand caressed his balls.

Oh God, they wouldn't! Not at this close proximity. They were like two teenagers; two heavy-petting teenagers. Please stop. This was much too much.

He turned her onto her side so she was facing away from me. His hands were supporting her round ruby bum. There was something undignified about her arse divided by that piece of string. His finger caught it, and moved it aside easily. She made no objection. He opened her thighs and slid down on the chair, so that he was eye to eye with her pussy. He leaned forward.

The little boy on the seat behind me started whining.

'There's a cat on this plane, licking milk,' he complained.

'Be quiet and watch the film,' said the grandfather, reapplying his headphones before the cat interrupted his enjoyment.

She had put her arm behind her head. She was exultant, abandoned, and so concentrated on her pleasure. His face was pressed against my thigh as he drank in her wetness and, as he dipped and dunked up and down, he knocked against my leg. She was panting like she was running a race.

'Do you mind?' I requested. Oh God, why was I so Victorian? How was I going to cope in Thailand? I would take photos, write postcards, collect souvenirs. I would be like those women travellers of old, lifting up my long skirts to explore rough terrain.

He pulled down the blanket, but still they bobbed around underneath. Her feet, in their perfect sandals, were splayed wide apart. One foot landed in the case in front of me, the other against the window. They squirmed under the grey blanket, hot pudding under

8

cold custard. Someone patted me on the shoulder. I jumped in my seat feeling guilty.

'Anything to drink?'

'No, nothing,' I said. The blanket continued moving, like a monster or like children scrambling around in a tent.

'Ice cream?' The stewardess looked peevishly at my wobbling neighbours.

'No, thank you. Oh, they're sleeping,' I added. The attendant moved on.

They pushed off the blanket, and now he was flat under her. His head was jammed right next to me, spilling over her seat on to mine, like an old man in the rush hour, who won't mind his space; only he was a young man, and his head was by my thigh. She got on top of him. She didn't dare sit completely upright, but she was small and tight, so she hid herself well.

I felt the boy behind smash my seat with his football kicks. Why was I in the goddamned aisle seat? It could have been me in the middle seat! Damn Roger and his aisle seat. Why did he always have to be so bossy?

She started her grinding movement on top of him, pouncing up and down, swaying from side to side. She looked beautiful. I could smell myself; sticky, smelly, unwillingly producing waves. I could feel the wetness between my legs. To be this close to the act of sex, it was like a dream or a hallucination.

The woman's face was serene and meditative, only she was dribbling a bit. A small dangle of saliva left her pouting mouth. They didn't have room so her head was scrunched on her chair. She was rocking up and down, her slim thighs working him, either side of him, pressing shallow and then deep and he was gasping, his face crushed into her breasts, as she held her head down, gnawing at his neck. They were whispering, but their arousal was still audible.

She fell forwards onto me, grasping for balance with her hand. It landed on my chest. My body was screaming

9

approval along with theirs, but I was frozen with embarrassment. Her fingers tightened around my breasts and, as she squeezed my nipples, my face burned. She was too far gone to know what she was doing, but I would have done anything then, to have someone, anyone, fuck me and to be free like she was.

She squelched into his lap, and her hard brown nipples slapped against his face. He lifted her arse even higher, and I could see from her rucked-up skirt, that his big hand was exploring her thoroughly, probing her. I could smell hot musty animal pleasure. And then she let out a short series of explicit moans and her whole body trembled like petals in a breeze.

I would never be able to let myself go like that.

'We are cruising at thirty-eight thousand feet.' The captain's voice boomed over the system. 'Our destination is hot, hot, hot. If you haven't already adjusted your watches, it's seven o'clock in the evening, local time. Please put on your seat belts and observe the no-smoking signs. We hope you all have a wonderful time in Thailand and we look forward to flying with you again.'

They kissed lingeringly. After the storm, now the calm. I caught sight of a big diamond on the wedding finger of her left hand. So they were honeymooners! And who could blame them for their lust? One day, I wouldn't be travelling on my own. Perhaps Roger and I would fly together, and we would be similarly struck by the urge to fuck, to free ourselves from all conventions. We would explore nature and our wild sides. Somehow I suspected that wasn't very likely.

'Thank you,' the woman said to me, 'for saying nothing.'

'You're welcome,' I responded awkwardly and then, because it seemed ill-mannered to finish our interaction at that, I added, 'What's your name?'

'Selma.' She shook my hand with her tiny sweaty one.

'And your boyfriend? What's his name?'

10

She smiled at me, studying my face as if weighing up my possible response.

'Him? Oh, I don't know. We've only just met.'

I tried to swallow my shock – oh, yes, complete strangers often shag next to me in aeroplanes. I tried to take it in my stride, but I fear my face betrayed me.

She swivelled around to ask him and then turned back to me.

'His name is José.' She took my hand again. I could feel the scrape of her wedding ring against my sweating finger.

'You look very pale.'

'Do I?' I asked, burning between the legs. I would have done anything to have done what they had done and I was disgusted with myself for feeling that way. I looked away, but she persisted, laughing.

'Do you think we will crash?'

'No, I don't think so.'

'Then maybe you are just afraid of flying?' she asked.

Maybe, I thought. Maybe that was what it was.

Chapter Two

*E*ven one night in Bangkok was too long. I was trembling with fear, certain that the taxi drivers were going to kill me or the porters were going to run off with my bags. The traffic into the city was a never-ending, bumper-to-bumper crawl. The cars were kissing, puckering and nudging each other along the highway. The twenty-kilometre journey to the hotel took three hours and sometimes we were parked for twenty minutes or more in the middle of the highway where the signs said the speed limit was 100 kmph. I was impatient to get out, even though I had nowhere particularly to go. The heat was stifling. I felt as though I was wrapped in cling film.

The infamous city smog hovered over the crowded streets like a bride's veil, obscuring everything within. On either side of the highway, the construction workers banged poles together forming precarious scaffolding around undressed buildings. There were whole families on motorbikes, adults and children suspended over the handlebars; there were open-topped wagons with farm workers sleeping on straw in the back. There were little Tuktuk taxis; small blue three-wheelers as though imported from toytown, but the drivers might have been imported from hell. They swerved through the non-moving traffic, careering noisily along the road, emitting a woolly black smoke. Here, the rules were different.

A man, spritely and dark like a woodland animal shouted as I descended from my cab. I lifted my hand to him, defeated. But then, from behind me, a crowd, his friends, emerged, and I pretended I was just stroking my hair.

A hotel room on your own is a strange place. I tried to turn the room into my own territory. I took out photos of Roger and put them on the bedside table. I unpacked clothes and toiletries. It was swelteringly hot and the air-conditioning didn't work. The windows were wide open but there was no wind. I ordered room service and, after an hour's wait, a young woman carried up a plate of noodles and spring rolls. She apologised about the broken air-conditioning.

'Perhaps it will be fixed tomorrow.'

'Perhaps?' I asked. She shrugged her shoulders: who knew?

There is nothing like an evening meal alone to drive home loneliness. Whereas breakfast is best alone, and lunch can go either way, dinner needs to be shared. At my goodbye party at work, some women said they were jealous of me. They wouldn't have been jealous if they had seen me that night, ineffectually swatting flies and picking awkwardly at the food with chopsticks. Why didn't I ask for a fork? I had to do everything the hard way.

I decided to go outside. After a short aimless walk I found myself in the notorious Patpong district. The streets heaved with greasy food stalls: chips and noodles, sausages and hanging chickens. And men, there were men everywhere: fat, sweaty Western businessmen, slim Thais and groups of suited Japanese. Everyone was hunting and gathering in streets lit with a thousand fluorescent promises. A rainbow of pleasure-seekers and where better to seek pleasure than Thailand? My guidebook said there was something for everyone: 'From the hill

13

villages, treks, and rice fields of the North, the tropical islands with their sun-soaked beaches and the capital city offering fun and excitement.'

I was drowning in the sound of drumbeats, not-so-personal stereos, people talking, shouting, haggling over fake Rolexes and keyring gifts. Tuktuk taxis were vying for road space, swerving around corners, swerving into trouble. There were jewellery sellers and groups of Italian women in bottom-enhancing black trousers. In the bars, women in skimpy vests and hotpants were gyrating to songs from the 70s. In some special establishments, the girls were performing ping-pong tricks; in and out, shooting balls at each other from between their legs. Even nice boys from England watched. They wouldn't go to see strippers in a working man's club in Tooting but they would see the equivalent in a foreign country.

There were backpackers all around. I suppose I was a backpacker, too, but I looked different. My hair was still blow-dried. They were all a cool matte and I was an over-pampered gloss. I thought they knew that I was a pseudo-traveller, a suitcaser. I would never get used to this life.

Footsteps sounded behind me, the same walking speed as me. A Western man, tall but not distinguished, wanted to accompany me back to my hotel. He would like to show me the way.

'I'm not lost.' I looked contemptuously at his over-eager face and the crowds soaked him up like spilt milk.

Back in my hotel room, I read my guidebook, like a detective hunting for clues.

'Thailand is notorious for prostitutes and lady boys. Drugs are also widely available; you can pick hallucinogenic mushrooms by the side of the road. But while some travellers come to Thailand for sexual or drug experiences the majority of them are there simply to enjoy the wonderful country and (inexpensive) way of life.'

I didn't imagine anything could be wonderful on my own. I had never felt lonelier. Why was I here alone? I knew why, though. I was waiting for Roger and telling myself not to wait because ... what was the saying? A watched pot never boils. And maybe a weak man never leaves his wife and child, no matter how much he loves the other woman.

I took off my clothes. I slowly unhooked my bra. It was as though Roger's hands were sliding on my bosom, sliding me out of the silky cups, caressing my small puckered nipples. Sitting on the side of the bed, I touched my breasts, just a little, remembering us together. I slid the knickers down, letting them stretch taut between my thighs, where they looked most sexy. I liked that 'caught in the act' image. I thought of masturbating, of toasting my absent friend, but I felt too tense to relax. I wondered about the hotel's other occupants, and how they would pass the time between now and tomorrow. I couldn't stop thinking of the couple on the plane: the slickness of their union, the ease of the slide and the descent. I recalled the expressions on their faces, the longing and the satisfaction of the longing. It made me hot and uncomfortable. I slipped my knickers all the way to the floor, where they looked forlorn and crumpled.

Throughout the night I heard the hotel doors slam. Guests were coming and going, drunken footsteps, stumbling along, clutching at the walls. A herd of elephants, maybe, or hyenas, were staying in the corridor above. Holding my memories of Roger to me, I finally fell asleep. The buzzing from the arriving aeroplanes interrupted hot and feverish dreams.

'The new governess has arrived.'

She steps nervously through the crowds of courtiers to the throne. It's a fantastic throne – gold and heavy, rich and ornate – but no one is there.

'Where is the King?' she asks nervously. The King emerges, walking down a grand stairway. His face is covered yet his presence seems familiar.

'Don't I know you?' she asks.

15

'It's a term of endearment in English your highness.' One of the courtiers jumps in, scowling at her. 'Speak properly to the King,'

'I'm the new governess,' she says as she should, and she curtseys down to her knees. She is wearing a wonderful gold and red dress of luscious material, and on her feet are tiny gold-leaf slippers.

'Wonderful!' The King claps his hands and his enthusiasm is so infectious she almost believes it.

Someone is playing the harp. There is a smell of vanilla and all around huge decorated urns are filled with flowers. The atmosphere is relaxed and gentle, but still she is edgy.

'Your highness,' she dares.

'You can call me "my lord".' He beams at her.

'Where are the children?'

'The children?' he repeats questioningly. He looks around at his courtiers for elucidation.

'She wants to know where the children are,' someone offers unhelpfully.

'There are no children here,' says the King and everyone peals with laughter. She hears them buzz, 'children, what a thought!'

'But sir, I am here to look after the children,' she says.

The courtier next to the King pulls out a long scroll. He unravels it with great show.

'You are here to look after the king's court. To obey the King's orders, to take responsibility, to always be on good behaviour, blah, blah, blah, at an annual income of three million baht including tax. And you have signed it here.'

'But I thought . . .' she murmurs.

No response. In fact, some of the courtiers look as bewildered as she does.

'Who the heck am I meant to take care of?' she says loudly, and her voice echoes around the room. A few of the women titter behind huge peacock feathers; a thousand little eyes watch her. The King claps his hands, and a huge draped velvet curtain is rolled back revealing a bamboo cage, the size of a garden shed.

There are men in there; about ten, maybe twelve. They are all *barely* dressed: they are smiling and waving at her. Open faces and friendly eyes. A pleasant view any other time.

'I don't think so,' she backs away.

'But yes, you are here to take care of these people,' says another of the courtiers loudly. He has a moustache so black and shiny it looks as though it's been polished.

He whispers to her, 'These are people who have done great favours for the King. Elephant dust, turtle juice, all kinds of spices, saffron, mother of pearl, their gifts must be repaid. The King has obligations.'

'Don't be ridiculous,' she says, and looks over at the men again. They are nice-looking males. All different shapes and sizes, all different clothes, or all different non-clothes: thongs, harnesses, strings, a range of sparse equipment hides their bulges. The only thing the men have in common is a certain eagerness about their constitution. Like lions before feeding time.

'How on earth can I look after grown men?'

'On earth?' the courtiers hiss, and then another stands forwards.

'On earth, it is not difficult to look after grown men, it is the same way as in heaven maybe.'

The penny drops.

'No,' she says, 'No WAY.'

'This is a problem,' says the King, 'But it is not an insurmountable problem.'

She nods gratefully at him. At last, someone to negotiate with, someone who could see her point of view. She is about to suggest that they call another employment agency. They didn't need an au pair or domestic servant. And the woman who dealt with this case had said she envied her, that this job was the best they had had on their books for years. Well, no thank you!

'Tie her up,' shouts the King.

'NO!'

Three guards jump forward. Two on either side grip her under her arms. The third scoops her feet off the ground. There are more people running towards her with material and ropes.

'Get off me, you ... you freaks.' She fights but she fights badly. She catches one of the guards in the eye with her elbow, but immediately a bigger more ferocious hulk takes his place. She is locked up, stilled and squashed, as if trapped in a train with irate commuters. Oh why did she ever give up her job?

'Tie her up,' commands the King clapping. 'I dare say, some of my friends will enjoy it more if she struggles.'

At 5 a.m., the roar of motorbikes woke me. I could hear young men shouting, whistling and laughing; they sounded nearby. The next hour or so was non-stop, trolleys running up and down the corridors and a sluggish elevator waking slowly. I was glad to leave that morning. There was something about this unsettling heat, this anonymous place, which seemed to have a bizarre effect on me.

Chapter Three

I was pleasantly surprised, if embarrassed, to see both José and Selma at the domestic flight check-in desk at Bangkok airport. I deliberately sat some way from them on the bi-plane but they didn't do anything untoward this time; they were probably both still flaked out after yesterday's exertions.

As we approached the island, we could see miles of golden beach ringing the lush green of trees; I could even make out tiny trucks, bikes and little people, going about their business. I felt better instantly. It was like waking up after a long illness and feeling yes, you can live again.

Selma suggested we take a boat to a little resort she knew. I resisted at first. My guidebook recommended another place. Selma wrestled the book from my hands and laughed victoriously.

'Come on, let's enjoy the *real* wildlife.'

I felt frightened without my guide, my bible; it was dark without it. I wanted to tell Selma that, actually, I didn't want to go off the beaten track, I didn't want a wild adventure, thank you – but I just took my place on the boat quietly.

I felt happier again as we glided across the water in the little cruiser. My holiday was starting. I felt like a schoolgirl in July. I slid my hand over the side, dipping tentative fingers in the warm sea. The sun was caressing my body and I felt my tensions evaporate.

José had freckles on his shoulders and I couldn't keep from looking at that flat attractive plain between belly and shorts. Whenever Roger and I slept together I kept my hand warming him there. José strutted around like a predatory peacock. I couldn't help feeling that he smelled of sex. When he and Selma disappeared for ten minutes, I guessed that was why.

Selma returned unperturbed. She sat next to me, our thighs touching, our hands dangling overboard. How glad she was that I was there. The two of us must become great, great friends. She said she was mad about boats. 'I lurve them,' she said in her accent so sweet that I wanted her to say it again. She told me the rocking motion made her feel, how do you say, excited? I pulled my suitcase on my lap and crossed my arms around me.

'I was lucky,' Selma continued, 'If José had sat next to you on the plane, I would not have found him.'

'Don't be silly,' I protested half-heartedly. But sometimes, as he prowled around, I caught him looking at me with the same look of open lust that he gave to her. I wondered how much coincidence had to do with it. I had always thought Roger and I were destined to meet. Even if I hadn't started work at the same company as him, I'm sure fate would have conspired to collide our lives. Although people in *lurve* always thank fate, don't they? They don't when it comes to divorce.

'I always had a fantasy about fucking on a boat,' Selma continued. 'You know, I'm crazy about the water. I wear a striped T-shirt and mini-skirt. Pirates take over our ship. They kill all the others but me, they laugh and taunt, and then one night they come and take me, they bend me over the side, and take down my knickers. Oh, yes, that would be fine.'

'Yes, um, where are you from, Selma?' I asked as soon as she paused.

20

Selma was married with two children. The children were with their father. She took her holidays separately from him and had a job at an environmental charity.

'How you say, out of sight, out of mind?'

After she returned, her husband would holiday for three weeks in Bali.

'It's fair, non?'

She said she had planned to have only Thai boys on this trip, but José was such a good lover that she was going to stick with him for the duration. I nodded mutely.

Selma put her hand on my arm in a sisterly way and said, 'You should try it. We only live once.' Then she added, 'In this body, at least.'

I thought Selma was lucky to live in that body. Her breasts were pointy like those of ballet dancers. Her arms were long and slender. She was wearing a tiny vest with a sunflower print and a short skirt – but then she could wear a plastic bag and still look elegantly sexy. I wrenched my eyes away from her, towards José who was spitting into the waves. He was wearing loose cotton trousers. If you looked closely, you could see the shadow of his dangling cock.

'I have a boyfriend back home,' I explained.

'A girl like you on your own, here, on this hot island.' Her eyebrows shot up. I thought she was laughing at me.

'He's coming here soon,' I said.

We arrived at the port. Crowds gathered around waiting to welcome us, and everyone was pulling at us to take their taxi. Selma took off her shoes and proceeded to pad along barefoot. I don't usually like feet, but hers were beautifully shaped. I had a silly urge to pick them up, to touch the pressure points for her, only I didn't know which point led to which.

We rode in an old open-top jeep. We sat in the back bouncing around on stony roads, palm trees waving either side. I held on tightly to my luggage as it could easily have spun out the back. When we went up some hills and then down again, I realised that Selma was not wearing a bra. Her nipples rubbed against the flimsy vest, and her breasts bounced around wildly. She caught me staring so I looked away. I supposed if I were that way inclined, which I definitely am not, then she'd be the kind of woman I'd fancy.

Occasionally a motorbike overtook us. One time, a man on a bicycle passed with about eight chickens in a basket. Children strolled along and waved. Their white eyes and white teeth were shining bright out of dark faces. We seemed to be driving deeper and deeper into the jungle. The sound of chattering crickets, territorial birds and leaves crackling under tyres grew louder and louder and the wind subsided. The driver's mate – a handsome Thai – was friendly, so I talked with him as José and Selma smooched.

'Does it rain a lot here?'

'Yes, very bad when it rains. The roads disappear and the jeeps get stuck.'

'Oh, I see.'

I watched José's powerful hand on Selma's thigh. He was drawing little circles on that creamy path.

'Your English is very good,' I added uselessly.

Selma put her hand over José's, locking him only inches from her sex. I wondered if she was wearing the same style of knickers as the day before; more strap than knicker. I unfolded my legs and felt warm perspiration between my legs. My underwear was inappropriate. I felt like I was wearing a corset. The fine lacing on my bra was making me itch. I imagined Selma on the deck of a boat, getting spanked, slung over someone's knees.

Selma applied thick suntan lotion to her luscious skin, and offered it to me. I splashed it on my shoulders. The lotion smelled faintly of watermelons. She offered to rub it in. I resisted initially but she looked offended, so I let her. I felt her hands power over my back. Lower, lower, just a little bit more. I was sweating all over. I liked the way she touched me.

'Like silk,' she murmured and kissed my shoulder. I giggled self-consciously.

Roger always gave me massages impatiently, and only when he wanted a back rub himself, but Selma caressed my skin as though there was all the time in the world and as though she didn't want anything in return. Her fingers trickled over me, and I couldn't stop myself from telling her how good she was at it. She agreed! I stared red-faced at my shoes. I didn't want her to stop, but José was scowling at me, so I told her I could manage myself.

The heat hung around, heavy with expectation. The sky was a muzzy white blue. I tried to focus on the road ahead, but I was aware only of their breathing and their touching.

When our jeep met another on the road, the drivers got out and started chatting. The passengers in the other jeep were going back to the airport. They had dark tanned skin and appeared dusty or faded. I felt embarrassed of my newness. I looked stiff and formal compared to everyone else. They looked over at us, and some of the men gazed admiringly at Selma's unfettered breasts.

'Shalom,' one of them said. Peace.

Selma stood up and waved vigorously, letting them have full view of her tumbling titties. José looked furious. When she sat down she giggled to me.

'Eh, he's jealous this one.'

José looked dark, like a little boy forced to share his mother.

'He likes looking at other girls, but he doesn't like anyone looking at me!'

She put her hand on my knee. I felt her fingers squeeze my flesh and I saw the storm break out across José's handsome features. I pushed her creeping fingers away. Selma reinstated them. She dug into my flesh with garishly painted nails.

'Don't.' I shivered. I didn't want to make a pantomime. Selma rolled up her T-shirt, revealing her flat girlish

23

tummy. She lifted it too high, so that the underside of her sweet buns peeped out at us. The driver's mate grinned at me, and licked his lips with a red lolling tongue. José scowled at him, his sensuous face full of unspoken threats.

Selma laughed for just a little too long. She had beautiful white teeth, but the two either side of the front ones were pointed and made her look a little like a vampire.

I forced myself to look away. I focused on Roger. We are nine hours ahead of you darling, so you are probably still sleeping; still sleeping in England under a grey sky. I wish you were in my arms. I could stroke your hair and whisper how much I love you, I need you, and all the other sweet secrets that I don't dare tell you in the day.

Chapter Four

My bungalow, or cabin, at the Sunita Complex was just one room containing a bed, cupboard area and some hangers. The bathroom – a barely functional shower and toilet – was down some cold stone steps at the back. From one window, overlooking the balcony, I had a view of the beach and I guessed I wouldn't spend much time inside. What a beach! Our view from the aeroplane was confirmed: it was a picture-postcard beach, a honeymooner's paradise with icing-sugar white sands and a turquoise-blue sea almost the exact same hue as the sky. As soon as I felt the sand between my toes and heard the waves caress the shore, I felt pinched with regret. It would have been perfect if Roger and I were together. I measured everything in terms of how much Roger would love it, storing things up for us to talk about when he arrived.

Every morning, I awoke to the soft sound of the breeze in the leaves – *sa-sa-sa* – and the waves on the sand. Nature's poetry. I thought the trees and the sea were having whispered love conversations.

From the other window of my room, I could see right into Selma and José's bungalow. Theirs was identical to mine, except they had an extra hammock swinging out front. I was happy they were nearby. They felt like old friends and, although I was sensible enough not to expect anything of them, it was reassuring that something was familiar.

The electricity clicked off every night at midnight and, just when I began to drift away, Selma and José had their physical nightcap. Regular as clockwork, in, out, in, out, they fucked. I pictured her face clenched with arousal; the tip of her pink tongue snaking between her teeth, the way she grimaced as she was coming, coming, coming. I covered my ears, wishing I could cover my brain. Jessuuss. They had more energy than a pair of athletes. As the nights went on, I grew more used to them: they were a soundtrack, that was all, like piped music in an elevator, or background music in a supermarket. But whatever I told myself, I couldn't stop my ears from pricking up, and listening for noises.

Selma asked me a few times if I wanted to go out with them, but I declined. I didn't act the gooseberry well, and their intensity alarmed me. Although she claimed she found him dull, she was always dragging him off into the bungalow. José followed her everywhere, and he didn't like her talking to others. But, rather than finding this annoying, she took his possessiveness gaily, and thought it a big joke. How very Bohemian of her, I thought, annoyed. She reminded me of smoky bars, big cellos and girls with bobbed hair who have loved too much.

In the day, the main street was like the dusty town in a western movie. There were chemist shops that sold mosquito coils, sandals, candles, sarongs, fishing rods and remedies for tummy troubles. There were takeaway food stores offering falafels, kebabs, sandwiches and noodles, or sit-in places where the travellers draped themselves over the chairs and watched the same old American videos churning out the same old lines: 'I'm leaving.' 'You can't leave because I'm leaving you.' Or, 'You're fired.' 'You can't fire me, because I quit.'

26

At night, the main street was bustling: gorgeous Thai girls shipped in from the countryside beckoned less attractive foreign men with bulging wallets.

Sunita Complex consisted of a café, a small store, and a small travel agency-cum-office as well as the bungalows. The café was under a canopy supported by pillars, and you could walk in and out freely. At the kitchen end, there was a pool table. At the opposite end, the tables and chairs outside led down to the beach.

The day I arrived, I had looked around the café apprehensively. There was just one other customer – a Western man drinking a beer and reading the *Bangkok Post*. He was wearing an outback hat and tartan socks with sandals and his face was an unhealthy pink. Selma and José had already fled for privacy, so I took a seat near him.

I looked over to the kitchen where a Thai man was methodically stripping a cucumber. Its skin lay in green curls on his chopping board. And then he cut the cucumber fast; the knife, one of those lethal rectangular ones, was flashing silver in my eyes. Chop, chop, chop.

A group of girls, English maybe, wearing headbands, bikini tops and flares slouched past shrieking with laughter. I saw the man in the kitchen look over at them. A couple of foreign men with pot bellies walked by. They were followed closely by two young Thai women with strawberry lips and cherry hips, swaying like flowers in springtime. I heard him tut.

'Prem hates westerners,' the man said knowingly.

Prem, I thought. What an unusual name.

'Who's that?' I said. Although I could guess, I was curious to hear more.

'The manager, him, over there in the kitchen.'

'Why does he hate them?'

'Why do you think?' he retorted, laughing. I shrugged.

Turn Prem sideways and he was narrow as a cork, but up close his chest and his muscles were defined. In fact, his front was so sculptured it looked like a cross was engraved on his skin. He looked like a thinker, a great thinker. I liked the way he resented foreigners; it showed he had attitude. Although I sometimes wished I could bend Roger to my will, I was always secretly impressed when I couldn't.

I read my guidebook.

'The Thais are the friendliest people on earth. They will go out of their way to make you feel at home. That's why Thailand is known as *the land of smiles*.'

Scowling, Prem emerged from the kitchen and poured a creamy milkshake. He had a white stripe on his wrist from where he once must have kept a watch or a bracelet. His arms were skinny-muscular.

Thank God I had found Roger. I didn't have to eye up men; I wasn't on the market any more. Roger may have 'commitments', but at least he was communicative. Prem's face simply conveyed his desire to be left alone.

As Prem solemnly passed me the glass, his shoulder was right against my face, and I wondered if he could feel my breath on his gorgeous skin. I had a ridiculous urge to touch him, to pinch him, to see if he was real.

'The Thai architecture is breathtaking. Take your time and look around at the shape and colour of the scenery and the landscapes.'

I kept my eyes on the manager's lithe body. Little pieces of cucumber were clinging stubbornly to his shirt. His shirt was undone, but I could only catch a glimpse of his skin. When he spun around to catch me spying, I busied myself with the book pages. Stupidly, I cut my finger. Not on a massive knife like the one he had used, or even a little one, but on a piece of paper. Ridiculous!

Prem took my glass away and tutted again when he saw the blood spill from my finger. He brought me over a tissue, and I wrapped it around. We watched as the white turned to a dramatic red but he still didn't say anything.

Chapter Five

*T*his is how they bathe her.

They soap her everywhere inside and out. The warm water trickles up her every crevice. They make her bend over, so they can see that everywhere, everything is clean as a pin.

This is how they tie her up.

She is spread-eagled on a wheel, a large wheel. Her legs and arms wide open. She is wearing a simple cloth that skims her thighs, but when they rotate her, she thinks they can see the place between her legs.

'Not here for long,' they say cheerfully. She hears someone say that soon, she will be in service.

She will sue the agency. That's for damn sure. If it's the last thing she does.

'Do you like doing this job?' she asks one of the men busily securing her left wrist to a wooden spoke. He points to his mouth.

'What?'

'He is mute.' says the man next to him.

'Gosh.' She pinches his arm, and he doesn't say anything.

'Before you start looking after the friends, we will see you tonight.' The one who speaks whispers.

'What? Why?'

'Don't worry.' He lowers his voice even more. 'We have come to rescue you.'

'Thank you, thank you, you are so kind.'

That night, the two return. They try to undo the bonds, but both of them are clumsy and are unable to free her. The mute one leans on her breast. A big greasy tear emerges. It flies away big as a balloon, bigger than a hot-air balloon.

'He is sad,' says the mute's friend, 'he wants desperately to save you from this, he is worried that they will spread your legs very wide and give it to you very hard.'

'Tell him not to worry,' she says cheerfully, 'honest, I think I can handle it.'

'There is news they are looking for the chosen one for you, the perfect fit. It is terrible. It will be terrible for you.'

'They will make you so moist, that the arousal will run down your legs, and then they will force you to endure hot shaft after hot shaft. They will whisper obscenities into your ears, breathing over you, kissing you with warm, needy mouths.'

'How awful,' she says, her cheeks burning.

'And not just your pussy either, oh no, they will touch all over your body, your legs, your buttocks,' he whispered, 'some may even touch your breasts.'

'My breasts?'

'And not just with their hands, they might use their tongues.'

'Oh really?' Her nipples are starting to tingle. 'And does the King have . . . have a go as well?'

'Oh no, thank goodness, that is one ordeal you will be saved from. The King is the King. It is only other men who may enter.'

'I see,' she says. A shame because there was something about the King.

'But we will help you escape.'

A little shiver runs through her.

'I really don't think you should. It's far too dangerous. Think what trouble you would get in,' she adds generously.

The men look terribly upset and the mute one is weeping as his friend leads him away. She lies back on the wheel and waits until morning. Curiously her strange nocturnal visitors have lifted her spirits.

My increasingly fantastic dreams fuelled the loving postcards I wrote to Roger. I begged him to come and I counted first the days and then the hours since we had last met. I said that I had made a few friends, but they were not my type. I had started to tan, but was keeping on my bikini top, to save some white bits for him to kiss. I told him explicitly what I was going to do to him when he arrived. I promised I wouldn't nag him any more, but that, well, I was growing desperate for him.

Days of heavenly nothingness wound their way onwards. Each morning, the sun streamed through the window with a thousand possibilities; I could go scuba-diving, snorkelling, or to the waterfalls. The world was my goddamn oyster. It seemed a crime that I should have felt miserable in such a wonderful place, but I was without Roger. Usually, I just put on my sarong and dark glasses and made my solitary way to the beach.

The masseuse had muscular hands, and grains of sand were stuck in the indentations. She began on my back with hard, up and down strokes. Then she added lotion, massaging the wetness into my skin. My muscles were heating up from her deep heavy strokes. Mmm. I felt drowsy, weightless, as though I were floating. A stone was digging into my ribs, but that didn't matter. 'Mmm,' I murmured. She unknotted the little twists in my back and unravelled balls of wound-up tension. She worked lovingly. She was an artist, a body artist, and my back was her object.

We were under a palm tree that filtered the sun's rays like a cascade of fireworks. The masseuse had approached me three times that morning, and three times I'd told her to come back later. Finally, I agreed to let her touch me. It was funny how reluctant I was about it, as though I were submitting to something terrible.

Next to us, her shadow was crouched over my shadow. I let my neck loosen and I closed my eyes. Every muscle that she touched zoomed into focus or, at least, was exaggerated a million times. First my neck, then my shoulder, and then the small of my back. She gave my arms Chinese burns, like we used to do at school. She pulled each of my fingers and they each clicked as though saying an individual thank you.

She moved and, for one horrid moment, I thought it was over. But she simply rearranged the towel, covering the top part of my body, setting to work on my exposed lower part. She worked my calves. I felt her fingers loosen my muscles, and I buried my face in the pillow. It smelled of other people's sweat, other people's faces, and that strange, almost spicy oil that she used. Every part of my body felt catered for and secure. Her hands travelled up the backs of my legs, arriving at my rounded thighs. She pummelled my flesh rhythmically. I felt her probing fingers nuzzle the tops of my thighs. On and on, she kept pressing me there, on and on, pestle and mortar. My groin felt heavy pressed into the ground. Her thumbs were swirling on my buttocks and then my bottom was pummelled. Unwittingly, my stupid pussy was stirring.

It was now three weeks, two days and eighteen hours since I had been touched.

Imagine if it were Prem touching me, studying my arse. I would love to show him the intricacies, a hole by hole account, of my body. No, not Prem. Imagine that it is Roger. Roger arriving at the airport. He is wearing a suit, heavy clothes, and he's every inch the young exec. I greet him, and we come straight to the beach. Where do we go? I know. We sit in a boat, not one out at sea, but a moored one. Roger has a parcel of silk underwear and asks me to model it for him.

I was wet between the legs. I couldn't help the responses my body made, the tightening and contracting of my cunt. I wanted her to admire my body, to search for treasure in my hole. Oh, God, if she only stuck her finger up there, just for a second, I knew I would come like a shot.

It's a woman, it's a woman, I told myself helplessly. For God's sake, don't get turned on by a woman – but it wasn't her, I swear, it was what she was doing to me. Could she see how liquid my lower body had become? The excitement poured through me, fanning out from my arse.

I told myself I was a whore, a dirty cow. She was only doing her job, and there I was, about to go off like a firecracker. What a slut! I once read that good manners were a question of 'appropriate behaviour at an appropriate time' – well, my slutty thoughts were completely uncalled for. Get a grip, I reprimanded myself, but all I wanted was for her to get a grip on me.

'Turn over.'

I laced up my bikini top with clumsy urgent fingers and rolled onto my back so that I was face up. I was glad that the sun was beating down on me; I could blame that for the redness of my cheeks. I hoped she couldn't read my mind as well as she could read the contours of my body.

'Nice breasts,' she said.

'Thank you.'

She rolled her fingers over my bosom, grazing my nipples through the flimsy cloth. Little sleazy arrows of pleasure fired between my legs. She worked hard, mechanically, as though moulding something on an assembly line. Her eyes were gazing out into the sea. Perhaps she was thinking about the money she would make. She massaged my tits perfectly but, exposed, I felt far too embarrassed to relax. Raising my head, I saw I had an audience; two skinny English boys were staring, openly admiring the rare spectacle of an open-air bosom massage. She continued polishing.

'That's enough, thank you,' I said firmly.

My nipples were hard little drills, sending flames to where they shouldn't go. I shouldn't have been thinking like that.

'How much?'

'Nice body,' she said, and continued gliding soft, hard-working hands around my mammaries.

'Thank you. How much?'

The English boy smiled. His skin looked tender, like uncooked chicken; he wouldn't be scoring tonight. He yelled that he would give me a massage for free. I saw that his shorts bulged ever so slightly; perhaps my response had had a stirring affect on him too. I wondered how he would fuck.

Gross! What sort of woman was I if three weeks of celibacy was beyond me? What did this say about me?

No wonder Prem hated us tourists.

Later that afternoon, some foreigners were playing volleyball on the sand. Slap! As I watched, the ball was carried over the net and then the wind caught it, spinning it in to the sea. I watched one of the men leaping about after it. He was proud of his agility, butterfly boy. He was a tall, straight up and down man with blond hair and golden hairs covering his body. He looked sporty, skateboardy. He would have been dismissive of my bungalow-beach-café routine. He looked the sort who, when he went to a country, whether it was for one week or ten, liked to 'do it' thoroughly. He looked over at me watching him. When he missed the ball, he shrugged in my direction, laughing.

I had fallen asleep, a letter to Roger half written in front of me. Maybe, he hadn't got the ones I had sent before. I was describing the time I'd been sent to his office to deliver a document, and he'd asked me to stay. I hadn't been wearing any knickers, and I'd flashed him accidentally on purpose.

Someone touched my back.

'You wan' massage?'

'No, I just had one,' I said sternly, but the finger continued on my backbone, stopping at the string of my bikini, fingering the line.

'No massage?'

The intonation was different to usual. I turned around wearily, and there he was, butterfly boy. Tall, blond and handsome; he was the sort of man you imagine when your horoscopes say that you will meet someone wearing blue on a Thursday night. He squinted in the sunlight. I noticed he had a gold hoop through one eyebrow and full, almost feminine, lips. He also had a tattoo of a dragon on his arm.

'You like volleyball? I saw you watching.'

'It's OK,' I said.

'I sure would love to watch you play volleyball.' He deliberately eyed my breasts as they crowded in my bikini top.

'I don't play.'

He sat down cross-legged. I noticed the other volleyball players watching, assessing my reaction.

'Trent,' he said holding out his hand.

'Are you American?'

'Canadian actually.' When he spoke, I noticed there was something glinting in his mouth.

'Abbs.' I held out my hand. He squeezed it for too long as I expected he would.

'Abbs?' he repeated, pouting deliberately. 'As in abdominal muscles?'

'As in Abigail.'

'Abigail.' He said the word slowly and he didn't let go of my fingers. I felt the whole world was looking at us. I tried to act appropriately.

'Excuse me for asking, but what is that in your mouth?'

He stuck out his tongue. He had a silver stud there.

'And I've got them here too.' He raised his T-shirt, revealing two chunky silver rings through his nipples. I don't know whether it was because of the rings or not, but those nipples seemed to me like the biggest I had ever seen. The outer bits were like pink saucers, and the nipple itself was swollen up like a baby's dummy. My eyes wandered down to a washboard stomach.

'Why did you get your tongue pierced?'

He lay next to me, his leg slung over towards me, on the sand. I could feel his body heat.

'Oh, I just thought it would feel nice.'

'And how does it feel?' I added shyly. I can be a flirt when I want to. Roger claimed that I flirted with his colleagues.

'You wanna feel?'

He moved to kiss me, but I backed off. Was he presumptuous or what? Instead, I felt it with my fingers. I had never touched someone's tongue before. It felt wet, comforting.

'It's nice on my finger,' I whispered.

'It's nice on other places too.'

'Oh.'

'I'll show you if you like.'

'What do you mean?'

His eyes were on my breasts, my belly, roaming between my legs. I hated it. I liked it.

'Put it this way, if oral pleasure is your game, then Trent is my name.'

'I have a boyfriend, thank you,' I said firmly. I held the letter up. Flimsy evidence, but evidence nevertheless.

Trent backed off, blinking. He was like a lizard in the sand.

'No, not here.'

'Oh, not here.' He smiled knowingly. 'That's all right, then.'

As he walked off, he did a thumbs-up sign to his mates.

Chapter Six

I was anxious for connection with Roger. I felt very distant from him. It wasn't the distance in miles though, it was the differences in our situations.

I entered the telephone shop. The girl who greeted me had beautiful hair stretching all the way down her back like black silk; like expensive bedding in stores where they hate you to bounce on their beds. Behind her were ten clocks, each set at different times, with the names of the capital city they represented underneath. It was ten o'clock in the morning in England. Maybe Roger would be thinking of me, holding one of my postcards in his hand, close to his heart.

You're probably not very sympathetic towards me; towards my seeing a married man. But Roger isn't really married. He does love me, he does. People wonder how we got together, you know, which came first – the broken marriage or the affair? The other woman chasing the weak man, or the adulterer chasing the available woman? I think it was a case of the chicken and the egg: I shivered whenever Roger came near, but he was the one who started the coming near. I started the touching – picking at non-existent fluff, rearranging badly tied ties – but he started the kissing. I initiated the groping – pulling at his back, his bottom, as we snogged – but he took off his clothes first. He had the condoms, which I unravelled and the rest, as they say was history; recently, it had been feeling like ancient history.

I heard the tone of his phone ringing. Playing the game: he loves me, he loves me a lot, he loves me, he loves me a lot. When would he pick up? He loved me a lot!

The girl walked into the back room where a Thai TV drama was playing. I was left with the stopwatch, the phone and a wall full of clocks.

'Roger?'

'Abby, darling.'

He was happy I called! His voice was smooth and melodious, a fine whisky on the rocks. Oh, Roger. Why aren't you here? Twenty seconds.

'Do you have your tickets yet?'

'Not yet, Abby, but soon,' he said softly.

I couldn't resist asking. 'When?'

'Not long. I said so, didn't I?' He hated it when I nagged.

I was wearing a skirt, and I looked down at my thighs, my wide-open legs. My feet were pointed outwards like a duck. I sat forward, pushing down on my pubic bone. Roger's voice turned me on beyond belief. I turned so that the corner of the chair was trapped between my legs, and I began to rub myself against it very gently. Thirty seconds. The seconds were clicking away from me, trickling through my head like water! Forty-two, forty-three. When it hit a minute, the price would go up again. If I could keep under three pounds it was still quite cheap.

'Darling, I miss you.'

How long would it take to come? I kept an eye on the clock, and on my legs. What funny knees I had! I needed an extra knee, one that I could straddle. When we slept together, I would often ride Roger's knees, like a horse, just until I was slippery. Fifty seconds.

'What would you do to me if I were there?'

Oh God. What wouldn't I do?

'I'd suck your fingers, and then your cock, and then, first off, I'd turn over and you could give it to me from behind.'

'What knickers would you be wearing?'

Roger has to have his underwear. He loves buying sexy lingerie for me. I like to twirl and whirl in front of him. He watches me change in and out – a private fashion show – until new knickers with freshly damp crotches lie dishevelled on the floor. Wrinkled stockings and lined suspenders are spread over the chairs. Bras with little flowers attached goodness knows where, or sometimes with little drops of pearl – once a little diamante, like a sun embedded in the silk – are thrown on to the shelves.

Roger is the only man I've met who knows my exact bra size. Where other men can tell the time from a sundial, Roger knows what time of the month it is by checking out my chest. He once said he was jealous of my bras – if after death, he could come back as anything, he would come back as my black silk one, and spend all day long clutching my breasts.

'But what about my bottom?' I said. 'Don't you want to come back as those tiger-print briefs and spend all day riding up my crack?'

'Alternate days?' he proposed.

'It's a deal,' I said. I liked the image, although I couldn't imagine living on without him, knickers or no knickers.

The only thing that made me angst-ridden was that he preferred fucking me with my bra on. Was that because he thought I looked ugly when my boobs dangled down?

He protested vehemently, hurt that I should say such a thing. 'It's only because you look so beautiful.' As usual, I ended up comforting him.

* * *

'Umm, the peach. That way you can just pull aside the string and the material will still rub my clit, while you're inside me.'

I couldn't help remembering Selma's arse. It really was a fine peach – just fit to take a bite from.

'What underwear are you wearing now?'

Oh God. One minute was up already.

'Guess.' Even on the island I dressed carefully. Even though no one would see, it boosted my spirits to know that beneath my casual clothes, I looked sexy. I didn't have to shout about this. It's enough to have a Porsche in the garage: you don't have to drive it everywhere.

'The light blue,' he guessed. 'The ones you were wearing when we fucked on the desk?'

A late Friday night, with fruitful overtime. Me sprawled out; him beady eyed, surveying me. He tied me up loosely with his red tie round the legs of the chair. He wouldn't blindfold me because he wanted me to see everything, but he gagged me so I couldn't be too demanding. He stripped off slowly and then pulled down my panties with a ruler. Cold plastic made me shiver. On the desk, I broke free, and came down on him hard.

Or did he mean the time I rode on him? No, because I was wearing red ones then, red rag to a bull, and it was before work – yes, it was Tuesday morning, just a regular day, but I knew he would be there early, so I got there early too. Surprised face, as he searched through his post. 'Coming to get you,' I said, and I did. Crawling over the desk, his hard-on bigger than ever. Roger and I had good sex, we did.

'No. Guess again.'

'The black big ones, you know, the ones I can put my hands up. You were wearing them at the cinema.'

At the theatre, actually, but who cared? He'd been given tickets for a Greek play. The story was dull, but he masturbated me through the second act. The knickers weren't big – that was just the style, gappy and flappy at the thighs, so the best route was to go up under my legs, fondle his way to the hollow. All these rich people around us were in pearls and gloves, and Roger was making his own glove of sticky pearls.

'No, I'm wearing the crotchless ones.'

Roger's absolute favourite: I first wore them at the Hotel Waterloo. Starting the job in the elevator. Stomach lurching, we must have gone up and down five times. Jamming the buttons so the doors wouldn't open. On the fifth time up, a very posh lady came in. I think she saw what we were up to – she and her thin-lipped husband talked bravely about politics. Roger said he'd never seen anyone go that shade of purple before. He didn't stop fingering my wetness. Continuing against the door of the hotel room, too excited to move, like waxy statues. Me saying, 'Imagine a pornographic Madame Tussauds, wouldn't that be fun?' Him saying that we could model for them.

I hardly ever wore these crotchless ones because they were bloody freezing but here, in Thailand, I wanted to be free. I liked the warm evening air whistling up my legs. I liked the wetness, lubricating my walk. It felt horny.

'Wow.' Roger gave a low whistle, and I knew that, all those miles away, his penis was hardening. It had to be.

Some penises just point skyward and don't grow much but Roger's really did change size. It was a wiener when soft but, hard, it was a magnificent machine. I pictured it, red and throbbing, seeking out its place. I loved its single-mindedness, the way it searched out its sticky goal, targeted and then, with those seesawing, back and forth moves, let go, madly shooting out its pleasure. I wished I were kneeling at it, worshipping it. I would let him guide my mouth over it, give him the power.

'Roger, are you touching yourself?'

'Yes, are you?'

'Uh huh.'

41

'You naughty little thing, you little slut. Where are you?'

'I'm in a shop.'

I looked guiltily towards the back room. The TV was loud and hopefully would absorb the girl for a while, and drown my groans. I slid on to the surface. I lowered my knickers, watching my own tufts of hair and my own fingers as they entered, wishing they were his hands, wishing you were here Roger. I was wetter than usual, wetter than ever. Oh God, it had been so fucking long. How could you do this to me, Roger?

My sex was so wide open to him; I loved him so deeply, so fucking deeply.

'Talk to me,' I pleaded. I wanted to come, to get off on his voice. I wanted to stick the phone up me, to have him talk directly to the source of my pleasure.

'Are you wet?'

'So wet!

Look what you're doing to me, Roger. Look at me, I'm helpless without you. Gulping and swallowing, I was being drawn down, down into a sticky, slurping, whirl-pool. Squeezing his buttocks in my mind. Scratching marks on his white cheeks. Riding on his cock, sinking his cock in my creaminess. Gripping him tighter and tighter to me, no escape.

'Please come.' I was whispering huskily both to him and to me. 'Please, please come.'

'I want to come,' he murmured, 'I want to make you come.'

I could only groan a reply. An incredible heat was consuming me. Two minutes and thirty seconds. Fingers doing what they knew best. I was tight, tight, tight around them.

'Come for me, darling – here, now, show me how much you miss me.'

'I can't . . .'

'Yes, you can. Come on, baby, rub yourself.'

'I can't stop,' I moaned softly. I couldn't speak. I

focused on the mound, my pubic mound. The pressure on my clit was unbearably intense, and he was willing me on. All those memories, all those times were flooding back, flooding in: wetness, the theatre, the elevator, the stimulation, his face when he came, the way his eyelashes brushed against my cheek, the way he gripped my legs, the way I convulsed around him. I couldn't stop, I couldn't stop. I was coming on the phone.

I slammed the receiver down in just under three minutes. Innocently, the girl re-emerged from the back of the shop. I shivered, as if someone was walking over my grave. Poor Roger; it was the same for him. He hadn't slept with Angela since their baby was born three years ago. He must have been feeling the strain too.

It was still early evening, the sun hadn't set, and I wasn't ready to be Rapunzel, yet. I strolled around the port, trying to appreciate the beauty around me. There were no car fumes, no mobile phones, no stresses, and yet, without someone to share it with . . .

The boats tugged away in the tide, but were tamed by their anchors. Proud owners had given them glamorous names: *African Queen*, *Cleopatra*. A few yards away, a group of men was fishing off the shore and I realised that Prem was one of them. He stood out from the others. His shoulders were too sloping to be macho, his build too slight to be a hero, but his torso was tight, well formed and natural. His white shirt, slung around his waist, emphasised the mahogany smoothness of his skin. His hair glistened black purple in the shafts of sunlight. The other fishermen were jeering, unshaven, and jowly. Prem was like a water sprite. Tears of water clung to his toned chest. His toes made sweet indentations in the sand.

Prem jerked his rod. At last, he'd caught something. He had hooked a fish and he reeled it in triumphantly. Even from ten yards away I could hear how the line strained. The poor creature didn't have a chance. Prem's biceps bulged as he worked the reel, and I wanted to touch him. Tears of water, little beads of sweat, clung to his toned chest. His skin was so smooth, so beautiful, almost inviting touch.

The fish swung towards him and he caught it deftly. Carefully, he unhooked it and then squeezed his prey. It flopped and jittered in his hard-working hands. I clapped approvingly, so that he would know that I was impressed. As usual, he only nodded solemnly at me. He kissed the fish, then plunged it into his bucket. For a second, I would have given anything to be that fish, to be caught, to be gutted, and served up for that beautiful fisherman.

I shook myself and walked away from the beach, red-faced and lonely.

I watched Selma wash clothes on her bungalow front. She was in a tiny dress that gripped her tightly, like a condom. She must have just taken a shower or had a swim, because her hair was damp and there were damp patches on the material around her bum, her tummy and her shoulders from where her wet hair flopped. She flicked back her hair and crouched on the floor. Her hair looked heavy and dark. She washed her bathing suit – aha, so she had been in the ocean. She swirled it in the water, making hypnotic waves. She rubbed the ends together, frottaging the cloth. Then she squeezed; wringing the neck. Her knuckles turned white.

When the last drops were oozing out, she hung it up. Her muscles tensed, the peg dropped down, and she struggled to pick it up. I noticed the skirt withdraw up her toned thighs. She saw me watching, and gave a cheerful wave.

Chapter Seven

*T*rent and I ate together in the eating area in front of Sunita Lodge restaurant on the beach. We sat on rickety bamboo chairs at tables covered with plastic tablecloths. The sea washed against the shore like bed-covers pulled up at night. In the distance were small lights from the local boats that brought fruit, cereals and flour, but mostly the island was dark. It didn't suddenly go black, it wasn't like when you switch off the light: it was just a gradual progression, a calm switching of shades. Candles were flickering gently in the timid breeze.

Next to us, a couple were playing backgammon. The counters clicked melodically against the board. I watched as the black and white were stacked up, and the powerful white ones gathered at the side. When the girl won she raised her fist in the air and knocked over her wine.

I was telling Trent about my life pre-Thailand. It was hard to remember my old job and my lifestyle; maybe the earth really is flat, and once you leave England you just fall over the edge.

'It wasn't that I didn't like my life, just that I thought there must be more to it than this.'

'So like most of us you're escaping from normalcy.

Travel is one of the best ways to avoid reality,' Trent said.

'I just wanted to see more things.' I thought yearningly of Roger. I certainly didn't *want* to leave him.

'It's always more complicated than that.'

'Well, yes,' I admitted. 'But I wouldn't have said I was escaping from an unhappy situation. My job was unchallenging, and I suppose . . .' I trailed off. I didn't want to tell him everything, not yet.

'Does anyone have a job they enjoy?' Trent asked rhetorically.

'Yes. Take my friend Sally . . .'

'Don't mind if I do . . .'

I was just getting used to Trent's inane jokes. It was impossible to have a serious conversation with him – but then, as Selma would say, 'we're on holiday'. Maybe serious conversations should be saved for other times.

'Anyway, she works for this great company and she loves her job. And she's pretty.'

'And I suppose she has a brilliant sex life as well?'

'Of course,' I said, aware that I sounded like a bitter old harridan. But the grass is always greener. Your neighbour's arse is always leaner.

'Rubbish! You never know what goes on in other people's sex lives. The best sex is on your own: just you, your imagination, your hand and your sex.'

'Hmm.' I was unconvinced. I had been doing a lot of that lately and I wouldn't have said that it was the best. The cheapest, maybe, the most convenient, and the least complicated – but not the best.

'Look, life is a vicious circle,' Trent said in that pseudo-profound way travellers acquire after they've been travelling for five months. He knew, as well as I did, that he had a secure job waiting for him when he got back home.

'Whenever anyone says vicious circle,' I said, giggling, 'I think of a circle of men. You know, five or six men tugging at each other, hands over cocks, leaning over to be accommodating. A ring of sexual fire: coming

46

together, spurting, and jolting one after another, like falling dominoes. What a joy that must be.'

'You're seriously weird. That's so gross.'

Trent made retching sounds over the side of the table. A cat that had been sitting there, minding her own business, jumped up.

The waiter came out with two greasy menus. We chose fish. I wondered if Prem had caught it. If Prem had slid his hands over its back. Maybe he had covered its eyes, fooling the fish into believing it was dead. Had he removed the hook from its mouth, held it up to the sun? Perhaps.

The couple on the next table switched from backgammon to Connect Four. I could see the woman making the wrong moves: she was doing things that gave her opponent the four counters in a row. I wanted to alert her to her mistakes, but I couldn't interfere. Backgammon was obviously her game!

The waiter brought out fish with sticky rice, salads, and soup.

'Enjoy your evening,' he said. The swing doors into the kitchen clattered open and shut. I thought I spied Prem up against a counter – so he *was* working that night.

I don't know how it happened, but Trent and I got chatting about sex again. I talked to him with the confidence of knowing that we were not going to have sex. If I had thought we might, I would not have been able to tell him any of the things that I did. Roger was a security blanket. I would have felt threatened without him but, knowing I was attached, talking intimately with Trent was nothing more than a bit of fun.

'Tell me about losing your virginity,' I said.

'I saw, conquered, came,' he said. He nonchalantly rolled a spliff. The way he folded the paper was sexy.

'No, the details,' I persisted. 'It's the details that make it interesting.'

'Alright,' said Trent amiably. 'She wore pink knickers. She wouldn't let me put on the light, so we did it in the

47

dark. No, OK, I'll start from the beginning. We'd been dating for about four months and I'd touched just about every part of her body. She had something clean and fresh about her, she wore this really nice scent, just under her ears. I loved that smell, still do. It was my birthday, and I had been nagging at her for weeks. I just wore her down until she got fed up – like battle fatigue, I suppose.

'I produced a rubber and she sort of nodded, like OK, tonight, for one night only, we could. I had practised putting the condom on for weeks. I mean, I had bought packs of the things and gone through them wanking, unwanking, whatever. I unravelled it gently but the bastard got stuck; I had put it on the wrong way round. I only had two left. I was so impatient, I nearly sliced my finger through it, but then it was on. I kept the curtain ajar and the moonlight seemed to bathe her skin. She had lovely skin, white as rice, beautiful she was. She started taking her clothes off. First, her skirt; I thought how odd that she would remove that first. And then off came her top. I was so excited when I saw her, I almost shot my load.'

'Oh, I like that phrase "shot your load".' I giggled into my milkshake, sucking up small shavings of coconut. Trent leaned back in his chair. He was enjoying it as much as I was. He passed me the spliff. I inhaled and felt the smoke crash into my throat and cruise lower, warming me thoroughly. Sometimes we need a dulling, a numbing of our sensations, when the reality is so bright.

'She lay down, and I removed her knickers. They had a tiny bow on the front. She had soft curly hair there too. I just wanted to grab a handful; but of course I didn't. I stroked her there as best I could, to make her relax. And then I just kind of launched myself. She had to guide me in. I was jabbing around willy-nilly –' I smiled at his choice of words, '– and then I found her hole. It was the tightest space ever, tighter than in my dreams, and I could feel the condom like a noose around my cock, but all the same it was wonderful. I started to stroke up and down with my cock. Gradually, she moved her fingers onto my butt-cheeks. I felt amazement; she was actually pulling me into her. She actually wanted me to go further into her, further into the unknown. I think in my wildest dreams, I had not anticipated that. I hadn't expected her to actually enjoy it. I didn't think she would want me to take my time. She was silent, though – not a murmur until the very end, when she gave this deep sigh. Oh, Jesus, I've never forgotten that.'

'So was she your first love?'

'Not really,' he said. 'There was another girl, too, Julia. She had massive tits. Good kisser, too. She really concentrated on you. The other girls were so easily distracted by the phone or the TV or something, but when she got started, she never stopped. It was devotion with her, nibbling the lips, peeping in her hot little tongue. She was lovely, but when you touched her, she sighed and groaned so. When I think about it, we were pretty cruel to her.'

'What did you do?'

'We called her "moaner", or "groaning Julia". We took the piss out of her. She just got so excited, so easily. You only had to slide your hand on to her bra, and she was wriggling around, making little noises from deep in her throat.'

'Why were you so unkind?'

'Because Carol was silent and Julia was noisy. And because we were idiots we had more respect for the girls for whom sex seemed a chore, a reluctant gift for the boys, than the girls who took the present for themselves. Deep down, I preferred Julia, but I wasn't going to tell anyone that. I once got my hand down her knickers, and she came. It was amazing. We were at this party, and everyone was making out, silently, but she . . . I touched her there, and everything seemed to melt. She was pure liquid between the legs, and she showed me how to touch her. I did like she said, and seconds later she was

49

throbbing and pulsating all around me. She wasn't like the other girls.'

I felt a strange jealousy about girls Trent had known ten years ago. I wondered what the boy I lost my virginity to would say about me. Would he say I was pure liquid, or that he remembered my sighs of pleasure?

'Now I prefer a woman who makes noise,' Trent went on. 'Oh God, I love those sounds women make when they're having a good time, when they're really up for it. You know, there was this man who had a sex change to be a woman, and then back again, and he said sex was so much better as a woman.'

He made a crude imitation of a woman coming. I was scared the people on the next table would hear.

'What noises do you make, honey?'

'The usual, I guess,' I said quickly, then tried to divert the train of the conversation: 'Don't call me honey.'

'Come on, be more specific.'

'It depends on the situation.'

'Let's say he's pulled down your knickers and is staring at your lovely bush. And he's slipping his hand in, stealing a feel, and you're all wet; it's like running water in there. Who put the tap on baby? And he's undoing his jeans, and he is harder . . .'

'I think that's enough,' I said, blushing scarlet. I flicked through the dessert menu. Fantastic pictures of ice creams, pancakes and cakes tempted me, but I resisted, ordering a sober black coffee.

Trent wouldn't drop the subject of sex, though, and I suppose I didn't really want him to.

'OK, tell me about your sexual awakening,' he pushed on.

I laughed. 'What makes you think I've been awoken?'

Trent looked at me sceptically, 'I think you know what's what. Am I right?'

I suppose I was flattered. I'm not usually such a push-over. I find it hard to accept compliments: 'You like my hair? Well what's wrong with my face?'; 'I look slimmer?

50

Was I so fat before?' Nevertheless, charm me about my sexual persona, and I'm anyone's.

'I think so, yes. You want to know about the first time I had sex?'

'Not necessarily. What about the first time you thought about sex?'

'I suppose you were six and did it with the babysitter.'

Trent had that look about him. You know the kind of face on American chat shows, which say, 'I've been shagging for years, I've won awards for it'.

'No, actually, I was seventeen.'

'Seventeen! What a waste.'

'That's why I'm catching up for lost time now.' He reached out and tried to hold my hand. I shrugged him off. I had realised that men, on the whole, were less sensitive about a bit of rejection than women were.

'My first kiss, adult kiss, was on holiday.'

'Hot weather can make you do funny things.'

'Yes,' I acknowledged, feeling the warmth on my shoulders and thinking, this time, it was not going to.

'I was fourteen. My parents took me to this little village in southern Spain. There was nothing to do there, *nada*. No discos, no clubs, no boys. It drove me crazy. Except, well, there was this one waiter, who was nice, and he always served us, and we always gave him a tip. And every night when we got up from the table, he gave me a kiss on my forehead. And then he and my parents laughed. I don't know why, but that just made me feel ... so humiliated.'

The couple on the next table were now playing scribbled noughts and crosses on the paper tablecloth. Each game resulted in stalemate.

I remembered the asexual tone of his kiss. The way he'd looked conspiratorially at my parents, mocking me for not yet being a woman. But, whatever my appearances, I had been ready. I'd wanted a kiss on the lips. I was determined that his soft palate and mine would meet. I imagined it would be like squeezing tubes of red paint together.

'So?'

'So, one time I followed him back to the kitchens. He was on his break having a smoke. I walked up to him and waited. He did nothing. I stood as close to him as I could and I stared at him. I was crying inside, desperate for him to make a move, to treat me as an adult. Eventually, we kissed. His lips were soft, friendly on mine, but turned into something more urgent when I weaved my tongue between his teeth. I remember the shock as his smoky tongue entered my mouth. It was the most amazing thing. I'd been so worried about it, Frenching, snogging – whatever we called it – and then here it was, and it wasn't so difficult; our teeth didn't clash, our noses didn't invade. I didn't feel stupid anymore.'

The way his tongue had felt inside me made me grow dizzy. Everything else had ceased to exist except for our bodies, our mouths and our tongues. This tongue had opened me up. Sure, my mouth had always opened and closed before, but not in that way, that secret way. I pulled his head closer; I was really aggressive, I mean, for a kid. I was charged up with adolescent passion, not for him, exactly, but for something. Remembering that feeling made me feel hungry to experience it again. Now.

'Then what happened?'

'That was it. He had to work. I had to go. When I got back to England, I told all my friends. They thought I was the most experienced thing – you know foreign man, foreign place . . .'

I trailed off. Perhaps I was particularly susceptible to desire in a warm climate.

Prem appeared from nowhere and asked if we wanted anything else. He was too cool to bother using a notebook; he just stored all orders in his head, and then went to the kitchen where he helped cook. I ordered another coffee and he took away my empty cup. I thought I could feel his eyes burning flames into my back as he retreated.

'That guy –' Trent pointed at Prem, '– thinks all foreigners are sex-crazed beasts.'

'We are, aren't we?' I kept my eyes low.

Prem dumped down my coffee refill. He then strutted off to another table where he spent about ten minutes chatting with the girls. I felt jealous.

I tipped up a candle and teased the hot wax over the back of my hand. It felt nice. My fingers were hot and tightly surrounded. The wax droplets hardened admirably fast and then I peeled them off. I carried on watching Prem out of the corner of my eye. He seemed very chummy with the other customers all of a sudden.

Trent stroked my non-waxy hand. He touched my knuckles and I felt my mouth go numb. Out the corner of my eye, I could see Prem looking at us. When I was young, I'd wanted to grow up to be a spy. If I really were a spy, this would be my moment to get into the speedboat and whiz out to the gulf of Thailand.

'I'd like to kiss you,' Trent said softly.

'No, I don't think . . .'

'Honey.' He corrected himself quickly, 'I mean, Abbs, I really would like to spend the night with you.'

He leaned back in the chair, his head down, little boy lost.

'I'm sorry, Trent, but I've been totally honest with you. You know about my boyfriend. I didn't mean to give you false hopes.'

'Abby, he's at home. You're in Thailand. Why not just relax and enjoy the ride?'

'That's not going to happen.'

The space, the oceans and the continents between Roger and I only strengthened our love. The distance confirmed everything I had always known; Roger was the right man. Being here, stranded on a desert island, all this was just killing time, a diversion before my real life with him began. I was more than in love with him. This separation was a test. And I was passing with flying colours. This was grown-up love.

53

I felt tremendously proud of myself. Hot, stoned, my skin gleaming golden, wearing my best underwear, and still I was faithful. My parents were faithful, but what was the big deal about that if you never met an alternative? Real fidelity, like mine to Roger, stemmed from having choices and options, but not exploiting them.

Trent hovered and then he left. Prem was cleaning the floor. He swirled the mop in the warm soapy bucket and then deposited the bubbles on the floor. Then he cleaned the floorboards, wiping round and round again like a masseur.

I hoped that Prem realised that Trent had left without me. Trust me, Prem, I am not your average tourist.

Chapter Eight

The following afternoon, Selma was lying, swaying, on her hammock. She was like a lazy animal enjoying the fading rays of sunshine before the evening. I waved and then took my place in my hammock – the closest thing to sitting on a cloud. I fell asleep.

Three days later, the King arrives to a fanfare of royal trumpets and flags unfurling.

'I want to see a good performance, you know. This is the Sultan of Persia.' He consults another long scroll, 'He brought me spices, oil, and er, veils. I'll be over here if you need me,' he says cheerily in that voice that sounds so familiar again.

The Sultan, the fourth man she must see to, is just a boy compared to the others. She is becoming an expert at this. The previous day they laid her on a marble table in the centre of the room and tied her down, legs bent. The first man who took her was big and gentle and cried when she cried. The second man was skinny and faster. The third man was big and rough, not selfish, but hurried. She was just about to come when . . . oh, it was all over. She couldn't wait for the fourth and she spent the night before trying not to satisfy the longing between her legs.

This time, they tie her arms, but they don't fix her to the table, so she gets on top of him while she has the chance. Some of the audience is muttering. She is going to break a few hearts tonight. She straddles him. Her arms are wrenched behind her back and movement is difficult but . . . he is more experienced than he looks. He jerks up into her, and then with one lone finger, he parts her lips and feels his way to her aching clitoris. She is shocked, no one has tried this before, and he looks so young and meek. The audience hasn't noticed the difference in technique, and she doesn't want them to. She wants to come, to come, she's been waiting, wet and horny, for so long. She bounces up and down as vigorously as she can.

'Still at it?' booms the King from the other side of the room, 'I have number five for you here.'

Ignoring him, taking pleasure for herself, she slams down on man number four and just as she is about to come, she feels him shoot up inside her. He stares at her in wide-eyed amazement.

Then a courtier is all over them; a complaining petty bureaucrat. 'We can't have you like that. I'm surprised they allowed you to.'

He sends the Sultan away, and rearranges her, so she's on her hands and knees like a dog. She can't see who's behind her but presumably it's Prince number five.

'How's that?' asks the King, wandering over to check out his property.

'Terrific, your highness,' replies the voice behind her. Someone decides to give him a helping hand. A hand is dunked into her vagina, and her lips are held apart. And then the Prince thrusts forward. His weight is pressed on her back. She feels like the ox with the rat riding on top. He has a medium-size cock.

'Comfortable?' someone asks, and she would have said 'no', but they weren't talking to her, they were talking to the Prince. She was a bit of furniture, oh a nice piece,

Louis Fourteenth, or something, but she was not someone to talk to.

'Can I? Would it be OK if I played with her breasts?' requests the Prince. He's breathing shallowly and his voice comes out all mangled.

'What does he want?' asks the King, amused.

'He hasn't seen a woman's tits before,' the courtier responds.

'If you must,' someone else says. She feels his hands come around and cup her breasts. He squeezes the nipples tight with both hands while pounding her from behind. She pushes back onto him, and feels him respond in kind. They're screwing rhythmically, confidently. She wants to scream.

The courtiers disapprove if she gets too excited. They say she's not doing it for herself but for the others. She should show some restraint. They'll be furious if an orgasm occurs, spontaneously, in front of the King.

His hands roam round, grasping her nipple, tight, hard; like tight marbles and he's shaking his hand, twisting the nipples, flames of pleasure bursting through her. She lets out a groan, and she can see that the courtiers are struggling up.

'Shall I put the muffler on her, sire?'

The King doesn't reply, and so the courtier adds, 'She does make some rather, how can I say, animal sounds.'

'Animal sounds?' repeats the King.

'Can I touch her clit?' The Prince sighs.

'What's that, what did he say?' barks the King.

'The small pleasure nodule, he seems to want to make contact,' offers a courtier. They shrug an assent.

His fingers are soft, tender on her womanhood. How does he know so well?

She comes in a rage of pleasure, a storm of passion. Oh Jesus, Jesus, how did this happen, jerking and flailing like a drowning sailor, and then she feels herself melt in the sweetest sensation of all.

'Is she alright? The last girl didn't look so, so animated, did she?'

'She's fine, your highness,' bleat the King's sycophants. 'I think she's affected in a positive invigorating way.'

'You mean to say, she enjoys it?'

'Well, yes, I suppose so.'

'I see.'

The King pats her hand through the chains, and smiles.

'Very good, dear, keep up the good work.'

I woke up maybe ten minutes later, at the sound of footsteps close by. José appeared from the café area, a bronzed little devil, with two plump ice creams nestling in golden cones. He held them over his dark chest and strode up the front steps to the balcony. He was staring at my breasts. Somehow, the very notion of him staring seemed to make them fuller. I didn't know how Selma could stand his tongue-out gazing or his hypocritical possessiveness. But I suppose their lovemaking was good enough to forgive a few transgressions. Who minds how much attention is given to others if our needs are attended to so well?

He sat down on the stool next to Selma – now ignoring me. Her eyes lit up when she saw him. She made a move to rise, but he told her to sit back, relax.

'What are you doing?'

'I got you an ice cream. Here, vanilla, like you. I put a flake in it; that's me.'

He dangled it over her mouth and she reached up for it. I tried to close my ears, but I couldn't.

'I love your titties. Let me suck them.'

She raised herself just a little, and struggled out of her T-shirt. Underneath she was wearing a fancy swimsuit. He undid the string. He toyed with the laces and then peeled down the swimsuit. She was brown all over, a woody colour; the peaks of her nipples were mahogany. He drew down the costume to her waist.

The ice cream landed on her pinky brown orb. She

shivered and her breasts wobbled like blancmange. They were both looking at each other, smiling.

'Suck me then.'

'How?'

'Long hard licks.'

Roger said that we didn't need to tell each other what to do. We understood automatically what we wanted. I agreed with him, except ... except sometimes, you don't need to tell each other, but you want to. It's nice to say it, so horny to hear it. Evidently, Selma didn't have to instruct José on how she liked her bosom touched, but they both enjoyed articulating the words.

He licked the cream off her breasts. The cream disappeared in his tongue, and then he moved to her mouth and kissed her. I felt a cold shiver. I buried myself deep in the hammock. I hoped they had forgotten I was there. I felt like a child pushing myself up against the window, squashing my nose against the glass pane, staring imploringly at the treats inside.

'More,' she said and grasped the top of his head, directing him to her enticing bust. 'Put my nipples in your mouth.'

Pushing him down to serve her. Would he have been doing this to me if I'd had the middle seat?

'Suck them harder. I want to see the nipples harden.'

He paused, grinning up with his pearly white teeth, and then he popped the nipple into his mouth. I could almost taste it, too. I saw her hands wrap around him. She held his back, hoisting him into her.

'I want you.'

'I want you too.'

He lay on top of her and the hammock drooped under their combined weight. It was almost brushing the floor. They couldn't possibly fuck there. Her legs clenched around him then, as he raised off to undo his pants, he slid out of the hammock and onto the floor. I tried not to laugh but I couldn't help myself.

Lying there listening to them was more erotic than

anything I'd experienced before. It was pornography without the screen, pornography without the fat ugly guy. The direction was superb. I could see a flash of her breasts, her legs, his hands claiming her and hers taking him. I groaned in anguish. I wanted them to hear me, but I didn't want them to know.

'Let's go inside.'

No, don't go inside. Please don't go. I want to watch you being fucked.

He was laughing. I could see scratch marks on his torso. Red lines from Selma the wildcat.

But she was lazy – thank goodness, she was lazy. She held up her arm. She was still wearing the loose sarong.

'No, fuck me here.'

'I can't do what I want to do here.'

'What do you want to do?' she asked sweetly. She edged apart her sarong as I craned closer to see.

'I want to pump your pussy, and fuck you on the floor, so that you come.'

Oh God, if only someone would talk to me like that. My skin was flushed, and I bit my lower lip so hard that soon I felt the metallic taste of blood on my tongue. My hands were on my breasts. I squeezed them tight, feeling my nipples. I massaged my tits, thinking of the vision in front of me. I could feel the liquid excitement in my pussy. I would soak the hammock through.

He pulled at his pants. Imagine the heaviness, the weight of an erect dick like that. It emerged out of his pants like it was struggling to breathe. It was such a big bold cock. It was assertive, too, knowing its beauty, knowing its rights. I wanted to see him stuff it into her mouth. Show her who was boss.

Damn. He walked inside and she followed him. The sarong stayed on the hammock. She was just wearing her bikini bottoms; one side escaped up her arse. She didn't look back at me. I was staring at her bottom. The hammock had made marks, small patterned indents, in her skin. How would they fuck? Would he kiss her there? I moved my hands southward, I slipped fingers between my legs. I touched a tendril of velvet pubic hair. I wished they were her hands, his, I mean, I wished they were his.

Her bare feet made padding animal noises on the deck. Did they know how lucky they were? The ice cream, deserted, left a creamy puddle on the floor.

Later, Trent and I sat out on my balcony. Trent drank three cans of Thai beer and topped them off with Mekong whisky. Yuk, it tasted like petrol. The heat was still sultry. I was wearing a light long-sleeved shirt because of the mosquitoes. I'd been bitten a few times, my own fault, I suppose. The insects loved my sweet, hot blood and my legs were covered with angry red spots.

We were talking about life back at home, and how, yes, it all seemed so far away. I was aware I was thinking in rough, ungenerous clichés. How would I feel if Roger were conversing like this? But I had no emotional attachment to Trent, so we weren't having a relationship. Goodness, Roger, you couldn't think that I would actually like the fellow! It was only talk, dirty talk. Like phone chat lines, only better – because on those you always speak to Gary from Essex who wants to know if you have big tits (or so I've heard).

Trent was telling me a fantasy about a girl he had seen that day.

'She works in one of the second-hand clothes shops near the port. When she bends over she makes this little "humph" sound. She doesn't need to, it's not much of an effort, but she says, "humph" and I love listening to that. It encapsulates her, and before I know it, up goes the old boy. I've got a hard-on. I'm fourteen all over again. Titty's bending over.'

'That's her name?'

'No, that's my name for her. I like it. It conjures up lovely images. The funny thing is, she doesn't have a particularly tight arse. She's a slim girl, but her arse is kind of spread like treacle.'

'Cellulite – tell me about it!'

'Loose folds of womanly flesh that I could lose myself in.'

I wouldn't be talking like this if I were in England. But then I wouldn't have been talking to him if I were still there. Only by leaving had I discovered people outside the small spectrum I had built. If I were in England, we would be conversing about jobs or mortgages.

'How about blow jobs? Is it really different in your mouth, so different, I mean, from sex?' I asked coyly. I would never feel so easy about talking like this with anyone else.

'Yes, it's different. Y'know those military graduations on the movies? Well, you know how excited they are when they throw their cap up in the air? Having a blow job is the same feeling as that. And then imagine having the hat come down and land on your head! That's the best. Somehow it's like being swallowed up, being consumed, taken over; nothing can convey the sheer pleasure. It's like being nurtured. It must be like the big bang that led to evolution, like, like . . . I'd been thinking about it for years. It would be as if you'd spent the last six years waiting for Christmas and then, when it came, it was even bigger and better than you ever imagined. There are so few things in life that live up to your expectations, blow jobs do though.'

'It was the opposite for me,' I interrupted. 'I hadn't thought about oral sex at all. I knew people did it, but I didn't know normal people did. I was so unprepared. I thought there was an order. A rule of what you should and shouldn't do. We were kissing; we had just started kissing. He wasn't a bad kisser, except sometimes he would stab his tongue in my mouth, like he was fucking it. The deepness of his kissing had enthralled me. He seemed to savour every last drop of me. It was arousing and at the same time, I thought I was in control. Then his hands were pulling at mine, getting me to tug at his jeans. I felt the stiffness inside, as if he was smuggling something. We undid the jeans together – they were dark blue, red tag, expensive and he was very proud of them. The pants, I don't remember so well; he squirmed out of them so quickly. Then, there it was in front of me, the big purple monster with its bold mushroom head. It was amazing. It was like ... like a dinosaur. I'd heard about them, but had no idea that this was it. "Lick me," he kept saying. His voice was different from usual. You can't imagine my shock.'

I trailed off, remembering. Until that day, I'd thought men were these great powerful creatures. To have one of them whimpering, pleading, begging me, was an enormous turnaround. It was a side to men that I hadn't realised existed.

'So?' Trent said.

'I didn't want to, but he was quite persistent. I agreed to touch it, but only with my hands. He showed me how to rub it up and down. I quite enjoyed it: the pulses it made, the rivers of veins, the tiny hole at the end, the freckles, the way it responded to me, like an eager puppy. But then he looked all forlorn. "What's the difference," he asked, "your mouth or your hand?" And he convinced me, so I got down. At first I just looked at it. I took in the hugeness, the heaviness, and I just got used to it. Then I stuck out my tongue and licked it. I felt his cock with my tongue, silky and hard. That was glorious: the mixture, the contradiction. It was like a hot snowdrop, or a slow Concorde. And I experimented with it, licking. I drew my tongue up the shaft and down. It hardened. He liked it when I nuzzled him. If I wandered down to those clenched little balls and traced the little throbbing veins on the underside, he went nuts. He was sighing and stroking me like he was delirious. I went about it like a science project. Let's see what happens if we add a little saliva.'

I'd asked him all the way through how he was feeling. He'd been more tender with me then than ever before. I loved him then; I loved the great debt he felt he owed me. The pubic hair itched in my teeth. The balls shrivelling and then growing between my cheeks. His hands tighter on my head, and he was whispering the same thing over and over again, 'Lick me, lick me, lick me.'

'Do you spit or swallow?' asked Trent.

I gazed back at him shyly under a non-existent fringe.

'Guess.'

'Let's see. You've got a beautiful body, so maybe you're calorie conscious.'

I laughed.

'On the other hand, I think you wouldn't let that worry you – not when it comes to enjoying yourself. But then again, I don't think you'd do anything just to prove yourself to a man. If you don't like something, you can't be bothered. You've no need to impress. You have a "take me or leave me" attitude. So, on reflection, I would have to say, spit. Although you are welcome to prove me wrong.'

I smiled enigmatically.

The first time I gave Roger head we were in his house drinking wine. His friend called him on the mobile, and he started wittering on. I squatted down and started fiddling with his trousers. He had no escape. Sometimes, seeing a man in a public place makes me want to put my head between his legs and listen to him speak on ... speak on while I minister to him. I drank wine, left it swirling in my mouth, and then covered his cock with my mouth. His cock was lovely, smelling all clean after his shower, and I began to writhe around the floor. Teasing his cock, flicking up and down the shaft, alternately gentle, passionate and persuasive. He twisted me round and repositioned me so that he could enter my hole with his fingers, while I soaked him with my tongue. 'Huh, huh,' he panted, his eyes were rolling and he looked gloriously defeated, as though he'd just lost a battle.

'We shouldn't be talking like this,' I whispered, suddenly ashamed. I shivered goose bumps.

''S'alright,' Trent comforted. 'Actually, I wanted to tell you something, Abby. I also have a girlfriend. She's back in the States. So . . .'

I could guess what he hoped for by telling me. He meant, 'hey we're equals, we can get it on'. No strings, both guilty, both sworn to secrecy. So that Adam was crazy for the apple too. It wasn't all Eve's doing. Nice play, Trent, but . . .

'I'm sorry I kept it secret from you,' he finished.

'I don't consider that secret,' I said defensively. 'It's not like you lied, or covered it up deliberately, did you? It's just information that you hadn't got round to telling me yet – like maybe you play football every Wednesday or that you went to Timbuktu.'

'Well, no. I didn't want to tell you because I was afraid it would affect us. If you knew, maybe you wouldn't want to talk. And I play football on Thursdays, not Wednesdays.'

'Why should I feel guilty about chatting? It's only words. Let's say I was a writer, and I was writing a love scene between a man and a woman. Should I feel guilty? Or what if I was an actor?'

'But that would be different. That would be part of your job.'

'So just because I'm not getting paid for this, it makes it less legitimate, you mean? Is that what you mean?'

Trent looked peeved. I'd won hands down. I noticed that his hands were down his trousers and probably had been for most of our conversation.

'You and I are nothing more than friends on holiday.'

He sat there shaking his head.

'I read you wrong, Abby, I thought you were brave.'

I interrupted excitedly. 'You were the one who said sex was best alone . . . beating the solitary meat, you said.'

'I would like to explore you.'

He made me sound like I was the shipwreck where they do their scuba-dives.

'You already know me, inside and out.'

'Correction. I know you outside, and would like to know your insides.'

'Well, I'm flattered. But you can't.'

We sat in silence, contemplating the world. Trent really was handsome in a fresh way. His eyes were green with brown spokes, like a sunflower, and his teeth were even. He looked very disappointed. I hate it when people are upset with me. I know everyone does, but I find it most disquieting. I could never have a job where I had to distribute bad news.

'I suppose I've got a secret too,' I said to cheer him up.

Intrigued, Trent sat forward, his chin in his hands. He was almost kissable.

'Let me guess. You don't really have a boyfriend. You're young, free and single.'

'No, nothing as interesting as that.'

'He's not a he, but a she?'

'What? No, actually my boyfriend is married. He's going to leave his wife soon, though.'

'Shit!' said Trent incredulously.

I was surprised at his reaction. I would have thought with all his piercing, his tattoos, and his supposedly outlandish lifestyle, that he would have been more open-minded. His mouth fell open dumbly, and I could see the little diamond knob on his tongue, twinkling like a little star.

'Do you really love him?' he asked finally.

The way he asked was as though he had never been in love himself.

'I love him to bits.'

As soon as I said it, I thought what a bizarre idea that was. As though my love would cause him to disintegrate into bits. But then it was better than 'love to death' a phrase I have always hated. I get this horrid image of shagging someone so much that eventually his or her body gives way.

'I love him, completely and utterly,' I said. Love felt strange without a rider.

I had never told anyone that he was married. I'd got so used to keeping secrets. But Trent wouldn't tell anyone. No one knew me here. That was the great thing about being on holiday. You can say what you like, act how you like, and it doesn't really matter.

We shook hands, curiously restrained after we had bared our hearts. Scratching my legs, I walked inside.

'See you, Trent.'

'See you, Abigail.'

I'd told Prem that I was having difficulty sleeping. That evening, after Trent departed, Prem appeared with an electric fan in addition to the one I already had. I didn't like to tell him that it wasn't the heat that kept me awake at night, but the noisy heat from next door.

When Prem stood near me in the room, I trembled. I stared at the floor; my face was in flames. He would never ever want to know me, he must have thought me a fool. When he spoke, I only partially listened to his words, but I looked deep into his mouth and wished myself there. I imagined lying on top of him, cram-feeding my tits to him.

When he left, I rewound the brief conversation we'd had and replayed it again and again. I gave myself better lines, and him more romantic responses. I had had this incredible urge to wish him goodnight by touching him on the chest, reaching out and feeling his ribs. Thank goodness I didn't. He would have thought I was mad.

I hated myself for my weakness. I wasn't someone who stepped off an aeroplane and declared love for the first man – or woman – I met. I wasn't like Selma – and I certainly didn't like Selma. The reason I couldn't stop thinking about her – them – fucking, was just . . . just proximity. I didn't just unbutton and shag every time I felt like it. Life wasn't a stag or hen party. I wasn't that kind of girl. Just because I'd left England didn't mean I'd left my morals behind. Without a structure, without self-restraint, where would we be?

Roger, please come soon. Before it's too late. Do you remember how we kissed on the pier at Brighton? The wind whipped my hair in your face, but you didn't mind. You hoisted me up on the railings, my legs were trembling and I thought I would die of happiness. I do miss you so much. Hope you miss me, just half as much as I miss you.

I lay on the bed, wrapping my sheets around me. I gripped the pillow between my legs. To be unfaithful because you fall in love is one thing, but to be unfaithful just because you're hot and horny is something else and I would not be so cheap. Surely, there wasn't long to wait now.

The arms of the fan whirred round hypnotically, but still I couldn't sleep until the sun began its unstoppable rise.

Chapter Nine

*A*nother hot afternoon. Quiet so intense that I thought there was something wrong. Maybe the island was wracked with typhoid, or malaria. Maybe everyone had run away. I read sleepily. Yawning over the pages, blurry eyed. There were plenty of sharks around the tropical islands, but there hadn't been a dangerous one for some time. However, the book urged caution, especially for women scuba-divers.

'Don't swim out too far. Sharks can smell prey from miles away.'

I was dozing, dreaming in my room, naked as Godiva. The odd fly or wasp was my only visitor. I rolled on the sheets drifting on a sea of strange dreams. The mattress was lumpy. Tiny ash-holes and little stains were the sheets' accessories. Empty milkshake glasses were on the floorboards with dead teas in brown glass cups.

And then José and Selma started their shagging siesta. Their pleasure rang through the walls, accentuating my isolation. No one wanted me. I was alone.

'Yes, baby, yes!' Selma was egging him on, and he was snorting his way inside her. I imagined him at work, like an animal snuffling for truffles.

'With your tongue,' she said loudly. It was as clear as if we were in the same room.

'Yes, just like that.'

So he was giving her oral sex. Tasting her sticky discharge, guzzling down her juice. Nose in that pretty pubic triangle of hers.

'Bite my ears.'

I lay in bed growing wet between my legs. Guiltily – I swear I didn't want to, I didn't plan to – I sneaked my hand to my sex.

'Hold me tighter.'

I played a tune with my fingers to accompany her rhythmic panting. They didn't know, of course. They wouldn't suspect. All the same, I felt like a thief, stealing part of their fun. I was groaning along with them.

'Yes, yes!' she bellowed. 'Do me now, screw me, you cunt, you fucking cock, do me now.'

If only I could see them. All I could see was the ceiling of my bungalow, the criss-crossing of the wooden slats. I opened my pussy, baring my red flame. I searched for my clit, and slipped my fingers up and down there. I could smell my own arousal. Under my arms too, I was giving off a strange damp scent.

I tried to fix Roger in my mind. Roger, do this to me. Instead, it was Prem who bounced in. Prem and I were on the aeroplane, fucking, and everyone was looking. Prem's dark hands were cupping my arse, lifting me on to him. We didn't attempt to hide it – we couldn't. No, I was hollering my pleasure, screaming ecstasy, and Prem was howling. He was fucking me so hard that his balls knocked into my loins. I felt the prick go higher and higher – the movement, the vibrations – and he pulled at my taut nipples, pulling them out, making them look obscene, like I was just a plaything, a blow-up doll, just there for the in-house entertainment.

Roger was watching me. 'Go for it, girl,' he ordered. Atagirl, give him it harder. I told myself not to rush, but I was like a shopaholic at the Harrods sale. Prem, Prem, give it to me, harder. Roger's cock was hard, and he was rushing his hands up and down at the sight of me. Wanking himself, jerking off as he saw me screwed by another man, harder, harder, more, until the white milky fluid flew away from him. I sighed and pressured myself further and then I was coming, coming. But they were still going on next door.

Eventually the noise subsided and my voyeur's shaking diminished, but still I found it impossible to lose myself in sleep. I'd betrayed Roger. If I was going to fantasise, then I should fantasise about him. If I insisted on fantasising about other men – which, of course, everyone does, so I'm told – then I should at least have the decency to leave him out of the proceedings.

There was a scuffling noise outside. I leaped to the window and saw there were two kids circling each other thunderously, then swiping each other with skinny ankles. The smaller one kicked and pow! He smacked the big one in the cheek with the side of his foot. I flung a towel around me and stomped towards them.

'Stop, stop. What on earth are you doing?'

The little tiger was strong. He swung around and bashed the bigger one again. They ignored me. Perhaps they didn't understand. I tried to grab the little one – although he was the more ferocious. Then I saw that Prem was there. Prem was encouraging them! The shock transition from seeing the dream-Prem to real life-Prem made me blush furiously.

'They shouldn't fight,' I said lamely.

'They're only playing,' Prem responded defiantly.

'It's not good for them.'

'Rubbish. They're kids.'

He picked up one of the boys and they began mock fighting together. Prem threw him up in the air. The kid loved it; he was clamouring for more. Arms out for his turn, the other demanding with bright button eyes, pleading, following him around. He tickled them, lifting up their T-shirts, revealing bellies brown as oak.

71

Giggling, slapping, he chased them and then, when he ran away, they chased him. The children relented, and Prem straightened his shirt and told them to scoot, and they disappeared laughing. The little one's laces were undone.

Prem faced up to a tree. He arched one leg into the air at right angles to his body. He looked incredible. His muscles were shining, taut and separate. His face was composed. I wondered if his expression changed when he had sex, or if he was equally impassive.

He stretched, bending, and then started jogging and skipping like a boxer. José and Selma were out on their balcony, to see what was going on. Selma was looking at me, a curious smile playing on those raspberry lips. She still looked high-coloured. Even if you hadn't heard them, from her face you would instinctively know how these two entertained themselves.

'Why do you teach children to fight?' I asked.

Prem looked at me contemptuously. 'It's about discipline and control over your body.'

I wondered if he thought I didn't have any. Perhaps he was disgusted at my fleshy arms and was proposing kickboxing as the cure. The towel, as an item of clothing, isn't renowned for flattering the fuller figure.

'If something's wrong, it has to be said.' I already knew I was losing this battle.

'By you?' he asked scornfully. I wished I had worn more clothes.

'Who else is there?'

'It's natural,' he persisted. He brushed a hair out of his chocolate eyes. I couldn't stop myself from staring at him. My chest rose and fell with the tension.

'A lot of things are natural but it doesn't mean we have to do them,' I said, facing him off.

The searing heat produced trickles of water on my thighs and the backs of my knees but, despite his exertions, Prem didn't even look warm. My towel slipped

72

down, revealing one plump, very white breast. I yanked up the unfaithful covering and rushed inside.

In the evening, I decided to call Roger again. I needed his voice, his reassurance. As I was walking down the main street, I slipped. Losing my balance, I reached out for the nearest solid thing to hold onto.

'Oww!'

I was groping hold of the most incredible person I had ever seen in my life. I had her by the bosom. I removed my hands.

'I'm so sorry.'

Her T-shirt was wet. It outlined her breasts gloriously. I averted my eyes.

'No problem,' she said. Her accent was soft Thai; her tongue cushioned each word. She touched the side of my face gently. Hers wasn't a smile; it was heaven stretched between two olive cheeks, ruby lips, and white pearly teeth.

'Beautiful.' I backed away, bowing. She was tall, she must have been about six-foot, and everything about her seemed elongated. The long calves, skinny thighs, elastic arms were all stretched out. She looked like a reflection in a crazy mirror. Her torso was a touch too gangly to be perfect, but she had a heart-shaped face; her large eyes were stolen from Bambi, her cheekbones pumped full of oestrogen. Her lips stuck out like rubber pillows. She too was teetering, on high heels, holding onto her drinks, as if they were stabilisers. Everyone looked at her – I mean, gazed after her – as though staring at some freak, or miracle of nature.

Two English men flanked her. At least, I guessed they were, from their Union Jack shorts. I recognised one of them from the beach.

'Alright, darling? Wanna join us?'

What was a woman like her doing with idiots like them?

'Beautiful, you are,' she said. She seemed in no hurry to move on.

I tried to speak Thai.

'*Kop kum cha*,' I said, mistakenly saying the male form of the words 'thank you'. This made her laugh. Her broad skinny shoulders shook. She was square-shouldered like a swimmer and fashionably narrow-hipped. Somehow, she was both defined and refined. She said her name was Lily, and I thought she was just like a flower.

The men's hands were on her possessively as they walked away. One pinched her arse. I watched as thumb and finger dived into her glorious butt. The other one rested his arm protectively over her shoulder, like a doctor giving his patient a guided tour of the hospital. She looked back at me and winked.

She should have been in the movies. I felt suddenly angry that a beautiful woman like her should have been with them. Not that I knew anything about the situation, but they were unworthy.

I went back to the same telephone shop. He loves you, he loves you a lot, he loves you. Roger picked up on the fifth ring. He loves you. That was all!

'I *am* trying to get away, Abby, but you know how it is,' he said before I even asked.

'No, I don't, frankly. You promised you would come straight after me. Why don't you keep your word?' I was irked. He wasn't going to push me around, not after the day I'd had.

'Darling, look, why don't you come back to England and we'll discuss it properly?'

'We've discussed it a million times, and . . .'

And then he was protesting, 'That's not fair, Abbs. Circumstances made my decision, not me.'

'It looks like you've made up your mind. I just want to know where I stand.'

'Abby, I love you,' he said fiercely, and my heart leaped. Oh, he did, he did love me.

Then suddenly his voice changed, and he grew all clipped and business-like. 'Thank you so much for your call. Yes, I'll be in touch.'

I knew what that meant. Dear wifey was in the room with him.

'You wanker,' I shouted as loudly as I could.

With hindsight, I suppose I shouldn't have called him that.

I walked away flushed and angry. My knuckles were tight. I suddenly understood why kids might want to learn kickboxing.

I didn't want to go out after that. Trent was putting in too much time. He was clearly angling for a promotion and I couldn't offer him a position. I didn't want to lead him on any further than he felt he'd been led. But he came over to my bungalow anyway and, since I was feeling bruised after the sour conversation, I was friendlier than I had planned.

I swung on the hammock while he sat beneath. I felt his eyes wander up and down my body and I couldn't help feeling flattered, if a little awkward. It was difficult to rearrange myself and, when I tugged clothes from one area, they only crept up from another. But it was idyllic, just the low hum of voices and the waves nudging the shore. Even the mosquitoes stayed away. Trent drank beer, swallowing loudly. I watched his Adam's apple flicker up and down. It somehow reminded me of a cuckoo clock.

'Heard from your man?'

'No – I, well . . . yes, he isn't coming yet.'

Was that a smile crawling over Trent's non-committal face?

'I guess he writes a lot.'

'No, but who needs letters?'

'Right,' agreed Trent.

We stayed there a while. I looked up at the stars in the sky, so much more beautiful here than anywhere else. OK, so they were the same stars that shine over England, but here . . . With anyone else it would have been romantic. I listened to the chirp of grasshoppers and the opening of cans and sighed.

Trent's eyes were closed and he was lying back, at home in the world.

'Tell me a fantasy you've had recently.'

'A fantasy?' I asked wonderingly.

'Yeah, the last time you masturbated, what did you think about?'

The last time I masturbated? A few hours earlier, actually, in the sea. No one could see me; at least, I thought they couldn't. There was something really weird, yet really clean about wanking in the sea. I'd actually thought about Selma and Prem. Selma made Prem have sex with me. He didn't want to do it. I was ashamed, although I had not collaborated in this.

'It's not my fault, Prem,' I say.

Selma is nasty and strong. 'Get down,' she urges, and I put him in my mouth. He stays resolutely soft. I admire his power, and then I feel his penis flicker and twitch, just like an eyelid at first, small as that, but I know I've found his weakness. 'More, more,' shouts Selma. Finally, he turns rigid, and I feel a lurching sense of satisfaction. 'Please, Selma,' I say, 'let's stop now.'

'No, you wanted this.'

'She wanted this,' she says to him, the telltale.

'Not like this,' I scream at her, hurling the words out. 'Not like this, not like this.'

'Do it,' she insists. Poor Prem is wincing and crying but he climbs into my heavenly hot pussy.

The water had lapped at my legs; the waves tossing me a little, just gently, up and down. And my fingers explored myself, growing faster and faster, like a flamenco dancer, whirling and whirling inside my space.

Trent was giggling. 'I can't wait to hear this!' he said.

He wanted to hear that I thought about fucking him. Well, he was not going to. I never thought about shagging him – except in passing.

'OK. I meet up with Roger at the airport. We go to my place and we fuck. Umm, he's on top, then I take over.'

'That's it?'

'That's it. Now, you tell me something,' I said. I'd got off the hook quite easily.

'Well.' He blushed. 'Mine's quite typical. Two girls, one guy thing.'

'Uh huh. Details please.'

'I don't . . .'

'Trent!'

'OK, OK, I'm a lifeguard. You know, the hunk that sits up on that chair, and all the girls fancy him. From there, I get this fantastic view. I mean, it's like walking along here, on the beach and all these girls, showing off their legs and their boobies, only this pool is better than here, 'cos it's women only.

'I convince the most beautiful girl to come into the changing room. "Oh, I'm going to have to teach you some moves privately," I say. She undoes her bikini and looks at me all naïvely, all bright-eyed and bushy-tailed. Well, then I kneel at her, trembling. I touch her pubes and part her legs. I'm ever so gentle. I say to her that I'll make her a good swimmer, that we both have to be comfortable in water. I gently finger her, and say, "Feel this? You're so wet. It's important to use this power." She allows me, and then I open her wider and lick her, I'm still kneeling, worshipping her, and I put my hands on her soft little titties and murmur what a good swimmer she will be.

'And then another girl walks in. She backs up, she's scared, and I say "It's OK, it's just extra lessons. Come over here." And she walks over, shivering. I tell her to get out of the wet suit and she does. I still nurse and nibble at the other girl, and she quivers when I touch. "Down here," I say to the new arrival. "Let's practise underwater swimming." So she gets down, and I let her take my place, licking at the other girl's fountain. And they are both trembling, and the one receiving is close to orgasming, and the one giving is getting all excited herself. I start wanking, I can't help myself. You can imagine the sight, these nubile bodies pleasuring each other, and not knowing what they're doing. Then the first girl whispers that she wants to sit on me, so I let her, cold on the changing room floor tiles. She presses down on me, but I make the other one sit on my face, so I'm guzzling her friend while I fuck her. Then we take turns, swapping, varying slightly, their pubises are different, equally fantastic, but different, and their responses are different. And that's it!'

'Very nice,' I admitted.

'I love giving oral sex,' said Trent, 'I mean, if I had to choose between fucking and that, I would chose the oral every time.

'Why?' I said, not just a little aroused.

'Well, you've got your head between a woman's legs, and it's a private place, right? She doesn't show this to anyone, not anyone, yet not only is she showing it to you, she's open. She's saying, "please touch me, spoil me". Fuck – and then when they start rubbing their mush in my face. Do you like being licked?'

'Um, yes, sometimes.'

'Tell me about the first time you had oral sex,' he said.

'No, you tell me, I've never heard a man's version before.'

'I suppose it's like instinct, really. What would it be like to put my tongue there?'

'And?'

'Well, I put my tongue there, and it was like, when the plane touched down at Koh Samui airport: fucking hell, I've arrived! This is my place.'

'What does it feel like?' I whispered.

'Soft, tender, open, and vulnerably mine.'

'Like fruit?'

'Like human fruit. Like flesh, like wetness, like open, like a mouth. And then when she started thrusting up into my face, grinding her pelvis into me, I couldn't believe it. I clasped her to me. I fixed her to me, like a facemask, and she was letting out these groans, and hot, fast, furious talk. The wetness – oh God, it was like the rainy season down there.'

'Did she come?'

'Honey, you're talking to Grandmaster Licky-lick.'

'Hey, the truth please.'

'I think that's a very orgasm–centric view of the world,' said Trent, pretending to be pompous. He made me laugh. 'I thought men were criticised for asking that question.'

'I just want to know!'

'You'll kill me, but I don't know.' Trent shook his handsome face. His hair was bleached all different colours by the sun – although I think he may have helped it along.

'Typical man!'

'Yes, I am a typical man. It's not that I'm not interested in a woman's pleasure – I would love to find it – but it's buried under so much. How was it for you? Did the earth move the first time you were pleasured orally?'

'Pleasured orally – sounds like one of those things on the menu, and the answer is no. I couldn't stand it. What? Go there? With all that slobbering! The first time I had oral sex was before I had vaginal sex. I was so surprised that I just kind of stood there wondering, "what's he up to now?" He pushed me down on to the settee, but he wasn't there where I thought he was. He was looking at my pubic hair, and then thrusting his face forward. And at first I thought, how sweet he's kissing me all over, so men do mean it when they say they want to do that, but then he was running his tongue along me, as if he were licking a stamp. What are you doing, preparing to post me? "I want to lick you," he said. I don't think I said anything. He licked and licked. It was warm and friendly and I felt like he was looking after me, but at the same time, although I felt the stirrings of pleasure and surging wetness, he was jamming his tongue into me, and moaning about how good I was, and I felt left behind. What was so good about that? I'd tasted my own juices before, and it was nothing special.'

How would Roger feel if I talked about boyfriend's pre-him to other men? Roger wouldn't know. I ached so much. I was sixteen again, wanting something but not knowing what. Only I wasn't sixteen; I should have known exactly what it was.

'I still have some hang-ups about it, even today.'

'Darling! You wouldn't with me.'

'Actually, there was one time . . .'

'I thought so.'

'He had a beard and thick glasses. Like jam jars, they really were.'

'Your taste in men is charming. You give hope to every ugly git in the country.'

'It was lovely. It was a one-night stand. We met in a pub, and I liked him immediately. He was so unsexy, unthreatening, not one-night stand material at all. But it was fun seducing him. And Roger had gone back to his wife, and I was still smarting from the pain of it. I positioned my hand on his thigh carelessly. It was summer, and I was wearing cut-down shorts, and I was spilling out of them, too, and then one thing led to another . . .

But, you see, when he took off his glasses, I knew he couldn't see much. Plus I was drunk. I kind of liked showing him my wares, like in *Oliver Twist*. "Who will buy my wonderful flowers?" He lay down and asked me to sit on top of him. I mean, on his face. I did. I'd been very careful with him before; I thought he was fragile, delicate, but now, I was like a bull in a china shop. I literally squashed down on his face. You know grape pickers? They stomp down on the grapes for the juice; well, I squeezed on to him; his nose, and his mouth. He loved it. He caught hold of my sides and thrust me back and forth over him. It was fucking amazing, his nose and his mouth were bobsleighing down my slopes. Mmm.'

I stopped. Trent was frowning bemusement.

'And the fact that he was short-sighted helped?'

'Ooh yes.'

I stopped. I felt terrible. No, I felt horny. I could feel the wetness form between my legs. My pussy was contracting enthusiastically, ready to welcome in a foreign body, a foreign somebody.

'Baby, I'll feign any disability you want. Did he make you come?'

'Er, yes.'

'What about your boyfriend?'

'Yes, he's pretty good.'

Roger went about his work there so diligently, so properly. Oh God, Roger, I need you now, more than ever before. Once, he popped me over the fireplace – no, there was no fire – it was Christmas time, and all the cards came tumbling down. He wrapped my legs around his shoulders and plunged his tongue up my pussy, and I meowed up the chimney into the sky.

'I am a cunning linguist,' Trent said, and nearly cracked a rib laughing.

I was aware, so aware, of Trent's breath, the rhythm of his breathing, and I wanted him to hold me, but I didn't want him to fuck me.

Do men ever understand that?

'Do you want to sit here?'

'No, I, I think I'll go inside. It's getting cold.'

I didn't ask him in, but he came through automatically as though I had. There was nowhere else to sit, so he sat next to me on the bed. I felt the warmth of his body, and the need to be intimate with it overwhelmed me.

'What about Roger?'

'He's a bastard,' I said and started to cry. It was his fault I was half way around the world without him. And now he was saying it was mine!

The lights went out, and suddenly there was darkness. 'Shit,' said Trent, fumbling. He lit a candle and a mosquito coil, and then he came back on the bed. The green coil let off this wonderful musky scent. In candlelight Trent looked gentler; soft and fuzzy even. I could pretend he was someone else. We kissed. And when we kissed again, I could feel his piercing setting the bed of my tongue alight. It tickled me, it promised me more, and I wanted to have more of it washing around me. I averted my eyes, focusing on a small section of the wooden ceiling. He slid his tongue along my gums, and I could feel my cunt dancing. If I didn't think too hard, I felt so good. It was nothing more than an extension of what we were doing anyway, just moving along the line of friendship. If anything, it felt mushy, natural, and nourishing. It was warm and tender whipping around my mouth. Oh Roger, oh Roger, you feel so good.

No, no, stop it. This isn't Roger.

'No. Wait.' I pulled back, dazzled, disorientated.

'Please, Abbs.'

'I can't. I don't want more.'

'Alright, on one condition. Kissing only. No more than kissing.'

We kissed again. He was both rough and gentle; I felt the warm bristle of his chin against mine. Pacing, his timing was good. Just when I thought I couldn't hold back on the gentle stuff, he would pulse deeper, more passionate, and then when I thought I'd had enough of that, he'd go softly; licking my lips, our tongues meeting outside our mouths, like an exotic snake dance. And instead of just one glorious feeling, the piercing seemed to exaggerate each sensation by a million times. I couldn't get enough of it. Even when the piercing knocked against my teeth, I was aroused, it only reminded me of the pleasure when it ran up and down my tongue.

I couldn't help from putting my arm around him and drawing him in. Kissing is one of the first things to go when you start having regular sex, and yet kissing is sometimes better than sex. Trent was drawing me closer and closer too and soon I was pulling at him, I didn't mean to, I had no ulterior motive or plan, but he did feel damn nice. The jewel on the tip of his tongue tickled mine, and I wanted more of it. I wanted it all over me, everywhere. He seemed to really savour me, he liked my taste, and I wanted to go deeper in him.

'I know you want to.'

He put his hand on my knee, as though tipping the scales further in his favour – which indeed they did. I felt delight surge through my skin at his touch. Moving up to my thigh, moving up, fast like a car in a high-speed race, sure the cops would stop him in a minute. Arriving at the damp protection of my knickers. He was a centimetre away from my crack. I was moistening up, warm and ready, and I hated myself for it. The knicker material clung valiantly to me, a lost cause.

Roger bought me these knickers, two Christmases ago. They belong to Roger as much as they do me. I wonder if Roger knew that if a woman is wearing the underwear that he bought that she is unlikely to wear it to screw another man. Does he give me underwear just to wield his power over me?

Trent fingered the crotch aside. I let out a sigh of assent – I said it was unlikely, I didn't say she wouldn't.

His finger was smooth and searching. He tickled my bush, fingered apart the hairs to find his entrance. Now the car had slowed down, he attempted to reverse into the parking space. The gap was bigger than it had looked.

'Huh.' I swallowed sharply, as he swerved right up my soaking pussy, feeling the encouragement of my slippery, engorged sex.

'You're nervous, aren't you?'

'Yes,' I said. No one other than Roger – and the jam-jar glasses man – has been there for five years. What if, after all this time, I discover I'm not normal? What if my body repulses him? What if my genitals are deformed?

'Jesus, you feel so good, so wet.'

'No,' I said feebly. Not in my Roger knickers. Take them off before you masturbate me, and then masturbate me to death – or at least 'til I come. Trent worked me like a professional. I was wet, slick and burning for more.

'Let me just kiss you there.'

'No.' I was embarrassed. But his fingers were climbing in and out of my sex. He added more fingers to caress my clitoris. Oh yes, he was working well. His pacing was so fucking right. He has his hand up my cunt, I thought absurdly. This man, this man I didn't know, was stroking my pussy, fingering my most private parts. He was on my clitoris, flicking me, making me shiver like it was cold outside.

'I want to lick your inner lips,' he whispered hotly in my ear.

Did he have to be so up-front about everything? Was this the American way? I heard that there was a university in the States where you have to get spoken consent for every sexual thing. Asking and announcing every stage. 'May I touch your boobies?' etc. etc. Well that's not my way; just get down and get on. I don't want you to ask me if I want my clitoris stimulated, you must know I do. I don't want you to ask me if I want my pussy loved, you must know I do. Did we have to have a committee meeting before anything was done?

'No,' I murmured, aware only of how strange I sounded. 'No licking, thank you.'

'Darling,' he nagged. 'I just want to make you feel good.'

'What about my boyfriend?' I protested. I should have known that that is the last resistance. When a man hears those words, he knows that after breaking through enemy lines, the enemy is readying to surrender.

'What about my girlfriend?' he retorted, before adding, 'Look, he won't find out. Besides, I won't lay a finger on you, I promise. Just my tongue.'

'Just your tongue?'

I wondered if there was a way round it. Was it adultery if we don't fuck? If I just lay back and thought of England? Surely in the overall scheme of things this wasn't a crime against humanity. It was just like going to the gynaecologist. Or something like that . . .

'You sure that's OK? No sex: you don't mind?' I said checking.

'Just my tongue,' he promised.

'OK,' I agreed reluctantly. Make me feel better, oh please, tidy up my life.

He moved over to me, on the bed. He got everything prepared. He pulled down the mosquito net, so we were cocooned in white lace. It looked wonderful; like a spider's web. I sank back, enjoying the fairy tale: Snow White's house and here, to treat me well, was my Prince. Who was I? I was the poisoned apple. Lick me, eat me, and rub my core with gentle fingers.

He opened my legs easily, like opening an envelope – an unstuck one. His face, his stranger's face, was hovering over me. The bed sighed beneath us, like a fat old man. The iron frames unsettled, wheezed. He told me to take off my sarong, and I struggled with the knot. Damn it. I wanted to ask him who the hell he was – I mean, really, who was he? – but I couldn't. He told me to take off my panties real slowly. I did, carefully, showing him the rude bits.

'You're good at that,' he whistled admiringly.

'I take my knickers off every night,' I said crisply, now all efficient.

Let this be functional, clearing the system. A sexual enema for my good health. This was purely a meeting of genitals. An exchange of fluid. Just getting pleasured – this would be great. Screwed without the chitchat. I was not going to have to talk to him. I just wanted to feel good.

But what kind of man would agree to this? I left the panties scrunched up on the floor, and lay back. Tonight we would christen the bed. The first spillage – not the first orgasm – the first coupling would take place. It was with the wrong person but ... I spread my legs as far apart as I could. Travel doesn't just broaden your mind – it can open your legs. I wanted to feed Trent's face with my pussy. I was a wide open hole, I didn't know what I was doing anymore, the sticky wetness, his unholy roughness was sweeping me, and his hands too were exploring my hips, my waist, my bottom.

I knew he was looking at me, studying my pussy. He must have seen loads with his experience. He was tendering the pink slit, sliding his tongue along the swollen cleft. I pushed his face down to me. I wouldn't let him escape; he could suffocate there, he could drown there, but I was going to come there, come hell or high water. He was nuzzling me, like a glorious suction, hoovering my clit. He was servicing my fanny. My clitoris was a quivering ball. I started rocking hard towards him, and he responded by licking and slurping on the up movement, and rubbing and making his hand tremble on the down. Up and down I rode. I had one arm across my mouth so I sank my teeth in: work me, like a piece of machinery, I will respond. Squeeze me, lick me, bite me. Make the back of my neck tingle, and the backs of my legs. Don't forget my nipples, yes, they need loving too, and my lips, and my ears, and my arse. Yes, please, give it to me, whoever you are.

I was almost on automatic pilot. I was so turned on; I was swaying back and forth, rocking on the bed. I am going to come, now. Deeper, get your tongue right up my cunt, lick me out, eat me up, taste my orgasm. His frantic action continued more urgently, and I responded by lunging my cunt to and fro, fast as forest fire, pushing him further and further up me. Oh God, it couldn't go on. It mustn't stop. I could feel the jewel in my crown, tenderly caressing my clitoris, stimulating my crease, working like a fucking charm. He sucked, and then he slathered over my clitoris, wagging his tongue. I could feel the whoosh and the incredible force of my orgasm. I could hear myself making sounds and saying words I had never said before. I was an embarrassment. Even the lovely Selma did not come as forcefully as I did.

Chapter Ten

*S*ix, seven, eight, nine, ten. All the Lords are leaping.
The best was number seven. How he managed to
prise her hands free she'll never know but he did, and he
put them on his prick, so that she could squeeze his shaft
every time he was near to coming, so that they could go
on for ever. The court cleared. The day crowd left and
the evening people looked bored as she and he rocked
together. The courtiers fussed around, disapprovingly
making enquiries, 'Are you thirsty, cold?' But he
wouldn't get up and leave her. No, he fed her sweet
grapes, while his cock fed her honey.

Finally, he said that he had to go, the sun was setting,
but first he wanted to see her blush and beseech him
with joy. Her hair was tousled and wild, and she tightened around him and she felt like a giant was coming in
her sacred tunnel. She could feel each throb and pulse
and the stream of wetness mixed with her own.

She serviced the remaining men over the next few
days. She came easily and that made the whole arrange-
ment so much more pleasant.

But then at the end of it, after number eleven, there
was no end of it.

'Just one round?' pooh-poohed the courtiers, 'Heaven's

no, there's plenty more where that came from! There are more things for you to do . . .'

She was still enslaved, she was to have no ideas above her station. She heard them muttering that she was an 'upstart'.

She's suspended from the ceiling, it's half hammock, and half rocking chair. Her pubis is at eye level. They can spread apart her legs, as easily as opening a newspaper.

It's like apple bobbing, but this time, they linger, their faces between her legs, not catching anything but enjoying being there. And this time, it's every day, not just Halloween. It makes her howl with pleasure, but also frustration, because however long their tongues are, and however wily they are, just as she gets going, just as she gets really horny, the hammock swings her away. They have made her come with their pricks, now they want to fulfil the promise with their mouths. She can see the disappointment in their eyes too. Even number seven can't perform his magic and number four is in tears of frustration.

'Jeez, Abby,' Trent said looking me up and down, 'What were you dreaming about? You were rolling and rocking like a ship in the storm. And all that yelling!'

I flushed crimson.

'What was I saying?' I inquired as casually as I could.

'Something about a king and stuff.'

'You're the one who was dreaming.'

Trent and I hadn't kissed when we woke up; nothing sentimental like that. First, I thought the body next to me was Roger's, the smooth mound, like a rock in the sea, and then I remembered with a jolt who it was.

He ruffled my hair and then, yawning and sneezing, stumbled around the bungalow grabbing his clothes. I squirmed beneath the covers, hugging my arms around me. How could I have done that last night? At that moment, I didn't regret the infidelity so much as I couldn't work out why, of all the beautiful people on the island, of all the people I had met, I had almost been unfaithful with Trent?

I grabbed a pillow to hide behind and flung open the door. You're not getting a second helping. One plate per person. I waited by the wide-open entrance. Just get out, will you?

'Sexy,' said Trent. The pillow could only cover breasts or pudenda. I had opted to hide my breasts.

Trent staggered down the steps, shoes and shirt in hand, and banged straight into Prem who looked up at me, amazed.

'I preferred the towel,' he said coolly and then walked quickly on. He moved so fast that he was at the café entrance in seconds, but he wasn't running. He looked like those people in fast-walking contests, only there was nothing funny about Prem. I cursed myself for letting Trent stay. It wouldn't happen again.

That night, Selma and José left the shutters open and I could see into the dimly lit room. Bathed in a tungsten light, it was like watching a tableau unfolding. I was swinging on the hammock. I'd just taken a shower to cool off but it was the wrong time of day and the tap produced only a trickle of water. No matter how much I scrubbed, little grains of sand were still stuck to my skin.

Do all women feel divided? I wanted so much to be back home, but I wanted to be here too. There was no such thing as having it all, because how can you be in a relationship and out of a relationship at the same time, how can you be faithful and unfaithful simultaneously? I felt as though I was being pulled in all directions: was it immaturity or schizophrenia? The guilt crept in again, and I shooed it away like a naughty child. 'Go to the back of my mind.'

Beyond the hum of insects came the exuberant cry of a holidaymakers' disco further up the beach. Selma and José had already made love once today. I had listened to Selma's familiar orgasmic shrill and the quickening of

José's breath as he thundered towards the finishing line. His low commanding voice. What did he whisper to make her squirm so acutely? I couldn't imagine what it was, but sometimes she whimpered like a frightened dog.

Selma was lying on her front on the bed. She was wearing her little yellow dress; the colour emphasised the warm tone of her skin. He stood behind her. I didn't want to watch, but I had to. It was like viewing a scary movie from behind the sofa. He lifted up her dress hem, very carefully, very slowly, almost as though he too was afraid of what he might discover. She wasn't wearing any knickers – she had been expecting him. He waited, gazing at her buttocks admiringly. She didn't move. Then he patted her arse a number of times, like he was playing pat-a-cake. She had the perfect rounded globes, separate from her thighs, not like me where one zone spilled into another. I tucked my hands away, out of view, up my legs.

I circled around the soft skin of my thighs. Oh God, you two, do you have to do it again? Do you have to do it so well, be so picturesque? I wanted to touch her there. I wanted to spread her butt cheeks and make her tremble. I would have loved to knock out José, replace him without her knowing, and then materialise, surprise, surprise; you've been fucking me, not him. I felt my way to my flooded sex: pushing fingers into me. How would our legs look wrapped around each other? Our shapely female thighs entangled? Breasts squeezed and squashed against each other?

The only contact they had was his light hands on her butt. But he was talking to her again, guiding her through his moves. He parted her legs, so they formed a giant V-shape on the bed. She was like a flower unfurling, unwinding. Her long hair spread out either side. It looked beautiful. My hole was flooded. I didn't need much to get me started anymore. Two fingers. I tried three, why not treat myself?

Then José's fingers went underground, down, down, so that he was finger-fucking her, splitting her inner lips with his fingers, and plunging his fingers in her wetness. She still lay on her front, but she craned to open her legs wider, she tried to open herself, she wanted him to take her. One hand was squeezing her buttock cheek.

I squeezed my clitoris, vibrating my hand, until I could feel my body shaking its pleasure.

She was begging him. I couldn't hear the words, but the tone was desperate, pleading and again his reply was soft and low, and turned her to jelly. Her face was pink. His colouring was the same, but his lips, his eyes, everything about him seemed to be shiny. He took his hand off her arse and unzipped his fly. He took out his perfect monument. It was just as I saw it on the plane, big as you like, bold as brass. I would have sucked him.

He leaned forward to place it in her. She still wasn't going to move. He slid into her core. He pressed it right up her, so that it disappeared completely. They started fucking. And her moans and squeals turned to cries for more, more, more. He stayed perfectly in control. He slapped her flanks. He thrust deep into her, his hands flicking over her silky back. Her lithe body rose to meet his hips, she arched her back in her eagerness.

I had two hands inside me. My body started to move weakly at first, but I would be spasming soon; the unmistakable signs were there. Then he faced up, gazing into the distance. Picking up speed, her groans increased. He was going deeper and harder. He looked directly at me. With the hand that wasn't holding her, nailing her to the floor, he blew me a kiss.

I squeezed my eyes closed, but I still saw their bodies, screwing in my mind. I went inside and shut the door.

Chapter Eleven

*T*he restaurant was high up in the trees, one room of velvety cushions, studenty bean-bags and low tables: a serious traveller's hangout. I didn't smoke any weed; I wanted to keep my wits about me. That night with Trent had been foolish, a lapse of judgement. The only consolation was that I hadn't really done anything; I had just allowed him to do things to me.

We sat near two women with matted hair and loose tie-dyed pants who were dealing cards. Other couples were lazily lounging around. I noticed out of the corner of my eye that one girl had her arms seductively around two men, and both seemed to be equally in her favour.

'Tell me a story,' Trent said. 'A bedtime story.'

'No,' I said. 'You go first.' Trent jumped as if he had been waiting for the chance forever.

'OK. My room-mate Paul started seeing this girl, Helen. Anyway, after about six weeks, he found out we were spying on him.'

'Oh, shit!'

'Only he wasn't annoyed. In fact, he really liked the idea. After we told him he said, "How about this Friday? When she comes next, everyone get ready for a real live sex show."'

'Of course we said yeah. Not only that, we got as many of our mates over as possible. There were about eight of us in all. We got the beers out, all ready for party time.'

'Poor girl. That's so terrible.'

'I know. It was a Julia thing all over again. He defied all logic. He made her sit facing us, open her legs facing us. We couldn't believe it. He licked his fingers and kind of fed them inside her.'

'Jesus! How humiliating!'

'But listen – she knew that we were watching all along. Apparently, Paul said that when he told her she said she wanted to do it. She actually volunteered. She was an exhibitionist.'

'Gosh.'

'That's not all. I started going out with her, secretly, behind Paul's back. She was attractive – like she knew she was attractive, so that somehow made her extra-good-looking. The first few times we had wild sex. It was not that I didn't like Paul; it was just spite I suppose, or old-fashioned competition. She was great; she slid on top of me, her head banging, and her hair at all angles. She really was my ideal woman. I would watch them together on Fridays and then we would do it on Saturdays. She wouldn't dump him. She said I could finish with her, she didn't care. We were locked together in our secret. I couldn't tell anyone. She couldn't tell anyone, and we were shut in this stupid game. The worst thing was, I got obsessed, I would make her do the same thing as she had done the night before, the same moves, the same every-thing. If she sucked him on Friday, I would make her suck me on Saturday. If she got on top on Friday, she had to straddle me on Saturday. Everything was the same, but I made her do it better. When she finished with me, she said that Paul may have been a lousy lover, but at least Paul was good; I was just a bastard pervert.'

'Blimey!'

'I really was in love with her for a long time. She was perfect, like a fried egg, sunny side up, but then I couldn't resist flipping her one more time. Boom it was over. The whole thing fucked me up for a while.'

We sighed and sipped our drinks.

'What about you?' he said. 'Tell me about your best fuck ever.'

I pondered the question. There were some things I hadn't even told Roger, and no, it wasn't with Roger. Quantity-wise, Roger was the highest scorer, but quality? There was only one incident that sprang to mind. Only one time qualified as the greatest ever fuck.

'Well?' Trent was impatient. He walked before he crawled – he licked before he fucked.

'It was from behind.'

'Give me some context, some history, anything.'

'Ha ha, now who's asking?'

'Please . . .'

'OK, do you remember I told you about the waiter who had tongued me so eloquently? Well, years later, I went back and looked everywhere for him and . . .'

'And the beast gave it to you from behind!' Trent interrupted.

'No, wait. I didn't find him, but then I was looking for a young man, and he, well, he must have been middle-aged by then. Anyway, on the last night of this frustrating odyssey, I met a student in a tapas bar. You know tapas?' I asked procrastinating. 'It's little bits of everything that you fancy.'

'And?'

I didn't want to tell him.

'Of course it wasn't the waiter. He was a University student, and he played guitar, flamenco naturally. Well, my Spanish is just poco and so was his English.'

'And?'

'It was strange. We undressed separately, you know, like very embarrassed. Him one side of the room, me the other. Then we stared at each other. All I registered was that his cock was enormous. We looked at each other for hours; that is, it seemed like hours. It probably wasn't very long. He had dark fuzz on his upper chest, the middle section was bald, but under his belly, the hair thickened again to this beautiful hairy foliage. My breasts were huge and swollen, and he was large! I mean hung like a donkey. I think, if donkeys saw him, they would want to be hung like him.'

I laughed, embarrassed at the memory.

'He came at me from behind. I literally melted into his fingers. He blew on my neck and then twiddled my nipples, all from behind. I couldn't see him. It was like being caressed by a friendly ghost. I could feel this great erection stood up against me. "I don't think I can", I said weakly. "Yes," he said, "you will."

'We stood there. He entered me, with his fat fingers. He told me to bend over the chair. I protested but he assured me it would be OK. Then he left me. I was so excited that I nearly dry-fucked the chair. He came back. He had some lotion – baby lotion, I think – and he oiled his cock. It was incredible watching it. Then he put it in.'

'Well?'

'It was fantastic,' I said. The words did not seem to cover the enormity of the experience. 'I was engorged, like a kebab on a stick. He didn't let up my tits or my clit, for a second. I just leaned forward over the back of the chair. It was so comfortable; I remember thinking this is heaven. He was groaning, forcing himself inside me. I mean, really screwing himself up me, like a corkscrew in a bottle, desperately, as though he was an animal, as though he was obliterating me.'

'Fucking hell,' bleated Trent. His cock was pressing against his trousers.

I wish I hadn't started. Me and my big mouth!

'Have you ever done it with a woman?' Trent asked.

'No,' I laughed. 'That's certainly not my thing. I need, you know, to be well and truly shafted . . .' If Roger was a woman though, I am sure I would still be in love with him. And if there were no Roger, maybe I would not have been so quick to push Selma away.

'Have you ever done it with a man?' I asked.

Trent laughed, too. 'No way. Anal sex disgusts me. It really does.'

The girl with the two men kissed one of them long and lingeringly while the other fiddled uncertainly with his glass. Then she turned back and kissed him deeply while the other one watched, a big dirty grin spreading all over his face.

Trent walked me back to the bungalow. We crunched noisily on the stones. I tried not to dwell on it, but I couldn't stop thinking of his fingers creeping over me, a million sensations. It was glorious being had, being taken advantage of. I recognised from his scent, or perhaps from his body language, that he expected me to invite him in.

'You can't.'

'Why?'

'You know why.'

He leaned against the door, covered my hand on the cold handle. 'You're just pining away for a jerk who doesn't love you.'

'Of course he does.' What the fuck did Trent know?

'He's married to someone else!'

'I do know that, Trent.'

'Just licky icky,' he murmured. He repulsed me, but I wanted him, someone, so much. I needed stimulation. I was gagging for it.

'Please let me come in, honey. I want to make you come again.'

'No,' I said weakly. It was dirty and silly, and I wasn't that kind of girl. I came to see great things in Thailand, great monuments, exquisite views, not my bedroom ceiling. Bangkok, not banging his cock.

'That's all I care about, rubbing you and giving you pleasure,' he said persuasively. He stuck out his tongue. The piercing glinted like lost treasure. I felt the blood rush to my pussy. I was fascinated. I nearly said yes, but I maintained my will power.

Maybe I could call this a holiday romance – but weren't they supposed to be romantic?

He touched my hand, and I felt moist excitement fill my hollow. Trent had been well behaved. He hadn't forced himself on me, but I knew that I wanted more. I loved oral sex too, but the last stages, I wanted to be rammed. I wished I hadn't done it. I wondered if the guilt I felt was how Roger felt the first time he and I slept together. But then that was different; we were in love, not lust.

I pulled my hand away and fiddled the key in the tight lock.

He lifted up my skirt and held me against the door.

'I'm warning you,' I said weakly. His hand rumbled around my thighs, and I stood still, frozen with pleasure. He pinned me against the door.

'Stop, stop, please. You know I can't.'

He found my knickers. White satin set, first worn to the Four Seasons Hotel. And Trent didn't mess around. He pressed the knickers against me, and from outside the satin, he proceeded to masturbate me. The juice flowed to my clitoris; he massaged me well. Just touching, no more than that, just holiday touching and fumbling, just at the door, not inside, just playing. It was not serious. Nothing serious. If I was an actress, I might have to film a love scene like this. If I were a patient, I might have to be felt up like this. Surely Roger couldn't object! We weren't even kissing. We couldn't give a toss about each other. Trent's fingers were split. One was paying attention to the front quarter, searching out the nub of my pleasure, the others were filling my hole, stimulating me up and down, like a prick would.

I pulled Trent's pants down. I fumbled to set him free. I took out his cock, and nursed it in my hands, coaxing it even bigger, welcoming it to the world. So we stood at my door, under the stars, wanking each other. His arms vibrated and I felt his fingers shaking inside me against my crack, against my precious clitoris. Oh, Roger, Roger.

If you knew how good this felt, you wouldn't deny me this pleasure. You would want the best for me. If you knew how excited I was, and how guilty I was. I'm too dirty for you. I'm a slut. I need to fuck. I need to. Trent's fingers were fucking me, prying me, taking over me. I was jerking in his arms, flailing, and clutching him close.

'Oh Jesus.'

'Yes!'

'Yes, fuck, fuck, fuck!'

I pushed against him frantically, digging for more, more, more. He lifted me up. My feet were suspended off the ground, and I was caught up, caught in the travails of his frigging fingers. I was wringing wet. I remembered Julia and Carol and all the girls he'd had. If they could enjoy this, why couldn't I?

'Yes, yes, Trent. Yes, don't stop, don't stop.'

Oh God. I was coming in short sharp gasps, pulsating against him, knocking against my door. My keys in the keyhole dug in the small of my back, and then fell to the ground. The whole little bungalow was rattling like skeletons in the closet.

His turn. I ducked down. I would show him. And he was growing huge between my fingers. I felt him shudder and groan. I held him in my mouth. I worked my tongue up and down his glans; the blue rivers of veins. I'm the best. I give the greatest blow job in town. He held my hair. He wanted deep throat and I obliged. Pushing his cock back to the wall of my mouth, so that the tip of him nudged my tonsils and I worried I would gag. I was pressing my lips down, making the 'o' of my cavity tight and warm. He was right in my mouth; he was fucking my lips, rubbing up and down my throat. I wanted to open up the tiny closed back passage, I wanted to enter him, and finger-fuck him. Why couldn't I? Why shouldn't I? There were no rules. I knew it would be pinky grey. Would there be hair?

'Owww!' He slapped my hand.

I gave up, concentrating on his front. His paws were

on my shoulders, and they smelled of my pussy. 'It's like the big bang,' yes. Drinking in his prick, sucking up his cock. I pushed back the foreskin and baptised myself in his spitting juices.

'Look up at me,' he whispered.

I looked up. I must have looked like every little slapper in every pornographic magazine, every desperate little cocksucker. Every unfaithful woman who won't let the man in her pussy, but will let him in her gob.

The come sprayed into my mouth like the water-fountains at Trafalgar square.

'See you, Trent.'

'See you, Abigail.'

After he was out of sight, I spat his juices out on the ground.

I'd been inside the room for only a couple of minutes when Selma crashed in, and threw herself on my bed.

'I'm hiding from José.'

She was out of breath and her slender throat was flushed. She took off her sandals, and brushed off the sand from her pretty feet onto my floor.

'Why?'

'He's so possessive. Plus he's a big bore sometimes, a big idiot.'

She peeped out of the window, just as José was walking along, his head spinning around, and calling her name. He looked an imposing sight with his face set. I wouldn't like to get on the wrong side of him.

'You know I'm on holiday, yet, sometimes,' she giggled, 'he makes me feel like I'm in a cage. Those English boys, he hit them!'

'What were you doing?' I asked.

'I was just teasing them,' she said sulkily.

'Teasing them?'

She giggled. 'The dark one has such nice eyes. Grey-blue with long lashes, and I melt every time I see him. It was very romantic. They had hired a car. We drove over to the waterfall.'

Ahh, the waterfall. I'd heard a lot about it.

'On the way back, the car broke down, and the less good-looking one went to get some petrol. I got on the bonnet, and . . .' She looked over at me smiling. 'It was so hot, I took off my dress, and just lay there on the bonnet, in the nude. First, the nice one started to touch me. I really liked it, you know, being outdoors in the heat, on the car, these two men. He touched my breasts. Oh, he was very nervous at first, not like José, and I said, "come on, it's fine baby." He slid inside me and it was incredible. And then the other one came back while we were fucking, and he wanted to join in too. He pressed my legs back, so my clitoris was really rubbing against his friend. Oh, God, pinned back like that, by two of them! He licked my nipples. I got on top of the one I fancied, and then sucked him until his juices ran dry. I like to have two men at once, it's my second favourite thing.'

'What's your favourite thing then?' I whimpered.

'A man and a woman, I think. Then there is both the hardness and the softness, the pussy and the penis. I like to lick soaking pussy and have a man give it to me firmly from behind. I like it when they hold me there,' she gestured the folds of skin above her hip, 'and drive me in and out hard.'

There was a crash from outside. José was striding around outside my bungalow, kicking things. He seemed to suspect she was inside.

'He's a madman. And how are you?' she said peering closely at me. 'You look good with a tan.'

'Thank you.'

She picked up my satin panties from the floor. Stretched them and let them ping back into place. She also looked at the size label. I wondered what she would look like wearing them, on her bed, no, on her hammock, swaying from side to side, up and down.

'Beautiful, very lovely,' she said, and continued to hold them. Her fingers searched out the crotch part and stayed there. They must have been damp.

'Thank you.'

'Does Prem like them?'

'Prem?' I said surprised. 'He hasn't seen them . . .'

'So nothing's happened yet?'

'Of course not.' Have you heard anything? I thought desperately, what did she know?

'It's obvious how you feel about him,' she said. About him, she said, not about each other. Damn, damn.

She came and sat next to me on the bed. She was still clutching my panties.

'And the American fellow who's always sniffing around you?'

'Canadian,' I muttered darkly. I didn't like her choice of words.

'What's happening with him?'

'Nothing.'

'You seem pretty close.'

'Well, we're not.'

Dear God, don't let my nose grow any longer. It's only a puppy lie, hardly an Alsatian.

'I haven't touched anyone.' That was almost the truth. I hadn't fucked anyone.

'But you let yourself be touched?'

She moved her hands to my breasts, and I lay there compliantly, half in shock. A woman had her hand on my breast. It felt nice, the same as when a man had his hand there. I felt her breath on my cheek. I realised that I'd been holding my breath, and that I was long overdue to breathe out. She circled my nipple with her finger. I wanted her to dig her shiny red fingernails into me. Did I arouse her as much as she aroused me? I dared not even think of it like that.

'You smell of sex,' she said, and buried her face in my neck. She kissed the small bone there, and let her lips open around it. Oh God, I felt my vagina twitch. I was frighteningly near to coming again. She wouldn't have to do much. Just stay there. I could masturbate; she wouldn't even have to move. Let me just show her, how much she turns me on. Just a self-massage, what's so wrong with that? She smelled fragrant, freshly mowed grass or flowers for Mother's Day.

'You don't do anything, but other people can do things to you,' she said. I thought, but wasn't sure, that it was a question.

There was a fierce knocking at the door. I breathed out slowly.

'Don't answer.'

She dragged me closer to her. Closer up, her hair smelled of the sea, her scent was dangerous. We were locked together tightly. You couldn't pull us apart. I felt the excitement ignite my pussy. I was scared she'd feel the wetness through my clothes.

'I should –' but my voice was muffled in her breast, '– tell him you're here.' I wanted to strip the clothes off her, to stuff her breasts in my mouth, to feast on her body, the way José did. Would she respond to me like she did to him? Would she nudge her pelvis against me, and then start storming her enjoyment, the panting, the screaming and the golden orgasms?

'No, he'll kill me.'

The knocking continued. Then there were voices outside. José was talking to Trent, demanding to know where Selma was.

'Why do you stay with him, then?' I asked. I knew nothing was going to happen now and, although part of me was relieved, and for Roger's sake it was the best thing, the other half of me – the lower half, I suppose – was devastated. If José hadn't turned up, she would have touched me. She wanted to touch me! All I would've had to do would be to attend.

'It's holiday, that's all.'

Was this a holiday too? Weren't her nipples as diamond-hard as mine were?

'Don't tell him you saw me,' she warned and slipped out of the back window, her long hair dangling over her laughing eyes.

Chapter Twelve

The ants invaded the following morning. Attracted by one of Trent's cans, thousands of the sweet-toothed buggers were marching over my balcony. It was gross; they even marched over my feet when they could. I could have killed Trent.

I went to the restaurant to seek out Prem. I was really upset about the ants. It seemed I had no control over anything any more. Prem was wiping tables with big circular strokes. His trousers held his butt just so. He strained to reach over the edge.

'I've got a little problem.'

Prem stood up and stroked the black hair from his face. Standing next to him made me tremble. He went to the kitchen and I heard him joking with the girls. They were laughing at me.

'What were you talking about?'

'Your ants,' he said still laughing to himself.

They're not my ants, I thought crossly.

'We think it's funny.'

'I don't.'

He boiled up some water, and then carried the saucepan across from the kitchen. He stumbled once or twice, and the water splashed over the side.

'Why is it so funny?' I persisted.

'Foreigners make a big fuss about insects. They think they are dirty. I think it's not the ants who are dirty.'

I watched silently, as the ants scattered helplessly beneath the scalding water.

And there was still no word from Roger.

That evening, Trent put his chunky hand on my arm and squeezed. And I felt how my foolish body leaped at the contact with another human. Jesus, I love to be touched. Maybe I have touch-deficiency syndrome, or feeling-affected disorder. I need it. I crave it. I was wet just at a hand around my waist. He pulled me out into the warm darkness, where he massaged my breasts from over my T-shirt and moved to lift it up.

I felt the shock of his fingers on my bra. I breathed out slowly. Yes, it reminded me of being a teenager one drunken New Year's Eve, letting everyone cadge a feel over my sweater. The men thought it was Christmas all over again, and me, trying to hide the pleasure, trying to act perfunctorily, when every zone, every hair was up on end, oh, yes. Squeezing me, like fruit pickers. Others touched with more reverence, just gliding their hands over my offerings afraid to offend, and others were digging in. One boy squeezed my breasts together, and I saw that his penis was erect, like a gun hanging down his trousers.

Trent's finger was right on target, rubbing my nipple, rubbing away my resistance.

I remembered the first time a man sucked my tits. He took me by surprise. We were in the toilets at a house party. Outside, our friends were drinking cider until they threw up, and hammered desperately at the door. He pushed me against the magnolia sink, scored three French kisses and then he was off, like he had seen green at the traffic lights, sucking and pulsing at my boobs. And I was ready to let him finger me if he wanted, the other girls had started letting their boyfriends do it, but he hadn't wanted. He was warm and friendly, and he seemed to think I was doing him a great favour. He freed me from my bra, and then nuzzled, his mouth pouting, puckering up. He sucked harmoniously. I felt great flames lick down to my pussy. I was on fire. Secret invisible lines, no one had told me about, were shimmering from nipple to clit, from clit to brain.

If he had wanted to fuck me then I would have opened my legs, let him in, and I probably would have come too. I liked it; I felt taken care of, occupied. But after ten, fifteen minutes of this had passed, and he was still just sucking there, sucking so contentedly, I got quite bored. My nipples were all wrinkled like when I spent too long in the bath. This wasn't going anywhere. I flushed the toilet, as a cover for our actions, washed my hands, and told him to leave. My friends asked what took me so long? Had I been fingered? I lied and said I had.

Trent was preparing to launch. I looked down. My breasts stuck out beautifully over the wire casing, full and succulent. He lowered his face. He pinched the nipples possessively. They were hard and taut and ready for his mouth. His tongue, the tongue that I knew to be so good on my clit, was popping forward like a snake's.

'I'm sorry, Trent,' I said and wrenched down my T-shirt.

'OK. Just talking,' he suggested.

But I didn't feel like talking anymore, because I knew what our talking was. It wasn't substitute. It was foreplay. And, besides, I had talked too much.

'I don't feel well.'

'I know a way to make you feel better,' he smirked.

'No.'

He continued to stare at me. The air between us seemed to freeze. Where was the happy-go-lucky volleyball player now?

'Actually, I have my period.'

I wanted to keep Roger; that was all I had to worry about.

'Well, if the red flag's out, there are other women here,' he said threateningly. 'Lots of other women.'

I was walking back to my bungalow, proud of my resistance, when I saw Lily in the street with three men.

'It's the beautiful girl,' she called out to me.

Sober, her compliment embarrassed me. She was beautiful. I wasn't. It was as plain as the moon over the Thai Sea.

'These,' she patted my hips, 'beautiful.' She said it like there was no doubt.

She studied my face sincerely.

'What's the matter?'

One of the men she was with, the most handsome one, was swathed in bandages. I smiled ruefully at him. Ahh, this was the one Selma had told me about. He had played with the wrong girl and got burned – Selma did have excellent taste in men.

The others jeered us. They raised their beer, pulled in their beer-bellies, and gestured at Lily – as if she would find them attractive! Poor Lily: wherever she went, she would be noticed. She would never be free. She reminded me of a caged bird, the plumage so beautiful.

'Why you so sad?' she asked concerned.

'Problems . . .'

It's hard to believe what she did next. She left the men, and walked with me, little me, down to the beach. I felt like I was walking on water. She had chosen to spend time with me!

'Tell Lily all about it,' she said patting her thighs invitingly.

I said shamefully, 'I miss my boyfriend so much.'

'He must miss you too.'

'But I feel so . . . dirty, I want sex all the time. With anyone.' I couldn't meet her eye. Could she guess that she was included in that anyone? Instead of looking repulsed, Lily smiled at me.

'I feel alone,' I added.

'But not alone with Lily.' She held my hand very tight.

She put her arm around me, and I snuggled up to her.

'I wish he'd never got married.'

She chewed at something, playing with a rock.

'So, you're his mistress?'

'No, I'm not. He's leaving his wife for me.'

'He must be a rich man.'

'You don't understand. I love him. We love each other.'

'It's a difficult life,' she said.

'Do you think local girls are exploited?' I asked thinking of Trent.

'Some are. Some exploit.'

'What do you mean?'

'Well, a hamburger needs to be eaten – that's what it's for.'

I didn't think the analogy worked. Who cared though? I was next to the most beautiful woman in the world.

'I like Western men . . . and women,' she smiled shyly.

'You're so very, very feminine,' I said. She took it as a compliment as indeed it was meant, and fluttered her long lashes at me.

'I try hard to be like Julia Roberts. I want to go to Amerikka.'

It should have been Roger and me on this beach but it wasn't. It was Lily and me, and I would make the best of it.

'Do you want to swim?'

'No, me no swim.'

She sat curled up tightly like an oyster, a delicious oyster, to be had with champagne.

'There are always ways out.'

She kissed me. I kissed her back. She wasn't a normal woman, she wasn't like a girl next door, and she was the most beautiful woman. Anyone would have kissed her. She kissed me, like I kissed. She closed her eyes. I watched her closed eyes and I felt it showed her faith in me. This didn't count as infidelity. It didn't. I couldn't be unfaithful with a girl, a simple girl, could I?

She liked my underwear. She had never seen a front-fastening bra before. She popped open the catch and my breasts popped out like surprised mice.

'So, so real,' she said with amazement.

She stroked them, but she didn't attempt to nuzzle them immediately. She seemed fascinated by them. She looked up at me, wide eyed, and she kissed and licked my lips.

'Oh God,' I said hollowly, 'Have you done this with a woman before?'

'Have you?' she said.

'No.'

Her hands were drawing down my knickers, drawing down my inhibitions. I'm going to lick her, lick her all over. We were going to fuck hard, here on the beach. Who cared who saw us?

'I can't.' We both said it at the same time, the exact identical moment.

'Great minds think alike,' I said.

And that made us laugh. We started laughing and laughing. I scrambled up, pulling my clothes around me.

'I . . . I'm too confused,' I said looking shyly at her. 'Thank you for not taking advantage of me. I don't think I'm ready. I'm not a lesbian, you see.'

'Wait for your man, I think everything will be all right.'

I didn't know if she understood everything I said, but I liked to think she did. I thought I understood her pretty well too.

Another game – just who invents these ridiculous pastimes? – of bringing her to the brink and back. Remember 'pin the tail on the donkey?' This time, she lies spread-legged in the centre of a dark room off the main hall. The contestant has just one minute to enter the room and to enter her. If he manages to find her, then he can stay for as long as he likes. So far no one has. She is gagged, otherwise she would not refrain from whispering out clues, 'Pssst. I'm over here,' but they can't even sense her

108

breathing. And she is soaking wet. Her bush is luscious, glistening, but in the darkness they can't see it. And they fumble around the room, banging their knees on table legs, and their elbows on harps, and they don't know how she waits and waits, egging them on. Once, someone grabbed her hair, and she thought, at last, thank God, the denouement, fulfilment, but it was at the final second, and the game was over. Her fruit unplucked and withering.

When the courtiers finally fetch her out, she is so frustrated, she is shaking with lust. Can't they just do something to her? Any of them; It doesn't have to be number seven, even number three would do.

'My Lord, this way is not to everyone's tastes,' she says, her heart in her mouth.

'What do you mean, governess?' the King continues, enumerating his gifts. 'A life's supply of honey, more peacock's feathers,' he sniffed, 'a zebra, male, moon-dust, and a personal computer, whatever that is.'

'I would like a change, I mean I don't mind doing this, it's just I've had enough.'

'Very good,' he says absently.

'I trust I've given good service? I would just like to be, to be freed.'

'Freed?' the King echoed. 'But my dear, we have only just started. It's time for the penis contest.'

'The what, sire?'

'This is what we've all been waiting for,' he says. He claps his hands and all the courtiers come a-running. The court fills with viewers. She can hear excitement in their voices.

Once again, she is positioned on her hands and knees, waiting for someone to ram her from behind.

'How do you decide the winner, sire?' she whispers.

'I think that will be quite obvious,' he replies, laughing.

Chapter Thirteen

*T*he masseuse was striding up and down the sands. I waved her away and retreated to the security of my book.

'The lobster moults, sheds its skin, once a year. They shiver, shaking and pushing, and then, after great exertion, the old skin is off. It takes about ten minutes to grow another skin. In those few moments, the lobster is most vulnerable to attack.'

The masseuse squatted beside me. I caught a glimpse of brown muscular calves. She was thick-legged, not like Lily, lovely Lily, sturdy from hours spent walking up and down the beach. She was not the one who massaged me before. She was probably about my age but her skin looked older. She carried a small wicker basket, like Red Riding Hood, and in it there was a thin tube of lotion, some oils, and cloths.

'You wan' massage?' she persisted.

'How much is it?' I asked. Taking the steps to defeat. Well, there were not many people about that morning. It was my duty to make sure she had enough money to survive.

'It's a very good massage, and inside, in hut, so that no one can see,' she said avoiding my question with aplomb. She had all the makings of a British estate agent.

'You want another girl?'

'Another girl. Why?' I asked.

'Two girls, five hundred baht.'

I considered.

'That's each,' she added belatedly.

I looked over to the huddle of masseuses, perched on the sand, only a few yards from us. There was one, petite, with a warm smile. She was no Lily but she was a flower in her own right. She saw us looking and jumped up. As she approached, I saw that she had a lazy eye. I thought that was good. I didn't think I could stand four eyes on me.

'She's my cousin,' said the masseuse approvingly.

Four hands in unison moved over my back. That was twenty fingers, twenty prying, caressing, smoothing digits, all working in harmony. They squeezed my backbone, tickled my sides, and pressed, pressed, heavily on my shoulders, just where my stress lies. My wonder about them disappeared like puddles evaporating in the sun. Who cared? Just enjoy ... cuddling up to their caresses. I purred, arching like a cat in the sun.

'You've done this before,' I said stupidly.

'Where from?' Masseuse B, I think, asked.

'England.'

'Very nice.'

I was anonymous, no history, no background, no reason to hold me back.

'It's nice to be massaged,' I said. 'In England, not much massage.' I was missing out pronouns, as though they were hard to understand.

'But you have a boyfriend?'

'Yes.'

'You are very beautiful.'

'No.'

Tickling me. I arched up. I could hear the sound of the

111

sea. Rolled over, useless as a corpse, I pinned back my hands on the bed rail. They work hard.

My face down, buried in the solicitude of the pillow. I felt far away from them. They have their language, their communication, and I have mine. I loosened myself, my arms stretched out to touch the iron rail. It was nice to be massaged. I didn't know it would feel like this. I was glad I chose to have my massage privately, I would hate the sunbathers to look at me, like I was a peep show – the way I looked at Selma and José. I was glad there were two girls busy with my body, sliding their hands up and down my torso.

Masseuse A pressed lower and lower down my back, squeezing the joints. I was amazed how pent up I was. She pressed lower and lower, and soon, she was on my arse. The cushion dug into me. Its tassels were tickling my ears. I felt slightly itchy. But I didn't move.

I pretended it was Lily and Selma.

She held me down in the small of my back.

'You like?'

'Mmmm.'

They didn't care who I was and I wouldn't care who they were . . . only how their hands felt on me, how they made me feel.

'You want more?'

I didn't want to say yes. I couldn't say yes. I just lay face down, gurgling into the cushion, allowing them. Permission by consent. Yes, I wanted more. Stop asking me. Just give it to me.

I felt my thighs budged apart, and I didn't tell her to stop.

I felt her fingers enter me, and I didn't tell her to stop.

I felt something slide up me, and I didn't tell her to stop.

The grease-coated bottle glides up me, the little lid nibbles at my side. I am impaled on the suntan lotion bottle. Oh God, yes, my sex tripled in excitement.

They worked it up and down me. I caught my breath,

112

amazed that this had happened so suddenly. They were still squeezing my rump, and I thought there was admiration in their clenches.

'You like it a lot.' They were laughing at the extent of my excitement. Laughing at my rude exhibition.

'Yes, I love it,' I admitted.

'He good boy,' they laughed.

I was climbing the greasy pole. How I longed to conquer the pole, to get to the top, to impale myself upon its peak to the cheers of the men below.

I bit the pillow to gag myself. Don't come, you had better not come. Dirty girl. Slag. No, there was a different word for people like me . . .

The more that I told myself not to, the more my body was excited. My skin rebelled joyously beneath me. My arse curved up to their hands, my nipples were rigid in between their rough and determined fingers, and my hole, my gloriously invaded hole, was swimming with wet arousal.

I rolled on my front, and lay there letting them pump up my space, feed and tame my cunt. I moved against the tube, letting the friction guide me, feeling the bulk excite me.

The masseuse leaned forwards and caressed my clit. She worked her fingers up and down, like I would myself, like no one has done before. Not Trent, not even Roger. How did she know how I liked it?

Roger – I was gurgling his name. I thought of him, when I was doing exactly what he would hate, exactly what would make him hate me. Prem, I wish it were you. Oh God! Losing it. Losing it. But, it was so nice to be massaged. My body hunched up tighter and tighter, my sex was clenching up tighter, until the great burden was released, and I was shaking, and I was still groaning and saying yes, into the sodden pillow, even after they'd left me alone to sort out the money.

I got my purse. The girl, the younger one, came back. She leaned heavily against the door.

'You want more?' Her cheeks were flushed.

'What do you mean, more?' I croaked – my best frog impression.

She walked over to me, took the money from my palm and put it down on the desk firmly.

'Four hundred baht.'

'What for?'

'Come.'

She lay down on my bed, on my bed where I had just let them do those things to me. She stretched out her arm across my pillow. I sat down and then lay down awkwardly beside her. I buried my head under her shoulder, suddenly worn out. She smelled sweet and her skin was hot.

I had gone too far, but I had crossed the line now. There was no going back. She put her arms around me, and I lay encircled within them. I felt hesitant, like I had done as a child when my parents' friends tried to kiss me goodnight. I didn't know what to do. She took my hand.

'I want to show you something.'

She moved my hand to her midriff. She had small fingers. She raised her skirt. I saw that she had very little pubic hair, just sparse tufts – plants in the desert. I could see the lips of her pussy. Her skin was pinky brown, stretched tight. How many people, men or women, had been here before me?

'I show you.'

'I don't know how.'

I had never touched a woman before. She led my fingers inside her hollow. She was slippery and moist: it was like getting into a warm bubble bath. I wanted to enter more. I wanted my entire body to disappear up that sweet, sexual cavity. My sleepiness vanished and I was awake, wide-awake.

I strummed up and down those smooth and soaking walls of her sex. My fingers were covered with mysterious sticky white stuff. I wanted her to come for me. I was consumed by that desire, make her come, make her come.

114

Roger could forgive me for this. One, because I was paying for it; and two, because it was his fantasy, me humping my friends to his applause. An age-old fantasy, like Trent's, two women: two women.

Oh yes! I couldn't think of Roger now; not at a time like this. She was making little meowing sounds – quieter than Selma, but louder than me. She was jerking her groin against me, and trying to reach my pussy with those small searching fingers. When she opened me up, I stared at her. We were inside each other, working the levers of each other's arousal.

'Can I?'

I unbuttoned her shirt and touched her little breasts. She did the same to me, and then she climbed on top of me, straddling me and I gazed up at her wide eyed.

'Good,' she said.

There was sweetness emanating from her hole. Her teeth were brilliant white, and her lips so big, they were more prominent than her nose. And her hands caressed me, let's not forget her frigging hands. I lay back with my legs wide apart as she fucked me with her hand, and I fucked her back. Then she rubbed herself to me, sharp and clean, like an eraser on a mistake, and purred. I clipped my legs around her, so my clit was pressed against hers and we vibrated against each other, neatly and efficiently. She was letting out cries, anguished cries in a language I didn't speak, and she pounded at me harder and harder. I didn't know how much longer before I would come. I wanted her to experience one first. Ravishing her, I dug my teeth into her slender shoulders, slapped her arse, as though giddying up a horse. And then she let out this wail. It sounded distressed but her face was ecstatic, her eyes were wide and clear as she shuddered her orgasm. Her whole body shook and then as the shaking fed its way against my clitoris, it set off a chain of shudders deep within me.

She got up, smoothed down her mussed hair, and pulled her clothes over her.

'That's five hundred baht,' she said dispassionately.

'I thought you said four hundred.'

'No,' she gestured her breasts. 'That more money.'

'Oh I see,' I said and took out the extra hundred willingly. My fingers were crinkled like raisins.

Chapter Fourteen

'*I* want to leave,' I said to Prem in his office the following morning. 'Can you get me a ticket out of here? To Bangkok and then on to England.'

I'd called Roger again and again but there was only an answering machine – and I wasn't allowed to blemish that with my voice. Why hadn't he written? Why hadn't he answered the phone? I decided I would go home. I couldn't enjoy myself here, not while I was thinking of him, and yet not thinking of him. Not when there was so much to enjoy but I couldn't partake. I felt like a dieter in a cake shop, or a quitting-smoker in a cigarette factory. Everything was out of my bounds. I had to go back.

As Prem typed things onto the computer, his tongue glided over his shiny lips, like a snake slithering around a tree trunk.

'When do you want to go?'

'Soon as possible.'

In my dreams, he says, 'Don't go.' He clutches me to him, and then throws me over his shoulder in a fireman's lift. He takes me to his hut, and undresses me slowly. I am wearing my stripy bikini and he folds to the floor, tells me he noticed me, undoing the strings, the triangles descend and he is left in the whiteness, the forbidden emphasised so much more for the rest of my body being brown.

In reality, he scanned the screen, scratched his head, and looked either pensive or pissed off, I'm not sure.

'Before the Full Moon party?' he asked, surprised. Every full moon there was a huge party on the beach. More backpackers would arrive for this. My book said that it was the essential traveller's experience, mind-blowing even.

'Yes.'

'There are no flights 'til next week,' Prem said sullenly, 'nothing at all.'

He swung a crop of papers in my direction.

I saw Selma on the way back to my bungalow. She left a trail of men gazing after her with glazed bovine faces. She told me she'd got a ticket. She was leaving in a few days.

'Where did you get the ticket from?' I asked, suddenly excited. Maybe she knew of a place, a second source.

'From Prem,' she said simply.

'Whaaa? When did you buy it?'

'About half an hour ago.'

'A single ticket?'

'Yes. José is going somewhere else.'

Bastard. My anger focused, I could only hit out at her. How did she get a ticket while I couldn't?

'You know, you should go for Prem. He's very hand-some,' she said.

She invited me to come and sit with her and warily I agreed. It was too hot for the beach and we sat in the shade.

'Abigail, what turns you on?' Selma asked suddenly. She flapped ineffectually at a fly. 'What really excites you?'

Just being asked the question was quite arousing.

'What do you mean?'

'Sometimes, José's a little too keen. Always hard, always ready. There's no challenge with him.'

I smiled, saying nothing. Imagine if Prem were like that! If whenever I walked into the restaurant he stood to attention. Hard shaft, pressing at his trousers. Coming over with the menu, offering his cock. I would nuzzle down to suck.

'I like some resistance,' she continued. 'I like to force people.'

'Force?' I echoed.

'I like doing it to someone when they don't really want to.'

'Oh, but José's not like that.'

'No, he's not like that.'

'I see.'

I got up. I wondered what Selma wanted me to say, but she was staring out of the window, so I assumed she was speaking hypothetically, and I had nothing to worry about.

'Do you have nice dreams, Abigail?' Selma said, and I shivered. Maybe she was reading my mind.

'Sometimes, yes,' I admitted hesitantly. I was thinking about the King and being held captive with my legs fixed wide, fucking wide, apart.

She said that she always experienced strange dreams in Thailand, and that was one of the reasons she came here so often. Because nowhere else in the world does she have as much fun sleeping as awake.

José was coming along the beach.

'Let's make him jealous,' she whispered.

José was coming up the steps. Why would I want to hurt José? I know that jealousy is painful, and those who suffer from it should be treated and not have their symptoms aggravated.

'I think that's cruel.'

'It turns me on,' she murmured.

'What does?'

'Secrecy.'

She kissed me. I felt her lips press on mine, barely touching at first, the way you kiss an envelope for luck,

119

and then heavily, a sensual kiss of prospective lovers. I couldn't move away. Her mouth formed over mine as naturally as the sea rode the shore.

'I think you enjoyed the massage though.'

She touched me on the cheek talking quickly.

'I was watching. You looked horny, yes, with the lotion running up and down your cunt. Yes, I never saw such excitement, your knees bent up and the way you wanted it. I was very impressed. Very excited. I saw right up between your legs, your pink slit, what a sight! But baby, a girl like you doesn't have to pay for it. I would have done that for free.

'José, what a surprise,' sang out Selma, and detached herself from me.

José looked up at us. His dark eyes registered no emotion, no surprise, and he nodded slowly.

Later, when the sun was at its highest in the sky, and the fishermen were coming home with nets full of their morning haul, Prem asked if I wanted to go for a drive with him. Of course I did. I sat next to him up the front of the jeep. His thighs were close to mine. I played chicken with his leg – first one to move away is the loser – he lost, but then he didn't know the game. On the way, we saw one of his friends who peered at me suspiciously. I don't know what they said.

When the man left, Prem said that today was a good day for fishing. The fish were biting.

'I'd like to learn how to fish,' I lied. I had visions of Prem's wiry arms around me, holding my hips as I leaned back into him.

'You need patience,' he said. His eyes were twinkling and I thought he was laughing at me.

I'd like to hold his rod, I thought, steady, steady, until something was biting on the line. Mmm. I wondered how it would be to kneel down in front of those thighs, embrace them, have him in my mouth. I wanted to gobble at his prick. I expected his balls would be hair-free, smooth and buoyant. I would lick them, and he would be taken by surprise at my audacity. I would stroke him back and forth, loving his glans, moistening the head with my tongue. I would swallow him, swallow him.

I stared out of the window, trying to cut the wicked thoughts out of my mind. What was wrong with me? I'd let the devil in and he'd taken me over. My whole thought process was devoted to chasing my next orgasm – while maintaining my duty to Roger, of course.

The shame of the last few days weighed heavily. What had I become? Paying for that massage? It was like paying for sex, or paying for not-exactly sex. Like Selma and José, two wild bucking animals? I felt crimson creep over my cheeks as I remembered. There was something wrong with me, something sinful and crude. Perhaps I just couldn't cope with this sultry heat. This place, so hot and hard to find; I heard that some of the travellers called it 'the erogenous zone'.

I asked Prem how he came to be at the island, managing the Sunita Complex. He said that his father had bought it against the wishes of his family. Prem had studied to be an engineer but when his father died he came to continue the business. His older brother was a doctor in the north, and his sister was studying to be a pharmacist in Bangkok.

'An engineer,' I repeated impressed. I know nothing about engineering, but the words suggest power and control. Twiddling knobs, men in hard hats.

'Yes, I loved engineering,' he said wistfully.

Prem seemed to know everyone at the marketplace. They thumped him on the back, and shouted out greetings. We wandered through, fingering the jewellery, the sarongs and the bikinis. I picked out a T-shirt covered with Thai writing from a stall selling second-hand clothes.

'Try it,' said Prem. He nodded encouragingly.

Behind the curtain, my reflection smiled back at me,

flushed and excited. My eyes were a little too bright. I pulled on the T-shirt and liked what I saw except that the finery of my fussy bra was visible. I unclipped it and stuffed it into my bag. I let down my hair from its ponytail. I had a suntan. Now, I looked like I'd been on the island for a long time. When I thought about England, it seemed black and white, while we were living in glorious Technicolor.

Prem insisted that I kept the T-shirt and I didn't have to pay. He said that he and the trader were old friends. The trader grinned at my cleavage, and I wondered if he could tell I had taken off my bra.

'What happened to your watch?' I asked. I was embarrassed.

'It was stolen by a tourist.' He said the last word venomously, the way other people say 'spider'.

'Not all tourists are bad.'

'Some are very bad,' he said.

'Thailand has never been invaded, has it?'

'Never,' he said proudly and then added wryly, 'Not 'til now.'

'Foreign tourists? Yes.'

He smiled. He looked so different when he smiled. I wanted to make him smile again.

'At least they bring money.'

'And other shit,' he said.

I chose a marble elephant for Roger and I paid the full price happily. Prem asked if it was for the American guy.

'Canadian,' I said. 'He's just a friend.'

'I thought . . .'

'No, no,' I protested weakly. 'I don't like him.'

For some reason, I didn't tell him that my true boy-friend was in England.

'Your friend says you don't go out with foreign girls.'

'I don't.'

I continued uncertainly, 'He said you hate the Western men who go out with Thai girls. Why?'

Prem blushed a funny shade of red. 'Yes, I don't like it. It's exploitation.'

He looked at me, and I sensed for the first time, that maybe, despite his wise talk, something was bugging Prem.

'Does that count for Thai men and foreign women too?'

Prem looked away. He had a slope of downy dark hair on his jaw.

We drove back in silence. Prem controlled the car masterfully, I liked watching his hands sit steady on the wheel. I wondered if the effort of speaking English or perhaps, more particularly, the effort of talking to me had tired him out, but once we arrived at the Sunita Complex he was cheerful again and he told me he'd try very hard to get me a flight. I felt confused again. I didn't really want to leave.

Chapter Fifteen

*T*he following day, I trekked three kilometres through the jungle to a sheltered beach the other side of the island. I wasn't disappointed. The beach was a glory of white sand, and the only other people there sat so far apart that you were fooled into thinking you were alone. I think some of them were naked. Although I kept on the simple black bikini that Roger bought for me, I too felt a great sense of freedom.

I swam lazily, long slow strokes, my face held above the surface. My body looked white, bright white underwater, and my feet looked huge. Little fish swam around my legs. I flapped around, amusing myself. I wasn't to worry that he hadn't got in touch. I had to have faith.

I turned around and there was Selma towing an orange lilo behind her. Everything about her was luminous, orangey light. Her long hair was streaming down her back and the freckles on her face were dancing in the sunlight. She looked like a mirage.

'Alone?'

'Uh huh.' I carried on bobbing about, because I wasn't bothered if Selma was there or not. I was having fun by myself.

'So how's life?'

'Fine,' I lied.

Selma's eyebrows would have raised the Titanic. She splashed water at me playfully, and I saw that she was topless. I splashed her back, but she was the stronger of the two of us and, as I didn't much like getting water in my eyes, I gave up first.

'I know that you look at us,' said Selma triumphantly. 'At night when we fuck, I feel you watching us.'

She was circling me greedily in the water like a shark. I was out of my depth.

'No, I don't,' I puffed, treading water furiously.

'Who are you most jealous of, José or me?

'I'm not jealous of either of you,' I said and I meant it. Maybe I had been, but not any more. I swam inshore a little.

'Ah, Thailand,' she hummed and then she climbed onto her lilo. As she levered herself on, I realised that she was bottomless too. Her arse was just a couple of shades lighter than her legs. She landed on the lilo and lay on her front, her chin in her hands, so her butt was on show to the world – if anyone else were about. Only the sun could see it, and the sun probably got to see a lot.

'So you and Prem, you're not . . . how do I say?'

'Don't say it,' I said. I came to the front of the lilo and started to drag it along. She was a queen in her chariot, and I her slave.

'But I know how much you fancy him. I'll tell him.'

'No don't.' We were grinning. 'Don't you dare.'

I swam under the plastic and pushed as hard as I could. The lilo lifted up, and then collapsed. Selma came struggling off, splashing into the sea. We fought some more underwater. She pinched my boob and I pinched her back. Selma really was a wildcat, unpredictable and feisty. Underwater, she tried to yank my knickers down, and since I had nothing to grab onto, I squeezed her buttock tight instead.

'Let's dance!'

So we danced like mad things. Shaking our tooties at

the bewildered fish. Swinging around, swivelling our hips until I was out of breath and had to hold onto the lilo.

'You're fun,' she said, 'and I thought you were just another boring English girl.'

'Oh thanks!'

'You don't look English. I thought all English girls were pear-shaped, but you've got those massive titties too. I bet Prem would like a suck on those babies.'

I pushed her and chased her. Then she showed me how to do an underwater can-can. She put her hands on her waist and kicked. I did the same.

'No, like this,' she said adjusting my hands on my side. It felt funny to have her holding me there, like a man. I did the same back to her, and I felt her waist was so tiny, I could almost wrap my hands around her, but I wasn't jealous. It was just a pleasure to touch her. She swerved downwards, shell diving. She looked beautiful underwater, graceful and poised. Her skin was electric white. She plucked seashells from the seabed and came up gasping for air.

'Listen.'

She held the shell to my ear, and I felt shivers run through my brain. Inside the magic shell were centuries of waves, sounds of the vast ocean, a hush that told me how insignificant I was – and how insignificant most of the things I did were.

'Lie on the lilo,' she commanded.

'No way.'

I knew she was going to tip me off. I was tired of it.

'I won't tip you off,' she promised. And playfully, I made her shake my finger in hers to swear that she was not lying.

I slipped along the plastic bed, and then I was lying in full sight of the sun. Its rays caressed me. Where was Selma? I was sure now that she was going to tip me off when I least expected it. I couldn't trust her for a moment. She came up, sea sprite, at my feet.

'Hi.'

I waved at her lazily; she leaned towards me, but not too much. She was careful not to tip us over. I wondered if there were sharks here, or just Selmas. She pretended to be a shark, she used her hand as a fin, and then she stopped and came back to my feet.

'Open your legs.'

I wondered what game Selma had in mind now.

'Go on, a little bit more; slide down a little bit.'

Very delicately, very carefully, she limbered aboard the raft. The top end rode up, but I balanced it down. I was scared we'd overturn. She was laughing, but at the same time seemed deadly serious. She touched my bikini bottoms and then, as I said nothing, she pulled them off gently. My pubic hair was exposed, but this was a beach, it was the most natural place in the world. And being with her was the most natural thing in the world.

She was up, her hair streaming back. Her beautiful, bountiful breasts were bobbing around in the water. I had an absurd wish that they were life jackets. If you could market life jackets like these, you'd be a millionaire.

She leaned forward, and she was kissing my pubic hair, exploring the bush.

'Selma? What about José?'

He was a figure in the dim distance, a dark outline on the beach so far away, that he was almost in the past.

'Shh.'

She opened my sex, and I felt a small trickle of wetness seep out.

'Abigail,' she scolded, 'you're already wet.'

I scissored my legs shut. I was not going to do this if she was going to laugh at me.

'Please,' she crooned, her face pressed in my thighs, squirming on the lilo. 'Open them, I'm not going to hurt you.'

But José would. José would go mad, and he was only over there. I remembered the man José had beaten to a pulp for stepping on his territory. Would he hit me too?

She nestled her face between my legs. I felt her thimble-like tongue weave its way through my hole. I felt how my sex lurched and responded happily to her. My pussy didn't care whether it was man, woman or beast, it just wanted to be loved. Selma was surprisingly gentle: she rocked at me like the waves. She lapped at my hollow. I saw that as she worked at me, she masturbated herself. Her bottom was stuck up in the air and under that her fingers were twiddling; she was a stealthy lover. Her tongue circled me. My arms fell either side into the warm water and the sun glazed a maple topping.

This was a dream. This was one of those experiences that do live up to your expectations.

Her sucking quickened and my moistening increased correspondingly. I was struggling now to contain my orgasm. That tongue of hers, that clever tongue was delving in and out of my crevices. Soaking me up. My thighs were rattling, and I couldn't stop drawing her into me further still. Her licking was so rhythmic and so knowing, that I needed to do something, I needed something to happen, and then as the soft melting was taking place, I remembered that was what it was, I needed to let go.

I was almost there, don't stop, Selma, don't stop. Let me go, come on, just a little more, consume me, mouth-fuck me – everything is clenched, clamped tight, squeezing the pleasure – and then suddenly, I was alone, floating on the lilo. The waves were pushing me in and out. Every so often I opened my eyes in panic that I was lost at sea, only to realise that I had barely moved at all.

José was swimming up beside me.

'Where is Selma?'

'Swimming, I think,' I said nervously. I lie so very badly. I groped around and felt for my bikini.

She was only ten metres away, and she was swimming her firm breaststroke. Her head turned up and down, breath, up and down. We watched her chop through the water, her little face upturned to God. 'Breast stroke'. I loved those words. José looked over at her, his expression was rapt like when you see a beautiful painting, or something that you know you'll never be able to afford.

'The island makes people act strange,' he said mysteriously. I wondered if José was sharper than Selma credited him. And then he did the crawl towards her.

Later, I sat in the cool shade of the café. Two dogs snuck under my table. Far away, I could hear some kids playing. Prem fixed me a shake and sat opposite me while I drank it. I moved my legs, afraid but wanting us to bang knees. Smiling shyly, he produced a postcard of Westminster Abbey.

'Is this what your name means? Abbey?'

I laughed. 'No, no. It doesn't mean anything.'

'A bee?' he insisted and buzzed around for effect.

'Nope, and it's Abigail.'

'A big Gail,' he suggested, 'Like when the wind is fierce?'

He was so sweet. I wanted to wrap my arms around him. Instead, I pushed him and poked him in his skinny ribs. I smiled up at him, pretending that what I was feeling was just plain old friendly stuff.

'Go and play pool,' he said. He didn't shove back when I shoved; I was glad he didn't. He wouldn't believe how hot my body got when he touched me. He just kind of leaned away with a grin that, when I dared look at it, looked almost as sentimental as mine.

'I'll join you when I'm finished here.'

I took a few practice shots and admired my own artistry. I was bent over the pool table, analysing the angles. I had chalky fingers. Already the cavity between thumb and index finger was swollen. I liked the game; I liked the thrill of potting the ball, the clunking noise as it rolled off the table into the pocket.

Someone was behind me, close behind me. Someone's hands were sliding up and down my arm. I felt my sex moisten and contract. Prem, don't stop. Breathing behind me, me leaning over to take a shot, my buttocks pressed

129

against his stomach, lower, pressed against his crotch. I couldn't take the shot like that, but I would enjoy the position a little longer.

Prem having me here, on the table, from behind. Sticking his cock up me. I would hold on to the sides of the table, stretch myself out and let him pump away. He's the manager, he can be the boss, and I would receive it like a good submissive girl. He'd better cover my mouth with his hands if he doesn't want me to scream.

The man behind had a very wide snooker cue or a very thick hard-on. He pushed it into the flimsy cotton of my sarong; I felt it jabbing me, oh, oh, God. Lift up my skirt and give it to me. Prem, you're under my skin, now get under my knickers.

'You look so horny like this.'

'Roger!' I screamed, spinning around.

Roger was there, behind me, beaming. His hair was darker than I imagined and he shook his long fringe out of his eyes as he held out his hands. He was so much bulkier and hairier than Prem, I didn't know how I could have confused them. He was wearing jeans, a T-shirt, and his jumper was slung around his waist. He had one bag with him. He wasn't the kind of man you'd notice when you first walked in a room, but when you finally noticed him, you'd see he was handsome.

'What are you doing here?' I screeched. 'I didn't think you'd come. Why didn't you tell me?'

'Would I ever let you down?'

Roger hugged me and we swung round and round. My feet flew off the ground, and I gripped him tightly for survival. Roger is here, Roger is here! The other customers looked on indulgently. The driver's mate nodded curtly at us, and then walked off to the kitchen. I fancied that he went to tell Prem the news.

'Roger!' I tried to kiss him but he gestured to the table.

'Carry on, baby, I want to watch you.'

'No,' I said weakly.

Now aware of being looked at, I felt underdressed. The

triangles of the bikini top were too small, right angles, over a circle. The skirt clung to my buttocks, leaving little to the imagination. Not that Roger would need to use his imagination. He already knew what I looked like down there. In fact, he probably knew better than I did. If there were a quiz . . .

'Put it in the hole Abby.'

Roger interrupted my weird imaginings.

'I can't.'

I saw Prem emerge from the kitchen with the driver's mate close behind. They had come to look at the new-comer. I waved ready to introduce them all, but they stayed back, consulting in a huddle.

Roger was laughing his face off.

'Come on baby, poke it.'

'Stop it, you're putting me off.'

I did it anyway, a little pose, arse upwards. I was an animal – I had turned my back on heaven – and I was leaning over the table, my boobs spilling out of their flimsy cups. Jesus, Roger was here. I wanted him to hold my arse, to separate my butt-cheeks and boom, shaft me. And he looked at me as though that was exactly what he'd come here to do.

Chapter Sixteen

'Wow,' he said.

I put my hand to his mouth, my fingers over his lips. I didn't want him to speak, to spoil it. I was going to be taken without conversation. I was shaking with the shock of his sudden guest appearance. He seemed so out of place, so out of context, a part of the city washed up on the shore.

'Are you pleased to see me?'

Bless him! He was uncertain of my reaction, unsure if my expression was pleasure or annoyance. What a sensitive darling!

'I'm so pleased, I've thought about nothing else.'

(Well, nearly nothing else.) I sat on the bed and then swivelled around my legs so that I was lying down. Roger watched, his eyes slowly glittering with understanding. I let my legs widen. I stroked my thighs. My legs were damp. I moved my fingers across to my pubic hair. I touched myself. The day had been my foreplay. Tonight was the match. Roger was hard as he watched me, probably hard from before he saw me. He undid his trousers, and his penis bounced up, immediately hard and strong.

'Oh, I missed you,' I groaned. I wasn't sure if I meant

him or that cock. It was beautiful. An impressive length, embellished by an even more impressive width. God save the pricks. He was straight and iron against my soft, fluidity. I liked his seriousness, the intensity of his demeanour. I flaunted, he admired. I melted, he screwed, and, all the time, his hands were over me. I stretched my arms behind my head, and as I did so, my T-shirt rode up higher, revealing the undercurve of my breasts. Yes, I was as good as Selma.

He opened my legs, and I let him look at me again. I liked feeling that he was assessing me. How do I do, sir? Is it good enough for you? I knew that by now, creamy excitement would be snaking its way to the fore, nestling on my engorged lips. My slit would be awash with liquid anticipation.

'Open your legs wider,' he told me. He certainly knew how to treat a lady. We had barely exchanged ten words since he arrived, and here he was getting back to basics.

I did as I was told.

'Oh, Roger, yes.'

(Can you tell that someone else has been here? Did they leave marks on my skin? Look carefully and you'll know I'm not innocent.)

'Come on, baby.'

Roger leaned forward and, very carefully, he handled his penis, gliding around between my thighs in search of my secret hole. He paused at the entrance, as I found myself groaning, hysterically.

Roger, I'm sorry, oh, but, Roger, and then I felt the penis fill my cunt, block out all my anxieties, as it pushed forwards up me. No more, I will make it up to you. I will make everything all right. From now on I'm yours.

'Yes!'

He groaned in response. 'Yes!'

Once I started, I couldn't stop.

'Don't stop, fuck me hard, oh yes, fuck me.'

I gripped him closer to me, slapping his flanks, pulling, and grinding him further up me. I was jerking myself off him. His finger was squeezing the tight nodule of my clitoris. I wanted to turn myself inside out. I didn't know what I wanted – to come like this, or like that, with his dick, with his finger, with his mouth. I didn't know whether I wanted to climb over him, take him how he should be taken, or to turn over myself and offer him my mouth. I didn't know, and my body was screeching that time was running out. Oh God, the past was forgotten. He was the only one in the world.

'Baby, you're so hot.'

I didn't move; I couldn't move. It was too late to change my position now; we were finalising the agreement. I felt the trigger of his come, the sullen growth, the clatter of strokes, the sighs of his completion. But I couldn't stop. I wasn't stopping. I moved him in and out of me, feeling the rub against my frenzied clitoris, the smooth friction. I wouldn't be stopped. He was still rigid, and I used him as I could. I exploited him, as he wanted and I wanted. Eating him, ravishing him.

I came, I came; shattered in his arms, ten thousand tiny pieces.

'My God, Roger, I love you more than anything.'

'Jesus, you're a hot honey, aren't you?'

Roger grew hard again. He has always been admirably quick at coming back. Soon, oh so soon, I too was filled with slippery excitement. I got on top of him; I wanted to pump him, to drain the come out of him, savour every last drop of sweet prick juice. I liked being on top. I liked to do it my way, my pace, my control. I fed him in and out of me, just as I like. No, I didn't care about him, just me, the right touch, the right angle. I sawed up and down on him, he'd better hurry up and get ready, sure I was taking him by surprise but why not, why wait? We're adults, we know what's what: do it to me, do it to me.

Pressing him down so he couldn't escape. I wanted Selma and José to hear next door. Yes, it was not only you who can fuck, I can do it too you know. I drove into

134

him. He was the nail that went into the wall, but I was the hammer, smashing us together. I was the provider, and I worked him like a dog. The harder I screwed, the more I'd forget all the nonsense of the past few weeks. The more that my womb contracted with pleasure, the more I could erase the others, the no-name masseuse, Selma, Trent. I could make them go away if I made him happy enough.

His fingers moved over to my clitoris. No, let me do it. I rub myself, showing him I could. I'm the champion. My breasts were floundering, and the mosquito net was shaking. I bludgeoned myself against his thick shaft, tormenting myself on him. Down, down, harder, harder, smashing him, writhing around on him, until I was drenched in sweat and the writhing was no longer mine, but my body's uncontrollable waves of passion. I buckled over him, my orifice filled, screwing out a hot and heavy orgasm.

I realised with some embarrassment that he still hadn't come. He lay back looking delighted. Absolutely thrilled – he always loved that. An ego trip I suppose. I can last longer than you can; my dad is bigger than your dad, nur nur.

'Darling,' I said appreciatively. His cock was rigid. I wondered how he managed to have such self-control.

'I'm so glad you're here.'

'I'm glad I'm here too.'

He stuck his finger inside me again and I jolted against it, as though a bolt of lightning was going through me. I was oozing silk wetness. I was a fish on a hook.

'You missed me, I can feel that,' he murmured. Oh God, he's so sexy. I went down, down, down, down, and sucked my juice off him. I tasted funny, like sour cream. As I laboured, he pulled me around, so that joy of joys, I was sitting on his face. Oh Roger, I was sitting on him. I might fuck him to death, but Roger was no amateur, his hands were lifting me, and although my buttocks were over his cheeks, his nose, oh God, pierces my hole. He was in control here. 69, 69 what a number! What a shape. There is nothing like this. Nothing. He could be anyone. I would do it with anyone, with a long pleasing tongue, and a long pleasing prick. It tickled me, it tickled me, and it made me jerk up and down. Harder and harder I squirmed, and his penis fell out of my mouth, but I didn't care, and he didn't either.

'Oh, thank God you're here, thank God.'

I was still shaking. I'd been waiting for so long, and still it was wonderful when it came.

'Jesus!' I murmured. 'I needed that more than anything else in the fucking world.'

The following morning, Selma smiled at me softly.

'Do you want to go to the beach today?' she said innocently. She had a new spray of freckles on her little nose.

'My boyfriend is here actually,' I pointed proudly to my bungalow where Roger was sleeping through his jet lag. How glorious it was to wake up next to someone you love. I'd pushed off the sheet, opened the window and whispered a thank you to the sun.

'Oh, yes, but he's . . .' she screwed up her little nose. I looked at her suspiciously. She couldn't know, she shouldn't know. How would she know?

'He's not so sexy, I think,' she said finally. I couldn't believe my ears. How dare she say such a ridiculous thing!

'I think you should sleep with Prem. Or me!' she added.

'What do you know about it?' I responded nastily.

'I know, eh,' she smiled with unashamed superiority. 'I know you. You think you love him, but you don't.'

I stared at the ground. I was amazed at the intensity she brought with her, in every thing she did or said. She was not the nicest woman I had met, but her feelings were perhaps the most passionate.

'And he's married,' she added venomously.

136

'How do you know?' I spat. Roger didn't wear a ring; there was no way she should know.

She stuck out her tongue and wriggled it around in imitation of someone I knew well.

'How do you think that I know?'

I stared at her. She flopped down onto her front step and told me to sit next to her. I didn't. I needed the advantage of height. I had nothing else to cling to.

'Trent told me all about you. What you like and what you don't like. He's a good boy, Trent. I like him. His tongue is very, how do you say? Very accommodating, yes? Can you believe it? He picked me up, and ate me like I was a pineapple. He actually held me over his head. Such strong arms, from the volleyball perhaps? Can you imagine? He made me come very quickly, like that. I was legs open, over his head, and his mouth was inside me, and he has that big piercing! What a superb jewel! What outrage! How it flickered against my clit, oh, I could not believe it when I felt it. It just seemed to exaggerate everything. I came all over his chin. His face was covered with my sticky come. I think his arms were tired out after propping me up like that. Poor José, he has to practise his technique there, now I am training him more. But Trent's cock is not so big as José's cock. I liked it inside, but it did not fill me completely, you know? I suppose I am used to giant ones, so I'm difficult to please. I'm small there, my cunt is like a teenage girl's, but I still like to have the great big ones. I told him if he wants to make me come that way, he will have to add his little finger to my arse hole. He said it was OK, but I wasn't to touch him there, he was very strict about that. I found him funny.'

I felt faint. Dirty. She knew about Trent and me. She even knew about Roger.

'I still have this fantasy about ... a woman –' she looked at me intently '– who is frightened at first, and maybe, I can free her. She wants, but she doesn't know.

So she comes to me. I think I would like to console her. Take José, he is too jealous, but I will cure him.'

She leaned very close to me, and I was afraid she was going to kiss me again. Her fingers turned into a pinch, a reprimand and then she turned away and was gone.

Chapter Seventeen

Roger didn't much like the island. He liked the sea and the beautiful people; he just hated everything else. He said the facilities were cheap. I didn't remind him of all the things he'd said to me before I left: that it was essential that I had 'the real traveller's experience. No four-star hotels for you Abby, you're going to have to rough it'. 'Be more open-minded, Abby.' Well, I was more open-minded now. He was the one who was complaining.

'But we don't have to stay here for long,' he said. 'Being together is the important thing, here or back home.'

'How long will we stay?'

'I don't know, but wherever we go we'll be together.'

The next time I saw Trent, he was swaggering out of a bar with a skinny Thai girl with legs like Tabasco sauce bottles. I tried to escape, keeping my head low, but he yelled at me to stop. The girl smiled broadly and stood back to give us the chance to speak. I was just relieved that Roger wasn't with me. Who knew what Trent would have said?

'Honey!' he bellowed.

I wanted to disappear; I wanted to turn invisible.

'Baby, ready for some hot talk?' he whispered into my ear. 'It's a shame this one doesn't speak English. Still, I remember your stories.'

'My boyfriend is here now.'

'He came? Shit, I didn't think he would.'

'Yes,' I said self-importantly.

'Honey, I can't stop thinking about you bent over on that chair, waiting for the giant to spread you.'

I started to walk away. He pulled me back.

'Do you regret it – us, I mean?'

'No, well, actually, yes.'

'No regrets, Abby, regrets are for losers.'

He bought burgers for him and his girl. I watched him stuff the meat in his mouth hungrily. The juice ran down in rivulets from his lips and I felt sick, remembering.

After a day of glorious getting to know each other again Roger and I went to eat at Sunita Lodge café. Roger was restless though. The longer the food took, the more he kept grabbing at my watch and grimacing.

'We've been waiting for so long!' he exploded.

'It's all right, Roger.' I put a timorous hand on his shoulder. 'Everything is slow here; you'll get used to it.'

But Roger insisted on clicking his fingers and eyeballing the waitresses. Prem was chatting with the driver's mate. The driver's mate was always there between us, catching our glances like piggy in the middle.

'Waiter, waiter, manager,' boomed Roger.

Eventually Prem slouched over.

'What?'

'We've been waiting for an hour.'

'Is someone chasing you?' Prem asked sullenly.

Roger was furious.

'When I order food, I expect it to come the same day.'

'We are cooking it now.'

'Don't argue.' I pulled at Roger's sleeve.

'I could have him,' he said darkly. I thought that was

140

unlikely since Prem was a kickboxing teacher and Roger well, let's just say he wasn't.

'No wonder the Thai women like foreign men. At least they treat them with some respect.'

'Prem has always treated me with respect,' I said defensively.

'Yeah well, you can see what he's after.'

'That's not fair. He's not like that at all.'

Roger put his hand on my thigh silencing me. I did the same back to him. Under the table, we played with each other. We scratched and scrabbled like burrowing moles, and before long, I felt the outline of his fine erection push against his trousers. I tried to look as though I was turned on too, but I was on edge.

Then Roger said, 'Let's go.'

I didn't want to. The food took time to prepare, and we should wait. But it wasn't worth a fight. I'd learned to bite my tongue about injustices long ago. We walked back, hand in sweet hand. I saw Prem come out with his arms full of our food and then he stormed back acid-faced to the kitchen.

Roger stopped at a kiosk to buy a passion fruit ice cream.

'I'm going to lick this off you,' he promised. I remembered Selma and José and I felt excited. Did Roger know how interesting they were to me? I couldn't forget Selma's words. The way Trent had carried her maybe, or the way she wanted a woman.

I was in too much of a frenzy to wait until we got back to the room, so I pulled him down onto the beach. We lay against the rocks, pressing against each other. His cock was hard in his jeans. Feel this Selma! I thought. I was going to fuck him to prove my point. He was good enough for me, he was leaving his wife, and if it was gigantic cock you were after, then he was the man. He took off his trainers, but I kept my shoes on. I loved the proximity of the water, of him. I was stuck between a rock and a hard place. I wanted to feel his boner.

'Well, are you going to do it then?'

'People will see,' he said coyly.

'They won't.' The beach was a shroud of darkness. Everyone was in the restaurants, or watching videos in bungalows.

'Lick me.'

He looked up surprised at my straight-forwardness. He liked flowery words.

'Please,' I added. 'I want it.'

'How?' he asked softly.

'Put the ice cream on my clit, and then lick it off.'

I opened my sarong. It was like drawing back curtains, and I liked the sense that as we went through one door, there were more doors yet to open. I was going to get sand in all my nooks and crannies, but it was going to be worth it. Maybe we would feel like sandpaper, crushing up my passage.

'I want you to put your tongue up my hole.'

First door, my knickers were pulled down.

Second door. My beaver was opened and stretched wide so that he could see the tender skin, the moist walls, and the little bouquets of white sticky stuff that I want him to feel.

'First look at me. Watch me play with myself.'

I touched myself, preparing myself. I loved the feel of my welcome. There were many things that made me happy, but this was the best of them. Silky smooth, honey dip. My fingers explored the whole forgotten continent and Roger watched me, 'just looking', he said, like an embarrassed shopper, a small smile playing on his lips.

'Now put the ice on my pussy.'

He held the ice over my expectant hole. It was going to drip down soon. I waited for the denouement cautiously.

I was throbbing there, hot and insensible. I wanted stimulation, quickly. I wished Selma were watching too, I imagined she was there, with binoculars, rubbing her teenage-girl-sized hole. I hoped she wanted me like I wanted her. I hoped she knew the way my legs were spread. I was hot and open for him. Look at me, Selma, José, I fuck too, I'm horny too. You only put the ice cream on your breasts, look where I can go with it.

We waited, and then Roger shook the cone gingerly. The ball of frozen cream slowly started to melt, and the drips started to fall; but, instead of falling away from the cone onto me, they slid along the side. Impatiently, Roger scooped at the ice with two fingers.

'Cold,' he said. I shivered with anticipation but instead of putting them on me, he put the boule in his mouth. I waited. My sex was wide-open and wide-a-fucking-wake. But Roger didn't swallow the ice. He did something far more erotic. He ducked down to my pulsating cunt and let me feel the ice together with his tongue.

'Shisisis.'

The ice cream was cold on my fanny. I'd been split in half. I was like the magician's assistant, cut in two. My whole body reacted. I thrust out my groin, but it was pleasure, a pleasurable frost.

'I scream for ice cream,' I said slowly, as though hypnotised.

Roger licked the cream off his lips. His tongue worked a small wicked circle around his full mouth. He looked incredible, committed and devout. He led another application. This time, my body leaped as though to greet him. My pussy was on fire; the contrast between the heat of my clit and the chill of the ice was too intense to endure, and I gripped the ground beneath me, taking handfuls of sand. Oh God, I had never felt so, so devoured before.

'Eat me,' I hissed urgently. 'More, lick me all over. I want to come on your face.'

Roger slipped down obediently, and supped sensuously at my cone. I spread myself as wide as I could. Legs conveniently either side of him, my pubic hair a hot triangle, almost like an arrow, signalling the way.

'Oh God. Lick faster, harder, I want to really feel your tongue.'

I wrapped my arms around him as he lapped at me. Everything was focused on my muff. The rest of my body bowed to the power of my genitals. I was nothing but a flaming sensation.

'More,' I begged.

He stuffed the whole ice up me, and I bellowed into the dark night, into the sea, into the beach, but then he was there with his tongue and prying fingers extinguishing the cold and bringing more passion. My legs wobbling, my fingers were gripping him tight.

'I've never tasted ice cream this good.'

'Now,' I said. I pushed him down to straddle him. 'I'm going to fuck you.'

He squeezed his eyes shut, and let his penis do the talking. I felt the bone hold me down, keep me in line. When I slipped from too much wetness, I steadied myself on his rod and I hammered him.

'I'm fucking you,' I said as though he didn't know. I wouldn't stop the rhythm. I couldn't stop the momentum reaching crisis point. I was really fucking him. I'll tell you why. I was scared I was losing him. If he knew, if he only knew. I fucked like an animal, the last sighs of a dying man. I fucked the lost cause, fearing this would be our last. He put his fingers up to my inner lips, and I helped guide him to my pleasure zone.

'Rub me there.' Rub me forever – don't stop when you find out, don't ever stop.

'This is what the Thai boys want to do to you,' he said hatefully. 'They want to poke your hole.'

I couldn't help being aroused by his dirtiness, his crudity.

'Cunt,' he barked. 'You cunt, you want those men to fuck you. But I'm the only one who's allowed, aren't I?'

I nodded mutely. I was appalled at his brutality, but I wanted him so badly.

'Feel these fucking huge buttocks.'

Liquid excitement pouring out of my snatch. He liked that, me doing it to myself, and I showed him how before fixing his hand there.

'Squeeze your cunt.'

'Yes, and my clit, I'm playing with my clit.' I massaged my breasts, squirming with pleasures. I ripped harder and harder, willing myself to a magnificent climax.

I looked at Roger's face and saw that he looked almost as bewildered as I did. He had sand all over his hair. For a second, he looked grey; older than he really was. For a second, I thought I was looking at our future.

'Jesus, Abby, you've changed a lot.'

'What do you mean?'

'I mean you're much more assertive now. You never would have opened up to me like that before.'

When we got back to my room, we lay on crumpled sheets, side by side, like merry schoolgirls at a slumber party.

'Angela would never have done that,'

I felt the same mixture of triumph and pain as I always did when I was proved superior to Angela in some way.

'With the ice cream, you mean?'

'Oh no, she did that. She would never do it outside though.' We were facing the criss-crossed ceiling. I was still soaking wet and proud. I felt his come squelch up inside me and I loved it there.

'No one else can ever have you but me,' he hugged me tightly. 'You're all mine.'

I told Roger that I was hungry and would just nip out for a burger.

'After all,' I explained, 'I didn't get to eat the ice cream. You did.'

'OK,' he said demurely and I hated myself for lying.

I needed air. I felt stifled. I was being crucified by my love for him. I went back to the rocks, beating my hands on them like drums, hands that only minutes before held him. My betraying hands. Why didn't I wait for him? Why was I so easily led?

Lily was once again the one who rescued me. Staggering across the sand on giraffe heels, she saw me, and laboriously made her unwieldy way over.

'What's the matter?'

'I lied to Roger.'

She looked at me. 'What about?'

'About everything . . . about . . .' I didn't know where to begin, 'kissing you.'

'It's not so important.'

'But I feel it is,' I said. 'When I said, "I love you, no there is no one else", I didn't mean, except for a six-foot beauty queen who I would die to look like. When you promise fidelity you don't make exceptions; you don't say, but it doesn't count on foreign soil, or people of the same sex, do you?'

'Were there others?' Lily asked perceptively.

'Yes,' I said, hangdog. I could barely look up to the force of her beauty. She could do you in with those eyes. 'Yes, there were others, not sex exactly, but yes, kissing, heavy kissing.'

She stroked my hair; I felt like I was receiving her blessing. The great Lily was telling me it was OK. Nothing to worry about.

'Be honest with him.'

'Tell him?'

'Yes. If you're too unhappy to keep it a secret, tell him. I'm sure, he won't be angry. It's normal to stray a little in a place like this. We're like the animals, eh? We need to mate.'

All I wanted was for him to forgive me. And then maybe we could go home, away from this place, this heat, this madness, this sex asylum and be together. Just him and me.

He was asleep when I got back. I lay besides him, my stomach rumbling a hallelujah chorus. I knew what I had to do.

Chapter Eighteen

I resolved to get it over with first thing, but I couldn't. The dream was so weird that I woke up unsettled, yet aroused.

She didn't know how many came to her that night. She was beginning to despair that the penis would ever fit. The others didn't fit, that is, they did the job very well thank you, but they weren't the perfect fit. She was looking for her Cinderella.

And then just as it's getting late, and the courtiers are beginning to panic, and even the eunuchs are flapping around, the one arrived. As soon as it entered into her, with a humph and a groan, she knew she had it. As soon as her vagina was filled, and filled it was, without a millimetre to spare, no place uncovered, she was almost coming. Shaking courses throughout her body, and the courtiers and the eunuchs who have been so blasé, stand up to attention, with amazement.

Someone cries 'it is the one', and she thinks, I know that, stupid, and she's grinding her teeth, and grinding against him, and little tears are prickling at her eyes, with pain, with pleasure and gratefulness. He brings her to completion, he doesn't have to do anything, but be there;

her perfect fit, his upright attendance is enough. She comes wildly, glad of the silks that bind her, because she could hurt someone if she were free, and this way, she rails, and rails against her imprisonment, safe in it.

'Who was it?'

They take off her blindfold but they won't tell her who it is.

She runs up to each of them. And then to the King.

'Was it you, my lord?'

She lifts up his face, and she can see tears prickling in his eyes.

Roger put his arms round me and I gradually shook myself from the mystery of the penis contest.

'Do you remember the first time we got talking?' he said.

I smiled, 'Of course.'

After work, we were in a pub. I'd seen him, and he'd seen me, but we worked on different floors. That evening, he had a cold and my every maternal instinct cried out to take care of him. I wanted to take his pain, kiss him better. I told him remedies I knew, and we grinned at each other between his sniffs. I could hardly dare meet his eyes, but when I did, I was delighted. Despite his cold, they were brown and soulful. He touched my hand, said I was a lovely nurse, and how about a bed bath? I was thinking 'yes, please', but I pretended I was just a concerned friend.

I couldn't live with the guilt for too long. It seared my flesh, the same way the sun burns your shoulders. We spent the day on the beach, oozing oil on our backs. It was the perfect day; my perfect cast had been assembled, only my unspoken script hinted potently at the doom to come. Late afternoon, we returned to the bungalow. The room seemed different, a cabin of concealment, of heavy secrets and white lies.

'Roger, I haven't been completely honest with you.'

'What do you mean?'

He looked at me curiously.

'What exactly do you mean, Abigail?' he repeated.

'I don't know what I mean,' I admitted, prowling around the room. I felt terribly sorry for myself, and guilty that I did because it wasn't me that I should have felt sorry for.

'Come and sit on my lap.'

I looked at him uncertainly.

'Come, come tell daddy,' he said, and patted his knees again.

I told him everything. I started with my arousal on the airplane, the noise of José and Selma's sex and how hot I'd felt. I told him how watching all the people in couples, smooching and fondling made me feel; not lonely but horny. I told him this had never happened to me before, I'm a Virgo remember? Kissing with Lily came out first. I told him about the evening on the beach and the way she touched me but we both held back. Then I talked about touching with Selma, the lilo, talking with Trent, masturbating with him, and then I plunged into the bungalow massage.

'It wasn't full-on sex, you know; not penetrative, at least, well, they were women so, in that sense we couldn't but . . .'

I blistered on and on.

The only thing I didn't tell him about was Prem. But then, there was nothing solid, nothing real to tell about Prem. We had never even touched.

When I'd finished talking, I wiped my eyes, blew my nose loudly, and dared to face him. Roger was impassive. I had absolutely no idea if he was upset, angry or anything. He was a blank. He was like a picture of a face before you draw in the mouth.

'Say something.'

He shook his head.

'Say something, please.' I pulled at his hands, kissing his knuckles. He took his hands away.

'Please.' I knelt by him, my face on his thighs, subdued and penitent. 'Please.'

Finally, he raised my chin, locking my eyes with his.

'Abby, do you realise what you did?' he said. He sounded sinister, Hammer House of Horror scary.

'Yes, I know. I'm so, so sorry,' I gushed. I'd really hurt him. The apology didn't work. Perhaps repeating it a hundred times would give the desired effect.

'No, do you really understand what you've done?' he continued slowly, pushing the words out painfully. 'I've given up everything to be with you, and now you're telling me this!'

I wanted to cover my ears. I wanted to be anywhere but there, listening to that.

He made me kneel on the floor. I struggled.

'Don't be silly, Roger. Let's talk about it.'

'There's nothing to say,' he hissed.

I got down and leaned over the bed whispering, 'I'm sorry Roger.' Everything seemed weird and out of sync. Roger was ordering me around, taking control. I felt squirming sensations of pleasure mixed with fear. I didn't know what was going to happen next, all I knew was that Roger was taking control of the situation.

He raised my skirt and angrily ripped down my knickers. I was murmuring his name, what was he going to do? Then he slapped my buttocks. I fell forward in shock.

'Roger?' He'd never touched me before like this, never so passionately, so fiery as he did then.

'Don't speak to me again,' he said. I could feel the wet arousal slip down my legs. I was so turned on by his power, his anger. I wanted to tell him how much I was enjoying it, but when I raised my head to look at him, I could see he didn't care. He smacked me again, and again. My arse grew red yet still my cunt was producing; hot sticky white juice, and my clitoris, quivering oh so impatiently. It wanted to be touched too.

I found it hard to hold my balance. I thought of school days and wanting to be smacked, wanting to be controlled, wanting someone to treat me like the naughty girl I was.

'Roger . . .'

'If you don't shut up, I'll do it harder,' he snarled and, because I couldn't imagine how he could possibly smack me any harder than he already was, I shut up.

My nipples were hard. I was a naughty girl.

Slap. Each impact created a big explosion. I imagined asteroids landing on the earth, landing on the moon. Great fat craters and shooting stars.

Slap. Give me your prick, Roger. Stuff me with your cock. Suffocate me with your manhood. Take me anyway you like. Just give it to me.

Slap. I was a naughty, dirty whore. I deserved punishment. Sent to the headmaster's study for talking in class. 'Please, sir, may I have some more.' I deserved far more than this.

'Roger.' I turned around.

Roger was taking off his leather belt. He snapped it in the air a couple of times, and then stood behind me as I knelt humiliatingly waiting for my punishment.

Crack. Help me, God. But I was gushing and my nipples were desperate for a mouth, his mouth. I wanted to slide down to the floor and squirm against the floorboards. He was the boss and I would show him that I knew that, I accepted that.

'Did they make you come?'

'No.'

'You're lying. Did they make you come?'

'Some of them did,' I whimpered.

'Let's start from the beginning, who was it? The neighbour, whatshername?'

'Selma – no, she didn't.'

CRACK, the whip smacked my buttock like a flame.

'Liar!'

'She didn't!' I wept. 'We were interrupted.'

'The one with the tongue piercing?'

'Trent,' I muttered.

'Louder!' SMACK. The belt soared over my buttock cheeks. He started doing it some times, and not the

151

others, so that I would draw in my breath, and then it wouldn't land on my cheeks. Other times, when I would think it wouldn't come down, it did. He was teasing me with a leather belt.

'TRENT!' I bellowed. Tears were washing down my face, and my nose was running too. I wiped it on the blue/white back of my wrist. My skin was raw. I feared the top surface would peel off.

'Hands down,' he barked. WHIP! His bark was not as bad as the bite of the whip.

'Did I say you could move?'

I shook my head. I suddenly thought what if someone could see me now? I must have looked like a total, terrible victim. And yet, how aroused I was. I wanted him to fuck me now, really give it to me hard like a madman.

'Did he make you come?' insisted Roger.

'I was thinking of you all the time.' I pleaded.

Crack! The leather fell on the roundest part of my arse. I writhed with agony and shame. I would be blue tomorrow.

'How many times?'

'We had oral sex once, and then with his fingers.'

'Did you blow him?'

'Yes.'

Crack! Funny how you don't get used to it at all. You'd think the body would prepare, would somehow ready itself for torture after four or five swipes. Instead my back and my arse were more surprised than ever. I thought of those sea creatures, turtles with a shell on their back. Imagine that you have a magical shell, I thought.

'And the masseuses?'

'Yes,' I whispered.

'With their tongues?' he said.

'No.'

He allowed me to get a tissue to blow my nose and wash my face. When I came back, he made me get in the same position as before though. His voice – and mine, too – was now controlled and regular. I suppose, if you heard us from outside the door, you would think we were just going on with our daily business.

'How? With their fingers?'

'Yes, and . . . with a suntan lotion bottle.'

Roger started laughing; he threw his head back and laughed. When I peeped around to see, I could see his metal fillings in their holes. And then he slapped me hard, with such force, that I almost tipped over.

'Fucked by factor five,' he laughed. 'Well, it's good protection against sunburn.'

He got me into the doggy position again. His fingers were all over me, octopus. How many hands, tentacles did he have, there he was between my legs, fingering my pussy, there he was down the silk road, there he was moving away from my fanny, moving backwards.

'No.' I shook my head. He was searching out my hole. The black hole between my buttocks.

'Fuck, it's been such a long time.'

Once, many moons ago, I let him have entrance there. Roger vaselined me. And then he licked me, tickling me. He made me lean over the sofa. 'This isn't going to work; this isn't going to work,' I was warning him. But I didn't mind because I knew she, Angela, Roger's wife wouldn't. And anything that made me better than her was not to be sneezed at. But it was hell. There was no room. It was like stuffing a sausage in a matchbox, a camel through the eye of a needle. I was frozen in agony. You know they say childbirth becomes less painful in memory, well this memory of getting fucked up the back passage became more and more painful as time passed.

'I'm going to fuck you up the arse.'

'No.' I leaped up but he judo threw me onto the bed, my arm behind me. Mouthing the words, no. Squirming, like a slippery monster, I twisted around onto my back and batted him away.

'You're so naughty, you know that?'

'No.'

'You're a bad girl, I didn't know how bad.'

The change in position didn't stop him.

He forced my legs up over his shoulders. For a moment, my guard was down; we were going to make love like old times, his cock, my cunt, romantic missionaries. Then his finger was digging at my arse hole, the way they dig holes in the sand, and my buttocks were giving way for him. He tried for access again and again, and then he found what he was looking for.

'No!'

I twisted myself out of his grip. Slipping away, we were both sweating, like two hurling sumo wrestlers. Outside, the sea fucks over the sand, and inside we fuck violently. His fingers were tracing me, tracing out my rim.

'Roger, stop.'

He wouldn't stop. Seek and ye shall find. He found. My anus was vacant, and he came inside. He separated my cheeks, and for one second, I felt the air swirl around and then his finger dived and plunged and everything became a lot warmer.

He knew I hated it, hated and loved it, hate and love, two sides of the same coin, two sides of his finger. He massaged my hole, stealing my decorum.

'Roger,' I gargled. And then he was working at his prick, rolling on the fuck skin, his cock was pressing against that small place, that comma, and he was impaling me on his stick.

The walls of my arsehole tightened around the foreign body. I felt my buttocks clench around him. My snatch was bubbling with joy.

I crunched back against him, used and exploited. I loved it. I did miss him. I was foaming at the mouth, rabid dog, pushing against his cock, having him blot out my being. Then he started to thrust. He was thrusting in a space that was not, and I was going with the flow, going with his movements, timing mine against him, rubbing, feeling his cock. His face was contorted agony, sweat rising on his lower lip, his eyes swimming with tears. He came; ejaculating in a series of sharp jerks, in my tightness, and God, I hated myself for it, but I let out a scream as my climaxing body betrayed me.

I was forgiven. I chewed the pillow, and inwardly rejoiced.

Chapter Nineteen

'You don't think I've forgiven you, do you?' asked Roger.

'What?' I was surprised. I was brushing my hair in the mirror with long powerful strokes. Electricity was flying. Outside, the sun caressed the balcony. I was going to sit out on the hammock, and perhaps stroll over to the café for some coffee.

'You don't think that you can make it up to me in one night, do you?'

'No, I . . .'

'Do you want me to leave you?'

'No,' I said without hesitation. 'I want you. I've always wanted you.'

'Well then, I'm afraid the punishment will continue.'

I smiled but he didn't smile back. His lips were set. I couldn't remember when he last smiled at me.

'I'm going to tie you up.'

I lay on the bed, aroused. I was wet with sweat. I wasn't allowed a shower. He looked at me, and said out loud – though I don't think he was asking me.

'Shall I gag you? No, I don't think so. Not yet.'

He left me with just my mouth and one hand free.

'What's this for?'

'I want you to play with yourself.'

I started tentatively. He was looking; how did I look? Spread on the bed, open, and easy?

I poked my hole, feeling my warmth.

'Yes,' he murmured. 'Touch yourself more.'

Exploring the wilds, the soft curly tendrils, the body-heat, and then the liquid walls. I was filling my cavity. I would have done anything for him. I arched my back, my buttocks raised. My legs were bent and my other hand squashed behind my head.

'Tell me what you are thinking . . . You're thinking of those men, aren't you? Little whore!'

'No.' I was thinking of him, watching me; him. The hard look on his face as he slapped me; the clenching of his eyes as he came up me; the shaft, the stimulation; bliss, satisfaction. As my orgasm subsided and I grew soft in my warm hollow, I wondered suddenly what reason Lily had for saying no. Did she find me unattractive?

'Slapper,' he said abruptly, as though he'd read my mind. He tied the free hand behind my back, and then marched out of the room.

For the first few minutes, I thought he was just playing outside the door, watching for my reactions. I pictured him waiting there, watching the world go by. Maybe he was chatting with Selma, watching her as she wrung out her wet clothes.

Then I thought he'd gone to the café. Maybe he was cooling off with a shake, rubbing a straw inside his mouth. Sitting staring at the too-slow staff. Or maybe he was playing volleyball on the beach. Waiting for Trent, waiting to beat him up, to smash him to smithereens, before telling him what a terrible dog I was.

After about half an hour, the time merged into one long forever. I sensed it becoming afternoon; the heat seeming to thicken. The sun pierced a slit in the curtain and made light patterns on the floor. I could smell meat frying in the café, and I grew hungry. My lips were like cardboard and my head grew foggy. If only I could have reached for the fan.

And then Selma and José returned to their room. They were arguing first, I don't know what about, and then they recommenced their fucking. It made me hot and wet, but there was nothing I could do. I swayed; dry humping, but to no avail. I let out a few sighs when she did, but that was all. Eventually, they fell quiet, and I was relieved, but lonely, like a mother when the crying baby finally stops. I supposed it was early evening. I began to bristle with tiredness. I studied my body in the dim light. My spread thighs looked like meat on a butcher's hook. My breasts were pale and pointless, obscene mounds.

Poor Roger, poor, poor Roger. He loved me. He came all this way to the other side of the world, only to find that the woman he loved couldn't wait. Why couldn't I have held out? Still, when I thought of Lily's hands on my breasts, Selma's legs and her tongue, and Trent and . . . when I thought of Prem . . .

Yet I was glad at least that I had told him, because I knew that only through suffering, would we arrive at a new understanding.

I held it in for as long as I could. I could feel my tummy fill out plump. Poor bladder was full to overflow. I tried to ignore it. Think of the world. Think of all the poor people who suffer lots of things. Worse things happen at sea. I thought of torture, and bad things. This was happening to me out of love, at least he loved me.

I let go. My own piss was streaming down my legs. I felt humiliated. I have not wet myself since the time when I was nine and the zipper on my jeans got stuck.

What if something bad had happened to Roger? Sinister things happened on these hot tropical islands. And no one would ever know. They were so hard to get to.

Roger came back when it was dark. I'd spent the whole day, a prisoner in a bungalow. He smelled of whisky, and he looked dishevelled.

'Jesus, what have you done?' he asked. He looked at me disgusted.

'I pissed the bed.' I tried to make a joke of it.

When he released me, I tried to hit him, but he was too strong.

'Be careful, or I'll tie you up again.'

'What do you want from me?' I asked. I was near to tears but determined not to go there.

'Lots of things,' he said but then his voice lightened, and it was as though I'd switched the dial on the radio, from the news to pop.

'Come on, babe, you must be starving.'

We had dinner at Sunita Lodge. Fortunately, the food was served promptly. Prem didn't say a word. And I was too embarrassed to meet his eye. What would he say if he knew? He'd say I deserved it, he'd say I was bad news, he always knew I was. 'Foreign women,' he'd say, 'slags'. We ate spicy soup and noodles. I did my best not to dribble but I could feel myself turning into someone who couldn't control herself. Roger's nose was red and peeling. When I touched it, the tender skin made me feel quite strange, as though I was touching something extremely private.

We talked about taking a trip to the waterfalls together. Roger said the sea air was doing him good.

'I'd like to have gone swimming today,' I expressed tentatively.

I was beginning to forget those lazy technicolor days basting on the sand. I was back in a black and white world again.

He cocked an eyebrow at me, and said. 'But, Abigail, that's a treat and you're too naughty to have treats.'

'What did you do today then?' I whispered.

'I went to see a bargirl,' he said.

I ignored him. I thought he was lying.

On the way back to the bungalow he made us stop halfway under some trees where spiders' webs glistened, and small insects were mating. Roger wanted to fuck again and I was more than willing. He loved me. He loved me a lot.

I couldn't speak. I could barely kiss. Oh yes, he was so in control of me. I couldn't stop myself from contracting around him, flapping my lips protectively around him, slurping back my own dribble. I was better than any bargirl. I raised my leg higher for more leverage; he had my thigh in his hand. I locked my foot around his back. We'd never been able to do this before, but tonight, tonight, we would. The air was still and heavy with impending trouble. The heat was incredible.

I had my hands on his buttocks. I gripped the underside of his cheeks driving him closer to me. Making him shaft me, ram me like a battering ram bringing the door down; up, up, we go, me smashing upwards, pushing my hole downwards onto him. Meeting his hammering, one by one.

'Don't stop,' I urged. 'I want this to last forever.'

He controlled his pulsing.

'OK, softly, softly, catchy monkey.'

'Oh God, don't move.' I was wrapped up him, he was wrapped up in me, he was a present and I, the pretty paper.

'This feels amazing. Don't, don't ever stop. Roger, you're amazing.'

I whispered things to him, things I'd never said before. I gave myself up to him completely. I was no longer human, but a fucking machine, his plaything. I wanted him to treat me like a rubber doll, take my hole and fill it up.

'Fuck me, fuck me,' I groaned into his ears, anything. But we couldn't go on forever. My mind was racing.

I remembered what Randy said about noisy girls, and about Melinda. It turned me on. I wondered how Selma felt when Trent did to her the same things he had done to me.

'Yes, yes,' I bellowed, hot in Roger's ear. 'I'm coming.'

He knew that anyway, but I had to say the words, for effect, for adornment. What's a Christmas tree without decorations? What's an orgasm without the declarations?

'I'm coming.'

He snarled between gritted teeth, and I held him tight. It was like restraining a lunatic, as he throbbed deliciously in my tight hole, yes, yes, yes!

The next afternoon, Prem was balancing at the top of a tree. I'd watched him climb up. Knees bent, then straightened, he hurled himself up the smooth trunk. He was swinging one-armed from the top branches. The King of the castle, surrounded by dirty rascals. Then the driver's mate joined him, and the two of them, monkey boys, threw coconuts at the ground. Pounding, boom. When one rolled near me, I picked it up and put it in the wicker barrel where some children were collecting them.

Other people were approaching, excited by loud noise, curious for a possible incident. Trent joined the crowd with two pretty Western girls in bikinis either side of him.

I said hello, but he didn't hear me, or he chose not to.

'This is the second main cause of death on this island,' he said to the women.

'What is?' asked the girl in a big sunhat.

'Getting hit on the head by a coconut.'

Everyone laughed nervously. Some edged away. I stayed watching Prem's big arms work loose a fruit.

'No, honestly it is,' he said, 'Unbelievable, eh?'

'And what's the first?'

'Motor bike accidents.'

I stared up wild-eyed. I felt the speed of my heartbeat treble. But it was not death I was thinking of when I looked up at Prem. It was not death.

'Abby, come here.' Roger was calling me. He stood at

161

the bungalow entrance, like a man ordering his errant dog home.

The next time, I was tied up against one of the wooden supports. As Roger fixed the knots a hiss of excitement escaped his teeth. He used a washing line.

'Where did you get this from?'

'The guy from Sunita Lodge. Your friend.'

Roger still hadn't bothered to learn anyone's name.

I was spread-eagled; bound even tighter than the last time. I was struggling and railing against the knots.

'It's a bit tight,' I said, my face shot with arousal.

'It's just right,' he said.

In books and films, they give room to struggle but Roger didn't give any hope of resistance. I too was breathing heavily, my heart was hammering at my ribs. I could hear the creak of the hammock next door. I supposed Selma was lying there, her long brown legs open to the world. Or perhaps it was José, rocking back and forth, his hands down his pants like a small boy in winter.

'You're going to stay here all night,' said Roger, tightening the remaining cord around my ankle.

'You're joking, aren't you?'

'No.' He lay on the bed and flicked through my guidebook, ignoring me.

The bands were tight around my breast. One cut across the top half, the other the lower half. My nipples were covered with tiny red bumpy enthusiasms. But already I was getting cold. And I was so uncomfortable, dangling from the straps like this with everything pulled up and in. I was bound up like a mummy.

'Roger.' I didn't want the panic to show in my voice, but a quivering note slipped in. 'I can't stay like this all night.'

'Alright,' he said. He flopped back on the bed, his arms behind his head and his big schlong coming alive between his fingers. I watched him hungrily. He held back his foreskin, and the bulb at the end of his penis seemed to be staring at me triumphantly. He didn't seem bothered about wanking though. He picked up and left off, started and then stopped, as though eating chocolates that were fattening but delicious. I'm different, once I start fiddling; I have to finish the job in hand.

'I'll suck it,' I offered wildly, offering him the world. My mouth felt dry, but he did look delectable, arrogant and in control. I was silly and wet. He worked his prick harder, and he groaned as though he were in pain. From where I was, I could see his balls nestling under his cock, full of sperm ready to shoot out on to me.

'I have something you can do. To make it up for me.'

I started to sigh with fear and pleasure. Deep breaths, deep breaths, Abby. I liked this game. When we were teenagers bursting with sexuality we used to play postman's knock and I remembered the thrill of waiting for your number, walking the death march into the room with a stranger, giving him your kiss.

He came at me, with a cucumber. I remembered Prem cutting the vegetables the first time I saw him.

'Where did you get this from?'

'Your friend.'

'What did you say?' I was suddenly appalled. What did Prem think of me? Cucumbers and washing line? Small splinters grazed my back. My buttocks were still sore from the other day's punishments. Plus I wanted to use the bathroom. I would have done anything to be set free, anything.

'Open your legs wider, honey. I can't see your hole.'

I leaned back against the post, letting it take the weight. He was down again at my fanny, peeling away my self-respect, parting my legs with a light touch, and I was allowing him to. My legs were shaking. He smoothed them like he was modelling from clay.

'You've got such lovely skin,' he said, and I smiled at the unexpected compliment. His hands moved towards my pussy. I grimaced and struggled, but he was gentle,

gentle, parting my lips now, and sliding along the inside of my tender sex.

'Please,' I murmured.

'Jesus, you're gushing already.'

'Now, please now, do something.'

I needed something solid. I was humping the air and I needed more, much more. Opening up, like a flower, I felt humble and small. He played with the cucumber, teasing me, and then inserted it. As it arrived in my hollow I felt my cunt fiercely throb its approval.

'This is the only waterfall you're going to see.'

This was great, playing greengrocers. My thighs were bent inwards, but were too tightly affixed to gain ground. I pushed and pressed. If I clenched my muscles, I could really get something going. I was anxious for friction, fluidity. He stood over me, and while he masturbated me with the vegetable, he fed his hard cock into my mouth. He held my head back, so he was pouring it down me, like a drink, down in one, it went right down me, it would surely hit my tonsils, and then when he removed it, I spluttered.

I groaned. I couldn't help looking at my hardening nipples incredulously, and he put his fingers there, squeezing me tight.

Suddenly, I didn't expect it then, he spurted hot cream gush all over my face and I fast-blinked it out of my eyes.

I needed more of the cucumber, I should have more vegetables; they are good for you.

'There,' I said. I really thought our scores were settled. They must have been by now. His come dripped down my face. I licked it when it arrived at my mouth, but mostly it dribbled past, down my cheek, cold onto my neck.

'That wasn't it. No that was just a warm-up, baby.'

'Let me off here,' I pleaded. I wasn't in a bargaining position.

'No, you have to say yes first.'

'To what?'

'There are two tasks,' he explained.

'Yes,' I said weakly. 'OK.'

'You can't go back on your word, promise?'

'Promise.'

I nodded. I would have agreed to anything. He unknotted my torture. I slipped off the post and slumped on to the floor.

Chapter Twenty

You must wonder why I agreed to what happened next. I suppose you think I was a stupid cow. I know if the situations were reversed, and it were you doing this, and I were reading about you, I would have no sympathy. Like at the pantomime, when all the kids call out, 'He's behind you', you're probably muttering silently, 'He's married'. Yes, he was. I admit that.

I could try and explain that I did it because I loved him. I felt guilty, and I felt that I had to make it up to him. But although that would be true, it wouldn't be the whole truth.

The island had changed me. I felt the heat in my skin, the fire in my heart, the freedom and the anonymity. I didn't need security, I didn't need protection: I was cool now. Everything I used to worry about had faded away to the trivial, now I wanted just to fulfil my basic needs.

Hey, don't tell me you wouldn't be tempted? If you had the chance to one, sleep with a woman, and two, sell your body for the night, don't try to tell me that you wouldn't be just a little curious.

That night, Roger rearranged me as though I were his baby doll. He placed me gently on the bed. I felt tears of pleasure and pain wrack my body, my heart ached with love for him. I could make him happy! He came to me, yes, he came to me, and I nursed him at my breasts, clutching his dark hair, and he gently pushed himself to my moist place, and heaved a sigh of pleasure when he arrived. I let him make love to me, peacefully, gently, and his kisses washed away the pain.

I love you, I love you.

I acquiesced to everything. I was hot and bothered and still dazed. He worried that I was dehydrated, but I said that I was OK. He was still sorry, so sorry about the cucumber.

'No, I'm sorry,' I said, grabbing his cheeks and making him meet my eyes. He apologised again, said that he just got carried away, and hadn't I enjoyed it, too? I had, I admitted, but it was the way he did it that hurt, without waiting for my consent. His knees were sore from rubbing on the ground. He had always had bad knees. He said pleasure and pain were two sides of the same coin. He said the opposite of love was indifference. He said I excited him too much, and I was thrilled.

I excited Roger too much!

He told me I had to wait in darkness. He would send Selma in. Yes, she knew all about it. She wanted to help, to be a part of the punishment. Roger would simply watch. He wouldn't tell me where from, but rest assured, he would see everything.

We struggled out of our clothes. She slid her hands easily into my dress, but I had problems with hers. Her clothes were so tight; there was no space for invaders. Her skin was translucent, luminous, and running my hands along her back was like stroking alabaster.

We kissed, and I felt the shock of finally having mouth-to-mouth contact with her. Her cupid-bow lips were determined, concrete. I felt she was in a hurry to get on to greater things, and I wished that she wasn't. I was nervous about proceeding and wanted to dally. She kissed well, as I knew she would, taking every segment of my mouth thoroughly, owning me, possessing me and, however much I tried to equal her, I knew she was in control.

She pulled the mirror down by us. We opened each other up on the bed enjoying the reflection. There were two of us, two hungry ovals, gaping for stimulation, arousal.

I had seen Selma with José so many times, but she was different with me. With him, she let him do it to her, but with me, she was active and, although I was not passive, it was her who initiated the proceedings. It was her who made me put my fingers into her cunt, first one finger, then two, three, then an incredible four, and it was she who licked around my arse hole, sending shivers through me, like I'd never had before.

Selma opened her legs wide and I had no choice but to touch her, not that I didn't want to, but she was shoving her hot sticky shape at me. When the first finger went in, Selma made this little noise, a groan, and then she started moving. She was half on her back, half-sitting, and she started winding herself up against me, her eyes black and hooded. She told me to do more, I got down, so that I could actually see what her clitoris looked like. Would it feel like touching down at Koh Samui airport? Would it be like a mushy fruit?

She groaned with pleasure, and told me to add another finger.

Her voice was hoarse, and her eyes were rolling.

She clutched me around the shoulders, the hair; told me I was beautiful. I believed her. I was different to her: bigger, looser, sluttier maybe. Perhaps she liked that. We kissed and fondled; fondled and kissed. She clutched my arse tight and when she felt the row of welts she seemed to excite more and she said she knew I was a bad girl, who loved punishment. I held her tight, viciously even. Biting her neck, her chest and rubbing my nipples against hers hard.

I was aware how we looked and that turned me on. Where was Roger spying from? I was careful not to show my excitement, this was my punishment after all, but maybe he'd be angry if I didn't express myself too much. (Imagine being on a stage, a concert in front of 10,000 fans cheering you on, as you bang, fucking up against the speakers. They howl for you, they Mexican wave for you and you fuck, fuck and fuck, giving the best show of your life.)

Knowing I was being watched added an extra dimension to being with Selma. In the place of intimacy grew showmanship. What did we look like, two clinging animals, tight and smooth? I loved Roger so much that I was screwing for him. I moved for him, my womb clenched for him. My buttocks were bucking up and down. I wanted to create a good memory for him.

'Is this alright? Is this good?'

She told me to stop asking, 'just do it.' Watch her and do, and tell her what I like.

She put her fingers inside me.

'Wow, you're soaking wet! Like that day in the sea,' she added. 'Remember the lilo? Springing up and down?'

That excited us more. We faced the mirror and we did it side by side, until she pushed me down to get on top of me. I looked wild, my face was like Selma's on the plane, the lips open strawberry, the eyes lit up, and the colour of the skin was the same as sticky toffee apples. I saw them in the mirror, my incredulity – our incredulity – that we were here, her hands along my thighs bringing me alive, my hands on that small flank, gripping her around the waist, exploring the buds of her nipple, her narrow silky shoulders.

I struggled my way to reach her down there. I could see the shiny pinkness, but I couldn't reach, and I didn't want to disturb the magnificent storm that was rising between my legs. Finally, she swivelled around, perching her pussy on my nose, leaving me to seek out her clitoris with my tongue. We were locked in a heavenly 69. I was breathing inside her cunt and she was facing mine. I pulled her silky thighs down either side of my head, and I slapped her buoyant cheeks. She did the same to me, tracing the lines of my scars, reminding me of the past few days and how I was up for anything. She pumped up and down on my face and I licked everywhere desperately, praying that she wouldn't stop licking me. We were crammed together, held in a sea of wetness, slathering mouths and moist pussies. Together, doing it in time.

'More, more, please.'

'Yes?' I was growing good. Yes, I knew how to flick on a woman's body, how to massage that small nodule. All for Roger. See how she sits on my face. See how she writhes, and her breasts bounce in time.

'Oh, oh yes, like that.' And she worked at me, diligently, fingers and tongues, tongues and fingers, shaking my world. My body imploded. A series of thrusting shakes, and then a quiet, a quiet spreading warmth.

'Trent said that you came very quickly; he said that you were so fast.'

Roger burst in, full of congratulations. He was very theatrical with his darlings and kisses. I saw that his zip was undone. Then he dropped his clothes, and without a shred of doubt, he climbed onto the bed, the Milk Tray man but instead of chocolates, he came, throbbing cock ahoy, like a policeman's baton, to take us in hand.

I was sandwiched between the two of them. I was facing Selma, my arms around her, on her beautiful slip-slimy skin. Roger was behind me, gripping us both madly. They were fighting for possession of me, fighting over me, with loving arms, searching hands, and their lips everywhere. Selma had the head start, but then Roger, of course, Roger had the precious cock.

Selma worked her hands over me and at each touch I quivered and whimpered for more. I was almost there again; it wouldn't take much. To be divided and to be loved like this was incredible. I was fought over; I was Helen of Troy. This was what travelling is, travelling to the end of my mind. Then Selma got off, and went to her bag. I felt Roger was going to win, he was preparing to enter me, but no, Selma had fished out a dildo.

She rammed the thing up me triumphantly. She was going to fuck me, not him. I felt my body bulge with pleasure, my cunt contracting like a flower around the strange possession of my sex. She started tugging it in and out. She had succeeded. I was a minute off coming, and I was so slippery, that the passage of the vibrator was too easy. Roger played diligently with my breasts, isolating the points, groaning over them, but Selma was in the position to get down and eat them. She stuffed them in her mouth, like a child eating strawberries and my nipples stiffened gratefully. Selma had won.

But Roger hung on in there, his legs clenched around me. His hands on my bottom, his hands squeezing my arse, so tight, that I could feel my cunt squirm against the dildo, and then he parted my buttocks, so firmly, so authoritatively, that I didn't feel that no was an option. He felt his way to my anus, my little hole, and with a swooping movement he plunged in a finger.

'No,' I hissed. I was sore and bruised there from the times he had brutalised that tiny wishing well. He was, literally, a pain in the arse.

'Not again, not now, please.'

I knew arguing the point would turn Selma on even more, and I was wary of resisting too much, because I knew how this excited her but I wanted to make my annoyance clear.

I felt the finger squirming up the familiar yet painful place, but I felt a terrible fear.

'No.' Selma was working the dildo up me. Her other hand was wandering freely over my clitoris. She vibrated her fingers knowledgeably. Expert Selma. Her face was dedicated, and urgent. His trespassing finger flickered up my arse now warm and lovely but . . .

'Yes,' said Selma, 'Do it to her with your cock.' The words were filled with intent.

'I don't want you to,' I wept. I knew I was speaking to deaf ears.

'Yes, Roger, do it to her up there, while I do her here.'

I didn't know who was more excited, her or me. I couldn't see Roger's face, but suddenly, I felt a terrible abandonment as he removed his finger, and my arse muscles relaxed. And then he was big and hard behind me, moving in for the action, and the dildo was making me so loose and so ready, that I didn't give a damn, I didn't give a fuck about them. I only gave a fuck. They were both working on me, on my pleasure. Every orifice was filled with stimulation. They were obliterating me. Real cock and surreal cock were consuming me, taking me out of my senses.

Our sweat mingled, as we three rubbed together, and our groans joined, we were singing our coming, like a village choir. I was first; the fucking trigger and as I came, my body trembling, I watched as Selma withdrew the dildo like a champion, and whipped it into her.

Roger was still trembling behind me, but I wanted to be a winner, too. I worked the dildo up and down Selma's honey-sex, and just when I thought she was going to come, I sneaked my finger around her back passage and took her up the arse as well. She moaned and winced, but I insisted. My finger felt warm and locked there, and as her body stirred viciously into an unwilling orgasm, I felt her body contracting around me, and I knew what sheer pleasure it was to fuck someone.

Later, Roger and I fucked while she took her turn watching us. She sat in the corner of the room masturbating like a naughty girl and I thought, this is heaven: me and my man, and the world watching. I wished there were more people in the audience, more people watching me writhe, secrete and turn. This was freedom.

Chapter Twenty-One

We were standing in the street, discussing what to do next, when the car drew up. I'd seen it go round the block once, hugging the kerb, windows down, but this time it stopped.

There were two men inside. Roger went over to speak to them.

'What are they saying?' I said when he returned rubbing his chin sheepishly.

'They want to have an hour with a woman.'

I licked my lips nervously. All I could see of the men was the back of their necks roasted pink. I didn't want to see any more of them. I swallowed. My nipples were hard at the prospect of an hour, just an hour.

'Do you want me to?'

'It's up to you,' he said, although I'm not sure that was entirely true.

'How much shall I ask?'

'Three thousand,' he suggested.

I opened the car door and, as I did so, I felt this amazing feeling of power. I sat down on the passenger, with my arm around him. Now I could see him, a spotty raw neck, flabby baby hands and gentle looking, thank God. My thighs looked awfully big flung over him like that. Pink faces, jowls and love handles. Neither nervous, nor arrogant. They had done this before, I decided, but not often.

'Where have you been?' I said breaking a cardinal rule about not speaking. They looked at me with surprise, so I said quickly, 'OK, I suck you.'

I got down to the corner of the car. It was clean; the way hire cars usually are, sparse and barren. No frills. All they had was a map; a guidebook, well thumbed – just like me; and their desires.

The guy in the passenger seat looked thrilled. I began unbuttoning his fly. He awoke all the compassion juices in me. Imagine if I could do this for everyone in the world. Imagine if I could cure them of their racism, their sexism, their pain, just by sucking on their knobs. Would I do it, would you? I shouldn't have. It was small, even erect it was small, but there was lead in the pencil yet, and it was stiff as an ironing board. I let it in, my cheeks pushed it to the side like a gob-stopper. I could put the whole length of it in my mouth, so that my face was pressed against the overflow of stomach. It was cute. The driver was waiting patiently. The two were speaking to each other. I didn't want him to come yet – OK, so I wasn't a very good prostitute.

I stood up and raised my Thai-writing T-shirt, revealing my breasts to him.

'How much?' he breathed.

'It's a treat,' I muttered back. The car was steamed up. As he sucked my nipples, I drew pictures of cocks on the window, and tits, round ones, like cakes and a cunt like an open flower. He wasn't as gentle as a real lover would be, but then he wasn't bad for a paying customer. It felt nice. He's paying me for this, I thought, and actually, I would have paid him.

Oh, yes, I was losing it. Didn't he know? I hadn't been penetrated for ages, for at least a couple of hours, I needed it, I would dry up without it.

I sucked the surprise out of him. Spit or swallow, surely prozzies don't spit.

He was clutching my arse towards him.

I worked on the other man's cock. They weren't big men. Powerless as driftwood. I was oozing inside my knickers. I slipped my hand up my skirt.

They were speaking in German, over my head, bewildered but pleased.

'Let me do that,' said the man gallantly. When he touched me, he actually went, huh, like from shock, and I could tell he was more than a little surprised at my arousal.

I liked the second man's dick better; cleaner. I focused my mouth on that and my hand on the other. He twiddled around between my legs, a look of sheer ecstasy on his face, and he was gabbling to his friend.

His friend wanted a turn.

He put his fingers up my passage and rubbed as though he expected a genie to appear any minute.

'Gentler,' I said and showed him how I enjoyed it most, 'Like this.'

He copied obediently. It was as if I was the paying customer, and he was offering a service. That wasn't right.

I ducked down to blow them both together. Alternating prick service, one hard cock then the other. Skin taste in my mouth, my hands slimy with rudeness. I was in control, and they were speaking gibberish. They had octopus hands, roaming all over me, squeezing, and grasping. The more I groaned, the tighter they clasped me, poking me, playing with me. I let them feel me up, let them do what they liked to my tits, my pussy, my arse, because everything was fucking glorious, everything was fucking meaningless, and Roger would love me more than ever. I sucked them alternately, I sucked them masterfully, and they serviced me, more than they needed to. Jesus, even by thinking about the situation I was nearly coming, never mind actually doing it. Two

175

cocks side by side, four balls side by side, and one mouth wet and horny covering them, hot and sticky until they exploded and then I slipped my fingers over my clitoris and rubbed, rubbed and rubbed again, until I too came.

I put the money back in the driver's trouser pocket. They dropped me off where they'd picked me up, and where Roger was waiting smoking a cigarette in the shadows. The dark made his face look twisted and I thought, for a second, that he was a ghost. Then he stepped forward, put his arm around me and said, 'Atagirl, you really gave it to them. How much did you get?'

'No one pays for my body,' I said.

Roger didn't say anything.

When the car headlights lit up the street, I saw that he was smiling.

Chapter Twenty-Two

*R*oger had gone out for a while but he'd promised not to be long. He was getting browner, the sun was at liberty to colour him while I was losing my tan and becoming ghostly. But I didn't care. I sat in the dark. He'd pulled the blinds but that good old chink of light persevered. At my request, he'd left the fan on. If I sat in front of it, my nipples grew hard like china, but aching and full. They needed attention. After he positioned me, he said I looked like a sculpture, from ancient Rome or somewhere, with my breasts upright, and my buttocks tight. I'd laughed. My wrists were behind my back, but I thought I'd be able to pull them over my head. One leg was attached to the bed, but with the other I was almost free.

This morning he fucked me ferociously. What we did last night thrilled him, thrilled both of us. I wondered what life we would have together, two perverts, two outcasts. Would we fuck people often? Would we consider ourselves bohemian? Open relationships had a rancid smell of the seventies, wife-swapping suburbia. I didn't want us to be like that, but yet, the threesome, the tripod, the tri-athlete is so much more remarkable than the bi-athlete.

This morning he fucked me in my mouth, my arse, and my cunt. He did so mechanically, and each time I orgasmed with shudders and terrible shouts, and nonsense words, a stream of fuckingness. I would not have believed my orgasms myself if I hadn't known them, the howls that came from my mouth, and when he grasped me by the hips, controlling my every contortion, I spasmed like a slippery eel.

I crawled across the floor to his travel bag. Crawling; he made me crawl this morning; dirty, he made me crawl to find him. I was humiliated. The floor was sandy, and had protruding nails that spiked me. A pair of smelly wet swimming trunks was in the corner. He made me lick his feet, there were baby stones between the cracks, and his toenails had grown long and misshapen, but I did so willingly.

I was bored. I reached the bag and with my mouth, I pulled at the zip. My teeth; I was grateful to them. I saw the Swiss army knife, and I wondered how I could open it.

The slim envelope of airline companies. His passport and ticket was inside.

'We are pushing the envelope,' he had said last night. That was it: 'enjoying the extremes.' My nest was moist just thinking of it. Pushing the envelope through the slot perhaps, my slot.

'Tied up in Thailand,' he said, 'We could make a film about it.'

'No one would believe it actually happened,' I said. I was proud of my experience. It wasn't one that I would repeat to the grandchildren (our grandchildren!) but it was one to keep forever.

Gingerly, I pulled at the passport with my teeth. With my hands still tied, I worked the pages apart, examining the photo of him. Passport photos; he looked sane and gorgeous. Why had they said I only liked unavailable bastards? It wasn't true. I had a ridiculous urge to stuff the photo up inside me, even his photo could fuck me successfully, even his passport photo!

I moved my mouth to examine the rest of the contents. And then Roger stormed in.

'What the hell are you doing?'

'Nothing.'

'Don't go through my things,' he yelled, and yanked them away from me.

He refused to explain where he'd been. I knew though. I put two and two together; he was with Selma. He had scratch marks on his back, and they hadn't been from me, how could they have been from me? My fingers were bound like criminals. He seemed to think my straying was licence for him to do as he liked. I suppose, in a way, it had been. I thought he was going to punish me again, but instead he untied me and we made angry love. We rolled violently on the sheets, pressing our bodies together. I liked fucking this way. I liked that we could do both, fuck and make love. He pulled at my tits as though they were enemies, dribbling and slathering over my neck, my throat, like he hated me. I wrapped my legs around his. I jailed him, locking him in ferociously. As he thundered between my kidneys, at the point of no return, I wondered what else he had to hide.

'How's Angela?' I asked coolly when we'd finished. I felt suddenly dirty, as though I'd had exquisite sex with a stranger. Don't be silly, Roger is not a stranger, I consoled myself, he's the love of my life. Even so, I could feel the heated atmosphere between us collapse like an overloaded sandcastle, leaving nothing to remind us of the glories we'd just felt.

'She's not bad. She's at her mother's for a couple of weeks.'

I felt awkward when we talked about her, but I wanted to hear about her, to hear how I was better than she was. Roger wiped down his cock and threw the tissue on the floor, where it joined the others like little discarded plums.

'So, that's how you got the time off.' I deliberately made her sound like work.

'Yes,' he said, 'although I don't know how I'm going to explain this.'

He pointed to his suntanned nose. What had been as funny as Rudolph between us, was now evidence of his entrapment.

'But how is she generally?'

A friend once said that she thought I would want Angela to be ill. I didn't. I didn't want her ill or dead. I wanted her to be healthy and strong, because otherwise Roger, bless him, would not have the heart to leave her. Roger's wife called work occasionally and I had to put her calls through to him. Polite, she didn't know, obviously, but she seemed a polite woman. We met once at a party, and we talked our way through vol-au-vents and high heels. She was very beautiful, very classy, but perfect people aren't necessarily perfect for you, I know that.

'Actually, that's what I wanted to tell you. She's pregnant again. That's why I came, looks like I won't get a holiday for a while now.'

His words, his phrases were spinning around in my head. I tried to make sense of the incomprehensible. Roger rolled nonchalantly onto his side, his hand on my shoulder.

'Let's go to sleep. It's been a long day.'

'Is it your baby Roger?'

'Of course it's mine. Who else's would it be?'

I shot out. I ran, tearing past the cafés, past the telephone shops, past the holidaymakers weaving their way back to their bungalows. If this was our honeymoon, then give me a moon made of cheese.

Angela was pregnant, pregnant! Expecting, having a baby, a bun in her stupid oven. And how did that happen? How are babies born? The stork? Well who screwed the stork? Roger's erection, his hard cock inside her, his orgasm.

At that time, all I saw was the sex. I didn't yet look at the consequences of a baby being born. Him and her, kissing, rubbing up against each other, the heat, the friction. Sparks flying. Him nibbling her there, did she scream? Did she know what he liked? Of course she did! She'd probably done it with him more times than I had.

And he'd made me feel so bad! 'You slut', he'd said. 'You whore', when he'd been equally, no, more, unfaithful to me. I hadn't actually had sex remember? Plus I hadn't lied.

But she wouldn't have got pregnant if I hadn't left. He must have returned to the marital bed in his loneliness.

As I walked along the beach I knew I would forgive him. Because I'd done it, I was not morally superior. I'd indulged, and so what if I never actually did the sexual act in its entirety? I'd met temptation and failed to resist. He too, had had one moment of weakness. Nothing is ever black and white: even the stars in the night sky were covered with a thin film of clouds.

I wandered further along the beachfront away from the bungalows. Other people were coming towards me. I heard a dog howling piteously and saw bodies under a blanket probably fucking on the sand. I stood and watched the sky. There were only a few days until the full moon. Tonight, last night, tomorrow night: nothing would alter the rotation of the moon. Whatever was said, whatever he did to me, I wished I could be as constant.

And then it started to rain. It rained buckets. The clouds opened and within seconds the earth was drenched. Rods of lightning flashed terrifyingly across the bay; thunder rocketed around the bungalows. All around me, people were panicking, pulling at the stupid clothes left out drying, grabbing amazed children to go inside. The wind was rising too; picking up loose things, a plank of wood there, a stray branch here, and smashing them back down.

I ran all the way back to my bungalow but I stayed outside on the balcony, sitting on the steps watching the water pour from the sky. Fat drops fell from the roof onto my forehead, and, from there, trickled down my nose. I saw large puddles form on the ground and then the rain made circles in them. I cried, I couldn't stop crying, maybe the rain had loosened something in me.

Prem must have just finished his shift. I heard his motorbike first and then I saw it. He waved at me and I waved back hesitantly. He rode nearer the hut, and then he parked and dismounted the bike. He didn't wear a helmet, and he wasn't wearing the right shoes either. His bare feet were brown and narrow in flimsy sandals. His white shirt was stuck to him, drenched shades darker. I could see his brown skinny chest and two nipples like shiny buttons through it. His skinny face appeared glowing in the wetness. I could see the sensitivity in his eyes even through the blur of the weather, even from those few yards back.

I got up from the step and walked towards him slowly, even as the rain pelted our bodies like a whip. I walked towards him, magnetised. When we were just arm's length apart, he stared at me for just one moment until I put my arms around him and clutched him to me. I felt his back through the cotton, and how smooth it was, how smooth. He stood woodenly, straight as an arrow. My fingers were on his soaking skin and I was never more aware of my own sense of touch as I was then. His hair was drenched and I was drenched too, but I stayed there, my arms around my Thai boy, my eyes swimming with tears. He said nothing. If he'd wanted to make love then I would have. If he'd touched my soaking vest, and searched for the hard nipples underneath, I'd have guided him there and further. If he'd just leaned down to press his cherry lips onto mine, I'd have kissed him back with ten times the passion. But instead Prem lifted his arm and put it on my head. He stroked my hair very gently, very sweetly as though I was a lost animal. And the rain continued to fall on us like a witch's spell.

Roger was already asleep when I went back inside. I

tore off my wet clothes and got in bed. I cuddled up to Roger and tried to block out the insistent patter of the rain and the exultant multiple orgasms from next door. Roger's come was still there, a comforting sliver between my legs. It reminded me that our juice, his and mine, were all mixed up together inside me.

He was all I had ever wanted.

Chapter Twenty-Three

The court is in chaos. And still she does not know who is the perfect fit. She stands trying to look powerful, dressed like a slave, chewing imaginary gum.

'What's going on?'

'Oh dear no,' says a courtier, 'This is no good at all.' Everyone has puffed up, worn out drawn faces like they have seen something they shouldn't.

'Was it the King's . . . member?'

'No, goodness me no.'

The poor man starts to cry. He gets on the floor and sits in a puddle of his own tears. Other people join him, soon people are sitting all over the place, cross-legged and weeping.

She is getting fed up with this. And her body, oh her body is singing for an encore. Who was the perfect fit, who was the owner of the magnificent penis?

She tries to guess again.

'Was it the mute man?'

This time, her courtier doesn't say anything. He buries his face further into his hands.

'Will no one tell me what on earth is going on?'

She goes over to the inner sanctum. She can see a fierce discussion is taking place. The wise men are stroking their beards; women are clutching suckling babies to plump breasts.

At least three men who had been waiting in line with their loincloths are scratching their hair and looking like their bid has been gazumped. She winks at one of them and he soon springs back into life.

'Your highness,' she says loudly walking into the chamber. 'Have I displeased you in some way?'

'No, I . . .'

'What was the outcome of the contest?'

'Ask my wife,' he says and, arms folded, he marches furiously to the window.

She turns to the queen. She has frosty make-up, long raven's hair, and a smile of great import. Yet even she doesn't speak. She dives into her handbag and removes something.

'Yes, yes, we are doomed,' groans the King.

'This is so fucking hilarious,' Roger said mauling me awake. He was reading my guidebook.

'Did you read this about the squid? They go on about their thing, and then one night they all mate together, they have a massive orgy, and they start reddening up, and then after all that effort, they lay their eggs and just collapse.'

I gradually came back to life. The sun was bursting through the window and heating up the room like a hairdryer on full power. There was a solitary fly buzzing around looking for food or perhaps a mate. Otherwise, there was quiet. Roger put his arms around me and held me tight against his body. I let him, trying to return to the dream, or at least trying to remember what had happened. Why were they doomed?

'And what about this; "the female fish lays eggs, and then the male fish chases her away."'

I was enjoying the cosiness of our heated morning bodies. I turned to kiss him, wrestling the book out of his

185

arms. He was so handsome and he looked so hearty and strong.

Then I remembered. I felt a dull ache in my heart.

'So when is Angela expecting the baby, Roger?'

'Abby, you do understand that nothing changes between us?'

Only a baby! A whole human person, Angela, baby number one and now . . . a new baby.

'Our souls are linked, Abby,' insisted Roger.

'Is that what you think?'

'Come back to England. I'll show you how I've missed you.'

I felt the press of his penis, the sunrise erection.

'First, tell me when the baby is due.'

Roger sighed deeply, as if I was a small persistent child.

'It doesn't make a difference.'

'I'm sorry, it does to me.'

'Why? What difference can it make?'

He said she was five months gone. So Roger junior was conceived a whole month before I'd started going on about travelling. Dizzily, I cast my mind back to us five months ago. There were three snatched Friday nights in the pub and in the car home, two Thursdays at my apartment, a Monday and a Tuesday evening in a hotel, and a whole weekend when she went to her mother's. I bet that was it, he spent the weekend fucking me, and then they had a welcome back fuck.

No. They'd been fucking all along. There was nothing black and white. Instead there was a kaleidoscope of colours. Red for anger predominantly. They were man and wife. They didn't fuck; they made love.

I thought of those fish who ate the eggs. Surely not the mother, surely it was the girlfriend.

I'd been sleepwalking. Holidays, like death, put things in perspective.

'Roger, I want you to go.'

He put his arms around me. Such lovely long arms.

'We have such good sex, Abby. What more do you want?'

I didn't know anything anymore.

'Baby, you need sex, I know you do. I know the contours of your body. I know you like fucking like a rabbit. You won't meet anyone like me. You didn't really think I would ever leave Angela did you?'

'It's over, Roger. Get out.'

'It's not over.'

'It's not your fault,' I said pleading with him, 'But we're finished. I don't want anything more to do with you.'

'You can't say that,' he said. He really looked surprised that I just had.

'It's my fault for putting up with you, but we're finished. There's a world out there and I want to see it.'

He came and put his face really close to mine, and then he spat those ugly, ugly words.

'You slapper. You whore. You think anyone else would want to go out with a headcase like you? You think I'd leave my wife for a slag?'

'I don't want you any more,' I said simply and walked away. He was sitting on the step, his head in his hands. I couldn't resist a parting shot.

'To think I nearly gave up all this for you.'

The blue sea was sparkling in front of me; the white sand was sprinkled like icing on a cake and . . . I was on holiday.

Chapter Twenty-Four

*T*he driver's mate was another of the city boys who came south in the summer, for money, for women and for a good time. He and Prem talked in low voices while preparing for the snorkelling. Their language sounded lyrical, exotic, but I was excluded from the club. Maybe they were talking about me.

'Does Prem have a girlfriend?' I asked when Prem went to fetch the fins. We were going scuba-diving.

'Many girlfriends,' the driver's mate said vaguely.

'Does he have a special girlfriend?'

He shrugged. 'Special, no, not special. I want to prac-tise my English,' he added (faint-heartedly, I thought). He didn't seem to like talking that much. He was too busy playing with mirror sunglasses. Each time I tried to speak to him, I got a vision of myself, an earnest weasel staring right back.

The fish whipped around my legs, criss-crossing between them, I stood still and looked down at them amazed.

'Don't worry,' Prem called. He looked fantastic. His hair was slicked back revealing his silken forehead. He dived and tossed in the water. One time he executed a perfect somersault.

I was sluggish at first, reluctant to trust the tubes. I came up spluttering a few times, inhaling when I shouldn't, but Prem was relaxed.

We had all day, he reminded me, as long as I wanted. He also said there were no flight tickets yet, not until after the party, and I said, don't worry, it's not so important anymore. I quite fancied staying, perhaps throwing myself whole-heartedly into all those things I had denied myself before. Why not? I thought, why on earth not?

I explored Prem's underground world, his underground kingdom. There were big pouting fish and skinny bony fish. Sideways-on fish, fish with eyes in funny places, fish that looked like they were smiling, fish that looked pissed off, fish that were all different colours. There were crabs on the seabed, crazy side-walking crabs. We flew in the water; it wasn't like swimming, we really glided. I followed Prem, as he led me around curtains of seaweed. Around us fish were living, eating, mating, dying, and getting on with it all in a fantastic overwhelming quiet. Prem showed me the underground coral, the colours, the texture, the life beneath. I hadn't known this existed, and something like eighty per cent of the world is sea, and I had not realised what that meant. I grew confident, cocky. I didn't need the tube. I held my breath for a minute maybe, gliding, underwater ballet, before gasping and heading to the surface to take deep breaths of real air.

That night, there was a fireworks display on the beach. It sounded like gunfire. A stoned traveller with Chinese characters tattooed on his shoulder, put his arm around Prem and Prem let him, so I looped arms the other side. We all grinned and pointed up at the sky together. And I thought to myself; Roger, I am coping very well without you. It's your loss, not mine. We stood there, my friends and I, and gazed into space.

Later, when the traveller left us – he was paranoid that we were going to get blown up – I brushed my lips against Prem. But Prem kept his lips soft and fixed. If he were less well mannered I think he would have wiped my kiss off onto his sleeve. He kept both hands in his pockets. Behind us, firecrackers flew and exploded, sizzling in the sky.

'Thank you for taking me out today, and for the other night. I just wanted you to know how much I appreciate it.'

'It's OK.'

I was hanging around him, like a teenager at the supermarket waiting for something to happen. I felt our auras squirm magnetically against each other. I felt such a frisson; surely he did too?

'This is the way we thank people in England,' I lied. 'May I?'

The fireworks exploded once more, only this time the entire sky was lit up red, like a flaming forest. I was carried away, moved by the beauty of the moment. I moved towards his face, my goal. This time, I succeeded in slipping my artful tongue in Prem's mouth. Prem moved back quietly.

'I think you misunderstood. Abby, I . . .'

'No, that's fine. Honestly, it didn't mean anything at all,' I whispered. I pretended that a little spark from the fireworks had fallen into my eye.

Roger was still there when I got back. Sprawled over my things, occupying my space, thieving me of privacy. The bastard! I had told him to sleep on the floor but he was draped possessively over the bed. I wanted him out as soon as possible but he wouldn't wake up, and I didn't want to wake him up because the arguments would start again. I lay on the uncomfortable floor, but I felt happy. Such relief that it was all over. Relief, like peeing after holding it in for a long time (and I should know).

I could hear familiar noises from next door. The padding around the room, Selma's wailing. I edged to my watchtower. This time, José had arranged her to be right in my line of vision. I could see right up her legs. She was only a few yards from me. Surely, she minded: but no, Selma appeared oblivious. I wondered about waking Roger, I was so horny, and just one more time with him surely wouldn't hurt. But I knew it would hurt. I couldn't be Roger's slave, and Roger was incapable of giving me the things I needed.

Later, a knocking outside roused me. I looked at my watch – 3 a.m. The knocking was gentle at first, then again with more urgency.

'Selma?' I called out. 'Trent? Prem?'

I had a dreadful premonition-like fear that it was José, already, prematurely, on the warpath. I didn't want to see that.

I opened the door tentatively. Light flooded the room. It was the driver's mate.

'What?' I was just wearing a flimsy T-shirt, and the moonlight made it see-through. I'd taken off my bra and knickers. I wouldn't give Roger the pleasure of knowing that he clothed me. My breasts were erect and beneath you could make out the suggestive dark outline of fuzz.

'Who is it?' murmured Roger sleepily, raising one ghostly white arm up at me.

'Go back to sleep,' I scolded.

The driver's mate was grinning at me, shining an old fashioned torch in my face.

'Come now.'

'Why?' I asked, but already, I was out the bungalow, the door closed behind me.

I had never been to the café after hours. The chairs were on the tables. There were cardboard boxes on the counters and a few plates from the staff's late suppers. It looked dark and gloomy but I felt strangely hyperactive.

'Where's Prem?' I asked.

'Not Prem. Prem no good for you.'

'What do you want?'

'Play pool?'

'Don't be silly,' I said, but I was grinning at him as he grinned at me. The man was mad, completely bonkers.

He tried a different tack.

'I know you love Prem,' he said.

'I don't think that's the right word,' I said. Love was a four-letter word.

'Lie down then.'

I lay down on the elevated table. I didn't know why the driver's mate picked on me. Was my appetite so transparent?

He raised my T-shirt. The driver's mate waited over my pubic triangle. He brushed the hair softly with the back of his hand. I was trembling.

'What if someone comes?'

'No one comes, not now. Only you and me.'

I smiled. 'Not even Prem?'

'Prem not make love with foreign girl. He don't like foreign girls.'

'Why not?'

The driver shrugged and then gave his heart-breaking grin.

'I like foreign girl, curly hair.' He stroked my mound admiringly. Then he pulled at the curly tufts.

'Owww.'

'Sorry, but it's like pad Thai.'

'Noodles?'

'Yes,' he said. He pulled at some hairs, twiddling with me, so that I had to breathe quickly. Let's take our time. Although his fingers haven't ventured any further than there, they will soon. They have to.

'What about you?' I said, 'show me yours then.'

I was licking my lips like an old queen. He was a slim, perfect specimen of man-hood. He undid his jeans. He was wearing Calvin Klein underpants. The driver was a city boy, with city boy tastes. He probably fucked foreign girls all summer. He considered that as part of his job. He probably regaled all his friends about it all winter. 'This one did this, this one said that . . .'

He'd probably done this a thousand times before. I knew, but I didn't mind.

'Show me.'

There was something childlike, almost innocent, about our encounter.

He pulled his pants down and indeed, his was a soft black fur, but my eyes were drawn to the enormous todge.

'Not all Asian boys have small cocks,' he said proudly.

'What about Prem?' I said.

'He fair size,' he said his head to one side, still grinning. Now I knew why he was always smiling.

'Look, he's crying.' A small tear dribbled from the mushroom end.

I put my hand out and started to stroke him. On the beaten track, up and down I went. The glans throbbed. He grinned broadly. Then I felt his fascination with the hair on my genitalia wane as he started to explore the hinterland. I was damp, no, thoroughly wet already, and he tickled my muff tentatively. He withdrew his finger as though taking out a thermometer, and held it up to me in the moonlight. Eureka!

'Look, very wet.'

I grabbed his wrist and restored his finger to its rightful place, up my hole.

I wondered if we were going to come like this, mutual masturbation. I liked the idea. He seemed too laid back to bother with anything else.

'I like G spot,' he said. I was impressed. He knew all the words. 'Feels good, feels good huh, I'm better than Prem.'

'Are you?' My breathing was quickening, but I wanted to speak. I was kneeling over his finger. 'How do you know?'

'You like playing pool?'

'Umm, yes.'

'I like watching you play pool. Prem and I watch you.'

So Prem didn't like touching, but watching was OK.

'You wanna then?' he said lazily.

'Wanna what?' I wanted to hear what word he would choose.

'How do you say this in English?' He made a circle with his index finger and thumb and then the finger of the other hand went up and down inside.

'Nooky,' I said, imagining with pleasure legions of girls after me who would laugh at this.

'You wanna nooky?'

I didn't know if I did. I was enjoying this, the distance, the cold mechanicalness. We were just like two pool balls gliding and knocking into each other.

'You wish I was Prem?'

'No,' I lied. 'Tell me about him. Is he a virgin?'

'No,' he laughed uproariously. He kept moving his hand very pleasantly, stroking the silky walls of my pussy.

'We had sex,' he suddenly said proudly.

'What? You and him?'

'When we were young men, we were too poor for the bargirls, and the other girls are too nice. So we sucked each other.'

'You sucked each other! Did you do that a lot?'

'Only when we needed to,' he said, very blasé.

I pictured the two of them needing each other. Prem ducking down to service his friend. Putting his friend's succulent cock in his gorgeous mouth, waiting for his turn. The friends, looking after each other's cocks. Was he surprised when his friend started ramming him and talking gibberish? When the juices began to flow, did he spit or swallow? I imagined his turn, his soft moaning, his pupils dilated and his hands sweating. How did he feel when he came the first time?

'He likes women though, he's not gay,' added the driver's mate.

'What sort of women?'

'He had one girlfriend. She was foreigner. She stayed here, five, maybe six months. She was the last tourist.'

I imagined her blonde, skinny and worldly. She prob-

194

ably loved having a Thai boyfriend. Probably thought she was the bee's knees. I pictured the two of them fucking, hot and fiery. Bet she wanted to take him home with her, trophy fucking: the native's head, stuff him and hang him on the dining room wall. Just to show off. Did she go down on him? Did he go down on her, taste the passion fruit?

The driver's mate stroked my arse and rearranged me. I was a bridge over the table. A fine sight. Doggy position.

'So what happened to her?'

'The one who stole his money, his watch? She, how you say? She broke his guts, his stomach. He hasn't had woman for five years now.'

He laughed adding shyly, 'I did offer sucking, but he said no.'

Five years! He must be busting, gagging for it! The first time would be brief probably, but the second, Jesus, the second time, can you imagine?

I rolled over. He was silent and profound. He started stroking my buttocks with his bigness, showing me what he was made of. Kneading me with his shaft of neediness.

'You have marks here,' he said smoothing my cheeks.

'Yes. I want it up the arse.'

'What?'

'This is my arse,' I said pointing. 'I want you to fuck me up there.'

'Here?'

'Yes.'

'How do you call this in English?'

'Arse hole,' I hissed. His finger curled around the tightest ring. 'It's also what we call someone when we don't like them.'

'Arsehole,' he repeated. 'Your boyfriend, big arsehole.'

'That's right.'

'Are you sure?' asked the driver's mate.

Sure? What was there to be sure about in this world? Nothing would ever be sure again. I liked it. I really did.

It was the feeling of doing something out of the norm. I got up on the pool table on all fours. My tummy sank low, but I knew that he didn't care. I saw his mesmerised expression, his concentration. He gift-wrapped his cock and got behind me. I could see the hands of the clock in front. The little hand was reaching the big hand: 4 a.m. The hour of my infidelity, the hour I would free myself from Roger forever. Here I was doing it for me, doing it for my country. Fucking revenge with my arse the murder weapon. The things Roger made me do, I will bestow on someone else, a stranger. My gift, my pleasure.

The driver's mate came at me. He gripped my flanks and opened me where the sun don't shine.

Once he arrived, he stayed still. Thank God he stayed still. He waited for my expansion.

'Is this OK?'

'More, push it in deeper.' I was shouting out orders like a commando.

The way it sank inside, the wrong way, once you adjust to that. It was like walking backwards: your view just changes. Sinks and then waiting for the adjustment, the expansion, the engorgement, like welding I suppose. I was being welded, drilled, and I couldn't get enough of it. I wanted more, hard cock, more sensation, a deeper penetration.

'Oh yes, like that, deeper, harder.'

I could accommodate him, yes. I scrambled back against him, mashing and grinding. He looked like a diver ready to launch off, into the deep blue sea. He dived. I felt the trigger, the chase, the splash, and I wanted to be fucked, fucked and fucked over forever.

'With your fingers, yes, yes, please.'

My pleasure surged forward with a life force of its own, as his hands moved around to meet my slit. He dabbled in my wetness, fingertips in first, and then a whole finger, then two and three. He vibrated against my engorgement, clutching at my genitals like a drowning man. Taking me down with him.

'You're so fucking tight.'

'Yes. Harder, harder, please harder!'

I was full up: there was no room left, not in or out of me. Completely full, overflowing full. I slammed back, and as I felt his hand work my clitoris, I couldn't stop myself from slamming back and back, again and again, pushing my bum on his cock, sighing and coming, and breathing hard, and promising I loved him, and yes, I was alive, I was really alive. Pushing on his cock, filled up with man, swollen with arousal. Just before I lost it, big time, I was sure I was with Prem.

'You're the best,' he said, shaking himself and then helping me off the table.

'I bet you say that to all the girls.'

I didn't care if I was his best or not. That was fun. There was a dark green patch on the table surface, but he said knowledgeably, 'Don't worry, it'll be gone by the morning.'

Chapter Twenty-Five

*E*arly the following morning, Roger had disappeared. I don't know how he managed to get off the island since the entire flight north had been booked up long ago. But I didn't see him again.

I slept late. About midday, José came over to my bungalow. He hovered at the door awkwardly. He was so big that he blocked out the sun, and my room was suddenly in shadow. Physically, he reminded me of the Incredible Hulk but with the melancholy of the hulk when he becomes normal again.

I chewed my lip.

'Done,' he said simply and turned to leave.

'Really?' I wanted to hear more. I didn't feel guilty or anything, I felt mostly relieved I suppose.

Last night, I had told him that Roger fancied Selma and that he would do anything to be with her.

'What exactly did you do?' I said remembering the way the boys who had looked at Selma looked after José's treatment. I wanted to hurt him.

He shrugged and began walking away. 'It's better you don't know . . . in case the police . . .'

And then he disappeared into the darkness of the hut.

I was walking back home along the beach when someone tapped me on the shoulder. I know it sounds stupid, but for a second I thought that it was Roger. I was still composing letters to him in my head, letters that I would never have the balls to send.

'Lily! How great to see you.'

'Kop-kum-kah.'

Lily took my hand. Her hands were unusually large and the lines were very strong. I would love to have been a fortune-teller, to know her future. I wanted to have my way with her. I was like one of those men in the movies, who have no doubt that the woman he wants will want him back. Lily didn't really want to come to my bungalow.

'Not now.'

She was patting her hair like a blue-rinse grandma. 'I look awful.'

Her resistance thrilled me. 'Don't be silly, you look lovely, Lily.'

She sat on the bed cautiously, the way I had when I was with Trent I suppose. This time though, it was me who lunged forwards. I was so thirsty, so horny for her and I knew I hadn't reached my limitations.

I reached for her. I'd been lazy, I'd been selfish, but no more. I would give pleasure wherever I went, yes; I was a veritable Santa Claus, except I would only give presents to men and women who have been very bad.

Lily let me touch her. I thought she was acting all coy and submissive. And then I realised that maybe she was genuinely coy. That night we kissed on the beach, she had smelled of alcohol. Maybe without that, she was as shy as I used to be.

I reached for a breast. I was ardent, earnest. I unbuttoned her shirt, and then pulled it off her shoulders. Big and up-front bosom, hers were like the ones they put on the front of men's magazines. I sucked her nipples. And the question that had dogged me ever since I had met her: 'How would it be to suck her breasts?' was answered. It was heaven, and I was soliciting the taste of

199

skin, and the texture; the nodule in my mouth like candy, the rest, and then the big cup. I wanted to consume her, all of her, at once.

Lily said that I was hurting her.

'Sorry.'

I rolled on top of her anyway, like a clumsy oaf, like a man, but I endeavoured to squeeze her more sensitively. Lily closed her eyes and let me do what I wanted to do. I started to take off her stiletto shoes, but then I thought that her sleek legs looked so gorgeous with them on – and she couldn't run away from me. She should keep them on. I fumbled around her calves, her elegant ankles. I would die for legs like these. I bent down and kissed her ankle, and she moaned. It was a weird sensation to kiss a woman's leg. I nibbled my way northwards, smooth and sensual. I liked rubbing my lips on her soft skin, spying the way onwards, only guessing at the hot pleasures nestling between her legs. I kissed and sucked her skinny calves.

I was going to do to her what Selma had done to me. I knew what to do; I wanted to do it. More than anything else, I wanted to. I wanted to finger her hole. I was desperate to lick her out, gagging to bury my face in her juice, then finally, we would move together, rubbing each other's skin. I was no lesbian, but I had to fuck her. I wanted to touch her pubic hair. I wanted to know how each individual pubic hair would feel caught in my fingers, caught between my teeth. Best of all, I was free. I was free to do as I pleased.

I was pulling up her skirt, uncovering those muscular thighs, magnificent gateways, for all the world to see. Oh yes, I rubbed her skin delightedly. After what I was going to do to her, she would love me forever. And if she didn't know what to do, if she'd never been with a woman either, then we would learn together, why not? Two women can be the best teachers of each other's pleasure. I was desperate to spend my last few days on Pleasure Island with the best girl Friday. Prem wouldn't

have me; Selma was impossible to get on her own now
José was bursting with jealousy, why not Lily?

I lunged for her panties and skimmed the surface.
Something was gnawing at me. Beneath her panties
something was growing.

'Jesus! Lily!'

'I thought you knew!' she cried.

Chapter Twenty-Six

Lily's ends were mis-matched, unexpected. How could I have kissed her? I wondered how I could have probed her with my tongue, run the track of her mouth? How could I have clutched her breasts?

I went to cool off in the ocean. I swam directly opposite Prem. He wanted to cast out a line, but I was in his way. He shrugged his shoulders at the obstruction and simply prepared some more bait. I was fed up with being ignored. I felt the water slip-slide around my body giving me courage so I came out of the sea, up to the edge where the water just about caressed my toes. Trembling, I stood up. The sun was behind him and I had to squint to see him. It had to be Prem. It had to be him.

I shook my hair, and put the finger of my left hand over to the strap on my right side. Slowly, very slowly, I drew the strap down. I pushed it down my upper arm, and then with the other hand I did the same on my left side. First my right breast and then my left was exposed. The sun caressed my naked flesh. Pretty tears of water clung to my tits. He was ahead of me, blurry and unfocused.

'Look at me,' I whispered. Please see me and want me.

The curvy clouds moved fast across the bold blue sky.

The swimsuit was down my middle, revealing little inside-out flowers. I slid the swimsuit over the chunk of my hips, down, to the first sightings of my pubic hair. I paused, feeling the dampness of the cloth stir my excitement. Down, down, down it went, to my thighs, to rest indecorously on my knees, and then I stepped out of it, leaving the material on the sand. I became aware of the tiniest sensations, the feel of my shoulders, my tongue between my front teeth, even the air from my nose. My hair was wet on my back, causing drops of water to land plump on my shivering buttocks. I could feel warm arousal flooding my sex.

I started to whistle, for attention. I don't remember the tune; all I remember is that the sound was lost in the wind.

When I looked up, he was still threading the worm through his hook. And I knew I had to see Lily again.

'I have an idea my lord,' a courtier cries.

'Hurry up, I'm getting cold,' she interrupts. Her arms are dotted with goose pimples.

'Annul the contest, my lord,' says the courtier.

'Anal this contest?' responds the King, his face brightening. 'What a brilliant idea!'

'I said, annul, my lord, annul. Oh never mind.'

'What do you mean?'

The blood seems to run from her face and disappear to her feet. She feels like an egg timer, upturned and devoid of sand.

'Anal this contest, anal the contest,' yells the King.

Everyone is chatting excitedly. The sound starts as a buzzing, like insects flapping their wings and then builds into a crescendo as if elephants are stamping their feet.

'No, now you go too far.'

She looks around for her rescuers, but they're nowhere to be seen.

'I have not yet had my turn.'

The King undoes his robe and the attendants fall silent.

'The King can't go with his own subject. It's against the rules.'

'Who would it hurt?'

'No one.'

'I think you should bend the rules, Your Highness,' she says. She is standing, bent over. She can touch her toes. All he can see of her is two giant globes.

At last, she recognises the King. She should have known long ago. He is her kindred spirit. His journey is her journey. He has been watching the proceedings for so long, watching and waiting his turn. Like the King, she is throwing off the albatross of duty and freeing herself from our thankless responsibilities.

'Bend the rules?'

They are still pondering, those moustache-rubbing sycophantic courtiers.

'Your Highness, you must fulfil your duties to yourself,' she shouts, jubilant at her discovery; the fairy on the Christmas tree.

'And if you can't find it within yourself to bend the rules, then you must rule the bends.'

I waited outside Lily's door the following day. I didn't want to hurt her feelings. She was perfect, yet she was so absurd.

'Lily, I'm so sorry. I was stupid, and ignorant, please let me apologise properly.'

Finally, she let me in. A naked red light bulb hung in the centre, bathing the room in red like the den of an Amsterdam prostitute. Even we were tinged like two red devils. There were photos of the Thai King and Queen on the walls. Lily said she was a royalist, she knew everything about the Thai royal family, and she followed the British one too.

Clumsily, I gave her flowers. I would have liked to furnish her with lilies but only strange flowers grew in that hot intemperate place. I picked the flowers off a dusty roadside, attracted by their long, long stems and their colourful eyes. I wasn't sure if I was right in giving them either. What may be a custom in one country might be impolite in another. Still, Lily looked thrilled with the gesture. She felt the petals, sniffed the flower, and said that no one had ever got her flowers before. (She didn't put them in water though.)

'I show you my life,' she said.

We went to a club. Dancing with Lily, the whole world was looking at us. I gyrated and swung my pelvis provocatively. I bent my knees and shimmered around. I felt excited and sexual. I got a buzz out of being looked at. I wondered if the people there thought I was a transsexual too. Maybe they had no idea.

Then we went to 'Dermot's'; her favourite bar was run by an ex-pat Irishman who plied us with kisses and free drinks. Other foreign men stood around trying to watch us. Most of them knew Lily. One of them reached out and grabbed my pelvis.

'Just checking,' he said.

Lily looked disapprovingly. 'Let's get out of here.' She pulled my hand.

Back in her room she said, 'I'm saving up for an operation.'

'What?'

'You know.' She played with her hands, her beautiful fingers. I wanted to touch her.

'You really want that?'

'I need it.'

She kissed me. I did care whether it was man, woman or beast, but this was Lily, sweet Lily. And whoever said that a woman had to have two size 32EE breasts, or that a man's balls had to be equal size? There are no rules, we're all unique, and if she was more unique than others were, then that wasn't our problem.

We sat opposite each other on the floor. Staring at each other like two chess players psyching each other out before a big match. When Lily smiled she was almost too beautiful, and, in a way, she was almost two beautifuls.

Her lower physique was that of a beautiful man, her upper belonging to an exquisite woman. I was job interview nervous, fiddling with my fingers; I wanted to touch her.

She was like a unicorn, or a mermaid with those two mismatched ends. I wished things were different, one or the other, not a little bit of both. I felt such a mixture of revulsion and excitement when I looked at her. It was like the first time I looked at a porno magazine. Someone at school had them and we joyfully passed them around. Page after page of ladies with their legs splayed, biting their fingers. Grown ladies dressed in baby dresses and sucking lollypops. These were the images I should have objected to, but at the same time, made me fill my knickers with so much creamy excitement.

Lily leaned forwards and kissed me again. I felt how her kisses fitted; they really did – like the perfect shoe, or a hand in a glove. She ran her tongue along my lower lip, and then my upper, and then when I was pressing for some action, her mouth was over mine, crushing mine, her tongue was conquering my hole, and all I could think was how much I wanted it.

'Don't struggle,' she whispered.

'This is too weird.' I guess I meant that she was too weird.

'Forget everything you've been told.'

I didn't remember being told not to do this. It would never have crossed my educators' minds to tell me not to sleep with lady boys in Thailand. It had never crossed my mind.

My heart was saying yes, it was just my head that was saying, whoa.

'Yes but . . .' I closed my eyes, just for a moment. This couldn't be right.

Lily touched me all over. She was tentative at first, as though fitting me for a dress, but then her hands became grabbing and selfish. She was enjoying herself.

Lily's skin was like velvet. I was collapsing, losing

myself over her. Playing with her great breasts, rubbing them over my face, can you imagine that? She allowed me to finger her tits, to grip them hard.

I opened my eyes, to see her face. The passion flooded forward, burning her cheeks.

'Oh Lily,' I purred into those outstanding breasts.

I slipped my hand up her skirt. Loving the feel of those sturdy thighs. She had such thick muscular legs. Now in my hand, I knew there was nothing feminine about them, none of that spread like treacle stuff. I adventured higher and higher, until at the top of the thighs, at the middle, I felt short spiky hairs. What's a penis between friends? I didn't know if I could go on. But I was a trapeze artist and I had walked too far along to turn back now.

The penis was in my hand. I held it tight, squeezing up and down. Only a penis, and yet so out of place. The penis itself was utterly astonishing. Not just because it belonged to a skinny woman but because the dick was a revelation in itself: fat, stubby and wide. It was the sort genetic engineers would look to for a shining example. It was the sort you see in the movies; people grab something like this when they're trying to smash a door down. I was falling, falling through the air, with no safety net.

'I don't think I'll be able to.'

Lily looked at me woefully. She touched my engorged nipples with a delicacy, in deep contrast with the great stonking penis that was poking my thigh unceremoniously. I desired her so badly but . . .

'It's OK, I understand.'

'No, it's not that, it's just so, so huge, how can I?'

'Please try.'

She resumed her meticulous attention to my tits. I was inarticulate from arousal. They say drunken men see women prettier than they actually are, maybe drunken women see dicks bigger than they are. But by any standards, she was huge.

'It's my last time to do this,' she said.

I climbed onto this amazing woman, and took her juggernaut penis between my legs. I was ready enough. I had got set and gone long ago. My sex was as wet, as alive, as the Ocean Sea outside the window.

'I don't know.'

Now that I was concentrating on the practicalities of our mating, the psychological barrier had almost disappeared. Yes, get inside me, stuff me up, truss me, and blow me away. I worked her cock up and down on the outside, on my pubic hair, on the trickle, on the slit. And she sat back, her fingers helping me, pampering my clitoris, giggling.

'I want one of these.'

'No, your cock is just the best, honestly.'

How many men or women would cut off their right arm for a third leg like that? Gradually, I steeled myself. I let the prick slide up me, closer and closer to the nest. I wriggled and gasped as it went in. I thought my eyes were going to pop out my head. I stared at her incredulously. It was too fat to fully enter. I simply couldn't take it right up me. It was gridlock like the worst Bangkok traffic jam. You can't put a camel through the eye of a needle, nor can you put someone hung like donkey through the lips of a pin.

'This is unbelievable.'

Never have I ever even thought about this. Not fantasy, nor in my wildest dreams. Yes, this was why women, occasionally, faint from the pleasure. Her cock was fully submerged, and I could feel it ramming my sex. I had to steady myself with sharp intakes of breath, as though I was running a marathon.

'Believe it baby,' said six-foot Lily, a crushed petal under me.

That enormous cock immediately created such a pressure on my clit that I was buckling and moaning like a raging bull.

'Oh God, help me, oh God.'

When the blood rushed to her cock, and she started to

thrust harder, I didn't know what to do or where to go. How could I cope with it? Do it to me, do it to me, I whispered between clenched teeth. I just stayed put, and let her smash me downward onto her inflated cock. I just let her do it to me with her fat penis until I was crying out with excitement and greed.

'You're unusual for a white girl,' Lily said, dangling a cigarette strangely from her lips. She was a caricature of femininity. She inhaled and then gave me foul delicious kisses.

'Why?' I asked. Fishing for compliments? *Qui, moi?*

'You really can fuck. But, you have too much hair. There I mean.'

She pointed with the cigarette to my sex. A bit of ash tipped off the end and left a grey mark on my leg.

'No one else has complained,' I said defensively.

'Well, it's up to you,' she said laughing. 'But if I'd wanted to fuck a gorilla I would have gone up to the mountain villages.'

I could have said something really nasty then, but I didn't.

Lily let me watch her take off her face. First she unthatched her wig. She put the hair on a plastic model of a head with no features. She had two other wigs; they looked like sleeping animals, one for parties, and another, the first one she had made. Her hair underneath was short and made her look gamine. She didn't look less feminine, her features were so light, but she looked different. I saw now, more even than when her penis was inside me, that she was male.

Her eyelashes came off and were placed in a little plastic box.

'You should wear them,' she said. She squeezed the bottles, a tube of cream, she squeezed and the white liquid spurted out. White cream smeared on her eyelids, then chased off with tissues. Then she turned to me, her naked face gleaming. Vaseline in her fingers. Bells on her toes. Transformed from female to male. The clown became serious. She looked young, so young. Neither man nor woman, but boy or girl about to leap into adulthood; that time when nothing else was simple again. Something about it, perhaps the nudity and the vulnerability, nearly made me cry.

Chapter Twenty-Seven

*T*here was a small wooden place like a doll's house, or a nativity scene, on a rock near Sunita Lodge. I had often seen it, but never found out its use.

'It's a little house for Buddha,' Prem explained. I looked closely. There were colourful flowers there, fresh fruit and, sometimes, there were sticks of incense emitting a smell that you don't just sense with your nose, but with all of your body.

'If you get up early, you'll see the women pray here.'

He grinned at me. He knew I didn't usually get up 'til eleven.

'What time do you get up?' I nudged him. He was in a good mood.

'Six,' he said. 'You hear the cock crow? That's when I get up.'

'And what time do you go to bed?'

'One, maybe, two.'

'You don't sleep much.'

He smiled, 'I have better things to do.'

Prem's smile was so contagious, so infectious, that I had to look away. My smile threatened to consume the island. 'He had better things to do!' What a darling, and so would I, given the chance to do them with him.

'Are you coming to the Full Moon party then?' I asked flirtatiously.

'No, no way,' he said. It wasn't his scene. He meant it was too full of foreign idiots.

When I tried to take a photo of him, Prem clowned around. He was wearing shorts and his skinny brown legs stuck out like a sparrow's. I would have liked a picture of him without his shirt but he hated posing. I made him stand still.

Click. He managed a watery smile.

'Let's have a photo of you and me,' I said, probably the most forward thing I would dare, 'Put your arm around me.'

He put his arm around me gingerly and I stretched my camera out in front of us. Our heads were close. Before I pressed the shutter, I raised my eyes to check his expression. He was smiling; his lips were closed and dreamy. He looked as though he were sleeping. Even as I took the photo, I couldn't wait to see it. I felt my insides twist and curl contented by his nearness.

We stood awkwardly together, holding the position for just a little too long, and then I asked Prem to get someone else to take our photo. He asked a young man who agreed readily.

'Stand closer together,' yelled the chosen one.

Once again, Prem slung his arm stiffly over my shoulder. My legs were longer than his and my waist was slightly higher, but he was a little taller than I was. I liked the feeling of his body next to mine, our hips side by side. I don't know if I was imagining it, but I almost felt his hipbone beneath the denim jutting into my thigh.

'We're ready,' I called. The elected photographer had slunk to his knees and was taking his task very seriously. Again, I raised my eyes to Prem's face, and then suddenly I realised that the expression I had taken for tranquillity was more like one of agony, or great discomfort.

It seemed to take forever for the man's finger to move,

and for the shutter to snap close. I had already started to give up. When people later looked at those photos, they would say how happy I looked, how healthy or what a nice couple we made, but I remember only how my smile was glued fast to my face and inside my spirit was dying. Poor Prem, he wriggled and worried. When I studied his face in the photos, I saw that every second with his arm round me was obviously a second spent in hell.

Trent didn't look too keen to see me either. I suppose I had rather wound him up before. And he'd found plenty of other girls to go all the way with. But he was still unfinished business and I've always fantasised about consummating my relationships with any man I am attracted too. I suppose my long ago trip to Spain was like that. A job worth doing is worth doing well, and I had to do him properly. I wanted him to spill his juice inside me, inside my womanhood. Was he as good with his prick as he was with his tongue?

We arranged to go to the Full Moon party together. Before though, Trent insisted on taking me to a café where, he said, they served the best omelettes in the entire country.

'I don't fancy . . .' I began, but he ordered over my head, grabbing the menu out of my hands before I had the chance to see what else was on offer.

'Mushroom omelettes, please.'

He tried to wink at the waiter, but the man wasn't having any of it, and instead stared professionally back (as professionally as you can when a bristly moustache obscures half of your face).

I know some women love it when a man masterfully orders for you in a restaurant, and I too have fantasised about it, but when it happened, it annoyed me.

'Don't I have a say?' I scowled at him but he, insensitive creep that he was, didn't reply.

'Why do we have to have mushroom?' I persisted. But I wasn't going to argue.

213

'No reason,' he said fixing me with innocent eyes, 'No reason at all.'

I remembered what the guidebook had said, about mushrooms which grew on the side of the road.

'Are you sure there's no special reason?'

'Can't a man just order mushroom omelettes without the third degree?'

He obviously didn't want to admit to me what was going on. That annoyed me. If I hadn't known about this particular fungus, then Trent would have been forcing me into something I didn't want. I decided to play the evening by ear. I couldn't work out his game.

The omelettes were grey and yellow. They didn't taste particularly horrible, just dull. Few colours do less favours for each other than grey and yellow. I smothered the concoction with red ketchup. And added lashings of salt and pepper. Then when Trent went to the bathroom, I waved over the waiter to take it away.

'That was quick!' said Trent looking at my cleared deck with astonishment.

'They were delicious,' I lied.

'Fantastic, eh?' he laughed and laughed. I wanted to slap his stupid face. Instead I asked:

'Why are you laughing so much?'

He stopped and gathered himself. Tightened his shoulders and said, 'Let's party!'

The beach looked fantastic. The full moon was enormous, a white orb. There were flashing lights, like Christmas decorations but more daring and a cracking bonfire, screens, scrolls and lanterns. There was a man on stilts, a burly oil-streaked fire-eater, and a juggler throwing bottles and balls. Some Thai women were serving waters and beers.

Every so often, a partygoer, overwhelmed by something, broke away from the crowd and ran into the sea, whooping and cheering.

Writhing dancing figures in the centre. A woman was dancing with her legs wrapped around a man's waist.

Imagine if they were really fucking and no one knew. For a moment, I missed Roger with a passion that made me shake.

'Oh God.'

'So, are you off your head?' Trent slimed his way over to me.

'Sorry?'

'You must be off your head by now.'

He had his arms around two pretty Thai girls in high heels and high hemlines. One of them had dyed and frizzed her hair so she looked like a country and western singer. The two girls chatted nonchalantly together.

I didn't know what to say to him.

'They do what other women won't do,' he said winking. 'Well, what some women don't do.'

'That's because you're paying them,' I said, although I didn't have the moral high ground that I used to occupy.

Some foreign men approached. Trent introduced the volleyball crowd. He whispered to a man that I recognised as the barman at Dermot's bar.

'She's so stoned.'

I was not! That was the joy of it, I was not. And he thought I was. I would act it, like when I was seventeen; I acted drunk, just so that I could flop, with my head on Luke's shoulder in the car home. I was sober as a judge then, and I was sober as a judge now. Yet, this, this was an excuse to misbehave with a capital M.

'She doesn't look it,' said the worldly barman.

'Yes, she is,' insisted Trent. I played up to it, acting how I imagined I should be. I gazed at the fireworks as they exploded over our heads, and oohed and aahed loudly. I watched the whirling figures in the makeshift dance area, and I commented how white their pale clothes became, and how white the water bottles were, and how amazing life was.

'See,' said Trent proudly.

There was a big crowd giggling in the centre of the

215

dance area, daubing each other with paint. I glided over towards them. I felt far less self-conscious than usual. Some girls started touching me, with paint on their fingers, using me as their palate. A Japanese girl with wonky teeth steadied me, then wrote something.

'Look, I've written the character for love on your shoulder.'

I turned around, chasing my back ineffectively. I couldn't see it. We were laughing, laughing, happy strangers. And then with my fingers, I wrote 'Passion fruit', across my stomach. The girl next to me was a big bronzed Scandinavian. She looked like a Viking, a Nordic warrior.

'Write something on me,' she said. I dipped my fingers in the paints and I wrote, 'Viking,' up her legs.

'I like it,' she grinned. She had a huge mouth like a frog. Then she knelt down beneath me and started to paint silver stars on my knees and on my thighs. I rolled up my skirt to make it even higher.

We danced together, the Viking and I. Glamour pussies. I saw a raised stage, near the speakers and dragged her over with me. We stood, side by side, showing off, competing with each other and putting on a show. My stars twinkled, and everyone stared at the passion fruit on my belly.

My bikini top came off, and so did hers. My tits were flying free and it felt wonderful.

'So white!' she exclaimed, and touched me. We were laughing and dancing too hard for it to be anything other than fun.

'Yes, look,' I yelled over the music. I started to rub myself, pinching my nipples and pulling them out. As soon as I saw how much I was appreciated by the crowd who had gathered at my feet, I started to rub her titties instead. Hers were bigger than mine, a little droopier perhaps. She reciprocated, so we were both up there on the stage clumsily feeling each other and jiggling about to the rhythm too. I suppose it was mostly men gathering

216

on the floor beneath us. They looked thrilled at the impromptu floorshow. Their girlfriends stood at the side of the action looking huffy.

The music changed, the bass was faster, and we moved faster, matching it. She was wearing thigh-high boots, and a short suede skirt, I suggested she take it off. I didn't think she would but she did. So there she was in just a white G string. I undid my skirt, letting it flap to the floor and there was I, in my black G string.

Some of the men took their clothes off too. I toyed with her knickers. She didn't seem to mind anything. She danced, her arms waving in the air, a big beautiful Viking. I pulled the sides of the knickers up and then lowered them. I lowered them, till they were level with the top of my thighs, and then I pulled them up, tight as I could, so that the thin material showed off the shape of her pussy-lips. She hugged me and we laughed some more, and then she did the same to me. We were still wearing them when we turned to face away from the crowd and then, showing off, we touched our toes. Our bottoms to the audience, just a thin strip of material between nudity and us.

Lowering, lowering my G string, I touched myself. I felt my way between my pussy-lips, and felt wetter than ever. The audience was cheering and then I touched her, we still had our backs to the audience. I wasn't interested in her, it was the effect I, we, could have.

The horny had taken over the disco. Someone had overthrown the DJ, and was shouting out instructions over the music through the fuzzy mike.

'Let's fuck, let's eat pussy.'

I jumped off the stage, and was in the middle of the dance area, smiling like a benevolent Buddha. Two boys raised me high, people were kissing me, and others were standing back, envious of our freedom. They carried me aloft, amid the dancers, and some of the men touched my legs or my breasts. The music pumped out, and the

217

dancing continued, some looked like wriggling spiders, sweating and jogging earnestly.

'Put me down,' I shouted. They got me a cushion, and I made the cushion case damp with my arousal. And how was I to decide who to have first? Why, the one who visibly wanted me the most of course.

The barman was the first. The pioneer, he spread my legs, open sesame. He had a handsome eager face. Everything seemed to go quiet. I know that the music continued at the same decibel, the crowds were still laughing and drinking, but in my mind, the place hushed. The barman was wearing soft Thai trousers, and he untied the string keeping them up, revealing a large shiny rod. The head was bulbous, light-bulb shaped almost, and it was shiny with pre-come. He leaned over me – very gently, under the circumstances – and I felt him in the first quarter and then halfway up my sex, and then with a final triumphant shove he was in. His knees were on the ground, and I was lying back.

Someone else put his finger between my lips, and I sucked at it, relieved to have something to do with my mouth. I could hear whispered talk around me. People were trying to work out if we were doing it for real. Maybe someone said that we were part of the entertainment that the organisers laid on. Well, we were the entertainment, but we were doing it for free. And then I ceased to listen to them any more, and I concentrated on the fucking.

Oh God, the relief of having someone inside me again, filling that hole. The barman soared up and down me, skating against me. He created an exquisite friction, rubbing my tunnel. My body was there getting fucked in the dance area, but me, oh baby, I was floating far away near heaven. What was going on? My clitoris was swollen up, and my lips were red, and I was so hot, so horny, so randy.

I saw another couple fall down on the floor and start screwing. Yet there were still people dancing. Some acidheads were waving and smiling or doing cycling movements. I realised the girl next to me was the Viking and she was writhing next to me with the fire-eater. Her legs jerked around him in the fastest orgasm in town, but he was still going on. He looked like a deep fuck.

I lifted my hips against the barman's pelvis. I wanted to shag him senseless. He sat back on his heels, and pulled me up so that I was eye to eye with him. I scraped my groin against him, making him sandpaper on my hole. The juggler was next to me, feeling my breasts. Was that enough for him? His penis was swollen next to his thigh like a fat sea lion.

The couple next to me ploughed on. Now, the Viking woman was on top, galloping home, riding the rodeo, I wondered if I looked like her too. Did I have the same wild unseeing eyes, the determined set mouth, single bloody-mindedness?

I was coming. There were three men around me. One, poor man, serving my mouth with his finger, the second, rubbing his face in my breasts, and the third giving it to me hard. No, there were four. The fire-eater finished, and had leaped in that small space, that tiny space between my vagina and the barman's prick, and he performed love on my clitoris.

I saw the Scandinavian girl was caught up with a different man in an undignified wheelbarrow. It looked like a manoeuvre from *Ground Force* – but that didn't stop her enjoying herself. He humped her hard, and she squealed like a laughing hyena.

I had so much energy, so much vigour. After the barman and I came, someone else took his place. I lost count of the orgasms; they merged one into the other, a stream of unconsciousness, and they continued, even when the man had stopped pumping, even when the man was out of me, my body seemed to be jerking thankfully for all the years it hadn't had this. Uninhibited was a wonderful state to live in.

The Scandinavian girl was the only one who could

match me. Her eyes were glazed, the white bikini bottoms now gaping over to one side. She was doing spoons with the barman, the other woman, the late arrival, was creeping an insolent hand between her wide-set legs.

I had a taste for the pumping fire-eater. He stank of paraffin, and some parts of his body were stained with black. He was wearing Speedos and now they stretched up and out like a fire stick. His kisses smelled of flames. His body heat aroused me, scorched my skin, and his dick was hot, hotter than any other man was. As he rubbed himself up and down my body, I felt like I was getting a lick of fire or was shagging Guy Bloody Fawkes.

I rolled over so that he was under me. I took him whole in my mouth. He let out a gasp of pleasure. I worked the skin back and forth. His prick pushed against the fragile inside of my cheek. I must have looked like a squirrel storing nuts. I continued, up and down, enjoying the power thing, enjoying the physical thing, but I wanted more; of course I wanted more. I got up on all fours, cleverly maintaining oral contact at all times. My bottom was suspended in the air. I wriggled my buttocks around. Come on somebody. There was no shortage of volunteers. A tall black man disengaged from his freckly girlfriend and stood behind me, as though waiting in a queue.

'Alright?' he asked, politely.

'Mmm,' I nodded furiously, my mouth was full of prick. I continued wriggling my arse encouragingly, what else could I have done to ensure he got the message. I don't know how I must have looked with my great buttocks waiting for some action, on my knees, another guy's dick in my mouth.

I once saw photos of groupies, doing a similar thing with some 60s pop group. I remember being shocked: long hair, wild eyed, contorting mouths, uninhibited and abandoned. As an outsider, a generation away, I thought it looked hilarious. Oh, we were so much more sensible than they were. I looked at the girls with their flowers in their hair, and their knickers down their ankles, letting goodness knows who slide into their lubrication, and I thought they must be stupid, brain dead. Yuk, I was far too grown up for an orgy. But now I knew, I judged too soon. Why didn't I imagine how it would be to suck some rockstar's prick and then French kiss his come with someone else? Why didn't I wonder how it must feel to have men clambering over you, while you don't care who does it, you just want someone to, not for the intimacy, the reassurance, the commitment, but for the sheer fucking hell of it. What a pleasure it was to be doing it, to be having that done for you. What pleasure it was, to live, to fuck for the moment, with no thoughts of a past or a future.

He was a big man, not too big, but big enough to make me stop and catch my breath. He slid up my passageway, and pulled my bum tighter into his groin. We were so tight that I couldn't tell if I was jammed up him, or if he was jammed up me. Then, once securely in place, right up me, he started moving stealthily, in and out, in and out.

The audience were clapping as though we were doing it for them. Their faces, their bodies, were a daze before me, as I tried not to pass out from over-stimulation. One man had got out his prick, and was masturbating; he was wanking at the sight of me, having it from behind, and giving it. I felt like a porn star. Some of the girls had stopped moving, and were just staring, open mouthed, and I knew that they were feeling how I did on the aeroplane, when I had been too coy to let go.

One man walked behind a girl, and she literally fell back into him, he was feeling her breasts, and she wrapped her arms around him. I guess she had no idea who he was, it was just his hands on her nipples. He lifted up her T-shirt and then started scrabbling down her shorts. Unbuttoned, I caught sight of a perfect blonde pubic nest. She just stood there watching me, watching

221

her, as he parted her lips, and entered her hole with his fingers. Adults; we are men and women, and we screw, no, not like animals, but like people. I had no fear, no shame, we were using our bodies for the purposes grown, yes, and we were like hamburgers, here to be eaten.

I tried to focus on the fire-eater's prick in front. He was balancing himself with his hands on my shoulders. I liked the desperation in his fingers. He wanted to ram his cock further, further down my throat, but he was too well mannered. Instead he encouraged me by whimpering and hissing.

'Suck me, don't stop.'

Nothing turns me on like a bit of appreciation. His penis was glorious, like a barbecued kebab, and I wanted to give it all the special attention it deserved, but at the same time, I felt like a bomb was going off inside me. Take it all, take me now. I pushed back further onto my man from behind, and wriggled tighter. I could hear him laughing, happy laughing, as he gripped my sides, and pulled me on and off his hot rod. I felt myself going into a trance quite distinct from the world around me. I was drooling. I was letting the penis in my mouth find my tongue, meet my tonsils, and letting the penis in my cunt find its way. I was but a receptacle, and I loved what they were pouring in. I relaxed completely, body and mind. Every muscle was melting, let them do it to me; down on all fours and enjoying it, oh yes. Fuck everything, fuck society, fuck education, most of all fuck me.

I held the fire-eater's tight balls, and explored the underside of his cock.

'More, more,' he pleaded, and he was speaking for all of us. I saw that the girl still hadn't turned around, was still looking at me as she sucked her thumb, was now getting licked out, licked up from underneath, and she was still mesmerised by me and my new friends.

My man from behind wouldn't stop. His pace quickened, he was nearing finalisation: he was groaning his contentment. The juggler re-appeared from taking the Viking from behind and he crawled under me. My body was a bridge between sucking heaven and fucking paradise. His view must have been terrific. I felt his ten fingers on me. Yes, do it. I felt them gallop towards my clitoris.

My mind was racing with sex. All the people I had fucked before? All those rude words I had said, the situations I found myself in. Now, the sensations of my cunt, the jamming of my hole were all that I knew.

I couldn't hold back. I couldn't wait. I sucked furiously on the fire-eater and he slammed his tight balls up me. I jolted. Thank God my man in front chose to shoot his load then. A rich, creamy almost yoghurt-like come spurted in my mouth.

The juggler gripped me by the arm. He lifted me onto his shoulders, only I was facing him, pressed tight against his grizzly beard. He proceeded to walk around the area.

'I'd give up juggling if I had one of you in my hand,' he said.

He nuzzled his chin, his stubble into me. I wanted to thank him, but I didn't know how. He took me to the net, like they have on army assault courses, and he turned me upside down. I was hanging from my knees. The blood rushed to my head.

The world was upside down, but I could see I had captivated my audience. I was the best entertainer in the world. The juggler wrought my furrow. He performed magic on my cleft. If he had conjured a rabbit from my pussy, I would not have been surprised, but what he did produce was far, far better.

I came; not once, but three times. Each time, I told him to stop. I yelled no, I couldn't follow such intense enjoyment through, but his fingers were disobedient. They massaged my pleasure nodule, like there was no tomorrow. Each time I came, my upside down body throbbed uncontrollably, I was sure my clitoris was going to explode.

They were stimulating my hole again and again. I lost track of what they were using on my slit: a petal, a leaf, a tongue, and soft treading fingers like little pads. I was coming again, and again. I was living in the erogenous zones; this place was utopia. I thought I might die and I didn't care if I did, I was in such an orgiastic frenzy.

And then someone shouted that the police were coming.

I didn't know who restored me, but I was up right way round, and a blanket was flung over me. Some people were screaming. Someone grabbed my hand. Someone else was pulling at my wrist. People were panicking, stoned bodies trod through the throng. There were scattered drinks all over the sand. I remember most the emotionless Thai women filling the boxes with the money from the travellers.

Chapter Twenty-Eight

*T*he first time the King did it to her, she was held down by five men, five men! And that was as well as the straps keeping her thighs apart. They feared she would struggle and holler like she did the first night. They did not know her well.

The King opened her buttocks carefully. She was a virgin there, and she shivered, chicken-skin arms. But the King was gentle and wise. He touched her body with trembling fingers. His touch was so reverent, so delicate, that she had to ask him for more.

The courtiers consulted books on her sexuality, and if they saw signs of her enjoyment, they would point them out to the King.

'Her pupils are dilated. Her nipples are hard, her labia is swollen, her skin tone is high.'

The King said he could manage very well thank you, 'he'd been with a woman before, didn't they know?' The courtiers scuttled away, her giggles ringing in their arrogant ears.

He waited for arousal to course through her. He waited until her cunt swam with excitement and then he pushed himself towards her. The King was inside her. And she was outside him.

That night, as she sleeps, still alone on the marble table, two visitors come. The mute boy's eyes are moist with sorrow. His friend, his translator, hobbles alongside him.

'We are so sorry, so sorry. It took so long.'

He cuts the strings around her wrist. He rearranges it, so it looks like she is still tied up, but she can feel she is not. It is an amazing feeling, like accomplishing a work that's been weighing on you for a long time, or reading your stars and learning that the future is full of exciting possibilities.

'Thank you, thank you.'

They unlock the chastity belt, they free her completely so she can shake her limbs and feel the blood flow through her in celebration.

They both stand with their shoulders hunched and their hands in their pockets.

'I should like to thank you.'

She crouches down to the man, and holds him in her mouth. He makes the most wondrous noises, like dolphin communication. She has never felt such an orgasmic splash as she feels when he explodes in her mouth. The boy's shoulders shake. He is Atlas, and his arms tremble. His friend, translating for them, says the boy has never experienced such kindness before.

'The boat leaves tomorrow evening.' In her floppy hand, he pushes some money. 'It's enough for the ticket,' he murmurs bravely. 'Farewell lady. May you have a safe voyage home.'

Trent was playing volleyball in the sunshine, a vision of innocence. I hated him. How dare he try to give me drugs without me asking him? How dare he? True I had had a good time, but then I could have got sick, I could have died, anything could have gone wrong. I didn't like it, because it assumed things of me. It assumed I was old-fashioned, old-minded. OK, maybe I was slow to join things, but that didn't mean I was anti everything.

I imagined twisting the jewel out of his tongue. I

226

wondered if he would ejaculate like they say men do when they are hung? Revenge was sweet. Revenge on a man who has wronged you is sweeter than sweet. Sweet without the calories, without the tooth rot, it is a saccharine – totally unnecessary, but oh yes, how satisfying.

And he had told Selma about me! Opening up all my private things to her. He deserved punishment.

I waved at José and Selma as they came back from the beach. They moved wearily like slovenly turtles, they had sand all over their clothes. She was wearing her rose red sundress. José's baggy shorts were so low on his waist, that his hands were constantly employed holding them up. He touched my hand in a more friendly way than usual. I guess they hadn't rowed for a few minutes. Selma flicked her wet hair at me. She was shivering. Since the storm, the weather had been getting colder.

I could tell José about Trent. I could tell José about Trent and Selma and then really let the rain come down. José would pick up Trent, throw him over his shoulder, smash him to the ground and beat him to smithereens. Trent would be boiled, scrambled and fried. José would show him who was the boss.

No, that was no good. I just knew Trent would probably find the experience exhilarating. I could see him, two days later, down the pub, telling his adulterated version of the story . . .

'And then this six-foot tall and six-foot wide wanker with a knife and a gun . . .'

Besides, I knew this was my fight not José's. I had to find some way to hurt Trent's manliness, to make him question his complacent image of himself.

As the clouds came over blocking the last rays of sunshine, I realised I had the answer. Of course!

He would be putty in our hands.

Chapter Twenty-Nine

'With all these gorgeous Thai women around, I'd forgotten how good looking Western women are,' Trent said smacking his lips approvingly. I caught a glimpse of silver promise on that long red tongue. 'I quite fancy a slice of white bread!' he added, patting my knee.

We were sitting together on the beach, on his towel. I was waiting for my sweet chance. A few chairs from the nearby restaurants were upturned forlornly. There had been another squall the evening before and the tide had brought in a load of waste.

'Did you fuck Selma then?' Trent asked. I nodded looking at his nipple rings. I was nervous to meet his eyes. Would he guess the storm I had planned? 'Jesus, you should have told me! I would have loved to have been there to see you two in action.'

'It was good,' I admitted looking out to sea.

'Tell me.'

He rubbed some oil in my back and pinged my bikini straps. I giggled. Jesus, Trent was more predictable than a sex tourist.

'Well, you know I'd never been with a woman, so I, we, tried some things for the first time. It was nice touching her and she was very responsive. Her breasts were a beautiful shape, and I liked nestling there, like a pillow. I enjoyed licking around her pussy. She was so wet and creamy, and really soft. I think it's a question of timing, and um, stamina.'

I remembered how her pussy looked. Pinky brown, the shaved bush, a single line, for better access. The wet hollow was fascinating. It was a work of art. Imagine a museum of sex objects. Imagine going there, and seeing the beauty of the female sex all lined up on display. I remembered the way she had bubbled over me and then the might of her orgasm. It was like being trapped in a volcano and an earthquake at the same time, streams of lava rolling down, and everything tossed around. I looked up at Trent suspiciously. He had been there too, he had the years of practice and the jewel, but had he given her the same experience as I had?

'What about you? I hear you've been getting around a bit.'

'I most certainly have.' Trent said happily, 'Remember I told you about Titty? She came, I don't know, four or five times in a row. In-fucking-satiable that one. Her underwear wasn't as nice as yours was, but boy, did she eat cock. She was ravenous. I couldn't wait to get inside her. I wanted to obliterate myself in her warm oozing cunt.'

'Did you get her stoned too?'

'Well yes, but she asked me too,' he admitted reluctantly.

'I didn't.'

'You loved it though,' he giggled. 'I heard all about you. You conducted a fucking orgy. They heard your groaning and sighing miles up the beach. The dogs were howling in response. So hot, they said, they nearly called the fire brigade. Jesus, when you were there, with your arse up, I thought there was going to be a stampede. You certainly changed your tune. I thought you were in true love.'

'Well, true lust and all that . . . Where did you go that night anyway?'

'I met a Thai dancer, lovely girl. Soft, tender tits and a little round belly. Every time I stroked her, she wriggled at my touch. She was fascinated with my chest hair. Wanted to taste it all the time. Her skin was brown as cardboard and her snatch as tight as a ballpoint pen. I didn't think we were going to get going. That's why she's so popular apparently. Literally, her cunt shrinks back to mini. Anyway, we were trying and trying, and my penis, well, when it couldn't take the ground, it was mighty disappointed, so I said, 'not to worry, let me lick you', and well, you should have seen the change that came over her.'

I smiled benevolently, I was aware of these changes, 'Go on.'

'From being all-professional, you know, in it for the money, she was begging me. She pressed herself all over me. It was like getting trapped in a lift shaft, with her box looming over me. Tight? I could barely fit my tongue between the lips. We're talking super-narrow. She said it was her first orgasm in years.'

'They all say that, Trent.'

'Women, eh? I love them all. My satisfaction is in satisfying you,' he said self-importantly.

Little sweat droplets were forming on my forehead. My head was fuzzy from sunlight. I got up to cool off in the water. He stood up too. He smacked me on the backside.

'Mmm, filling. Like a steak dinner after many spring rolls.'

I scowled at him, but we walked to the water edge together.

His words excited me. I knew with Trent it wasn't just talk, he had the trousers. He was an experienced and an enthusiastic lover. He just wasn't such a smart guy.

I strode into the sea holding my breath. Trent whimpered and rubbed his elbows. Only when I was fully submerged and laughing at his cowardice, did he dive down to the waves. He emerged, teeth chattering and his hair dripping. We pulled cold water faces at each other and hopped around. Gradually, the parts of us out of the water were colder than the parts of us that were in it.

He pulled me close to him.

'Do you remember?' he asked triumphantly, 'how you came? You were struggling, head from side to side, howling.'

I hated myself. I hated him too, but all I could think about was the way his head, his blond hair had bobbed around like a buoy between my legs. The way my thighs had clamped around him almost involuntarily and the way my pussy had clenched around his stupid fucking piercing.

We trod water. I loved that feeling of lightness. There was nothing beneath my feet; only water, only me, working my body. He came at me from behind, grabbed my bikini and deftly slipped out a breast.

'I thought you would have gone topless by now.'

His fingers tweaked my nipples possessively. Oh why did they respond like that? Turning pink and hard as though no one had touched me for days. I worked at staying afloat. When my arousal overwhelmed me, I forgot to paddle. I sank, lower and lower, and he put his hands on my waist to pick me up. He was sliding hands down my panties and there were other swimmers close by. I knew he wanted to make a fool of me, show them his power over me. Could I come underwater? I grabbed one of his nipple rings and pulled just a little too hard. Imagine ripping it, a line, making a small scratch, Trent in agony. We stayed wrapped in each other and the sea. Flesh slapping against flesh.

I suppose I looked good with my greased back hair, new freckles. The sea was the perfect backdrop and we were framed by the sun. I was turning liquid. He kissed the back of my neck and blew in my ears. I could feel my pussy echoing his call.

'Trent.' I struggled and swam away from him. 'I want you to come to my room now.'

I was a mermaid, luring my sailors to drown, luring him from where it was safe into the deep dark sea.

'Why?' he said, making me beg for it.

'For coffee?' I laughed, 'Come on, I haven't got all day.'

'Ready for a little –' he stuck out his tongue, ' – oral massage?'

When he wrapped his legs around me again, I felt the surge of his generous cock and I decided on a subtle change of plan. Lily would come to my bungalow as arranged, but she would come after I had tied him up, not before, and after I had got him to whisper his (Canadian) excuses into my (English) fanny.

Of course, we had to walk past Prem. Typical! Prem was getting on to his bike. He had a small thin glaze of hair over his upper lip. I didn't like it. I fantasised about taking him to my room, holding a knife to his throat, and riding him, firm, and hard, deep, deeper, pressing into his saddle.

Prem nodded curtly at us, so curtly that even Trent, who was more self-absorbed than most leading brands of kitchen paper, muttered, 'What's the matter with him today?'

I peeled off my wet swimsuit and looked over at him. I suddenly remembered his two-woman swimming fantasy, and it made me smile. Dreams can come true, but often in a way you least expect.

'You've shaved your pubic hair,' he said.

I didn't tell him why. I was happy with the result. My genitals looked naked. It looked rude; there was no other way of viewing it. I enjoyed shaving myself. And now my nakedness was exposed: my sexual hub was out in the open. There would be no more navigating around spaghetti junction to get there.

Trent squirmed and sighed. He held his hand out to me as though asking me for a dance.

'I preferred it hairy,' he said, 'like a coconut.' I shrugged. It was my bush; I trimmed it how I liked.

I rubbed sun oil on my tits until they were greasy. I rubbed myself while he watched me, his eyes popping out. His boner was already rock-hard, and I hadn't even bothered to stroke it. Then kindly, I lubricated him, oiling up and down his great member, wetness all around us.

'Tit fuck me,' I requested. I massaged his cock between my breasts. The shaft went up and down, the skin held back. I squeezed my tits together, so that the route was tighter. Trent was delighted. He loudly sighed his pleasure. My breasts looked gorgeous, slickly squeezed around his rod; my whiteness, and his purple. My femininity pressed against his masculinity.

'Come on then darling, sit on my face.'

I opened my slit, and tendered the wetness inside.

I hovered over him, then feeling his tongue stuck out and wanting me, I sank down, bringing a barrage of pleasure. I had never felt so welcome as when I sat on Trent, as if I was the most important guest. He really loved using his tongue, and why not? I felt the tiny jewel stimulate my clitoris. As his tongue searched out my crevices; the little device was just like a tiny well-adjusted extra tongue, with a mind of its own. He began slowly at first. It was like being tickled by a feather, and then the flapping and slathering began in more earnest. I used him, as you might a TV or a microwave; he entertained me. I grasped at his muscular shoulders, intent on my own pleasure. I couldn't stop grunting, grunting like a fat old man, wheezing with anticipation. His tongue whipped around my vagina, slid along my exposed genitalia. Yes, the piercing hit the spot. Yes, every spot was hit, again and again. He licked and explored my wet cavity, until I was ready to come.

'I want you to stick your finger up my arsehole,' I whispered.

He opened my buttock cheeks and found the small trigger of my anus. I leaned forwards to give him the full benefit of the experience, the real fruit of my passion. I felt him enter the ring.

'Christ,' his voice was low. 'This looks fantastic.' I couldn't see his finger sliding up the dark passage, but I could imagine the view. I rocked and pushed against him. The small nodule, the hole, and the dainty well like an eye clenched shut. Very good. Slap me around.

He was beaten and we had only just started.

'When does this little man get some action?' he moaned. His penis was bent towards me, hard as nails.

'Afterwards,' I hissed and continued mashing against his face.

Afterwards, I got off him and went to the window. I opened the curtains wide, and then drew them across again, the spy signal. Lily was going to be Lily the Pink when she saw this. Trent looked like he was about to be crucified, and I was Judas about to betray him. His arms were outstretched. Project Trent was underway.

Lily sauntered in wearing a skin-tight dress. It looked gorgeous, like it had been tattooed onto her. She sashayed around the room showing off her delights. She could have been arrested for inciting disorder.

'Hello baby,' she said. Her voice was pure sex.

I was red and dishevelled. There was no hiding it. Only a few activities make you this red: being interviewed; drinking, exercising or shopping. But I was more than red; I was Scarlet O'Hara.

'Hi Lily,' I said nervously. But Lily, lovely Lily, just gave me a wink. She knew which side her bread was buttered on, as it were.

'Is this Trent?' she asked demurely. As if he could be anyone else!

'Who are you?' he said and his mouth was open wide, catching flies.

'Lily,' she whispered huskily.

'You're the most beautiful woman I've ever seen in my life.'

Lily fluttered admirably. If I hadn't known better, I

would have to say that she liked him. But I did know better.

His eyes were transfixed on her golden skin, the shape of her breasts, pushing at the shirt. She was exquisite. If Selma was attractive in a tight, tiny 'Audrey' way, Lily was gorgeous in a Liberace way. Her teeth were whiter than white, and as indestructible as building blocks. I imagined her opening bottles with them, ripping out the corks.

Trent was in ecstasy; he lay on that bed like the cat that was about to be creamed. His big todger stuck out a reminder like a flag on a golf course.

'Two women,' I said, as if he needed reminding. 'Here's your fantasy baby!'

Grateful? He nearly spunked all over us there and then. His penis was squinting at us both.

Lily didn't just strip – she did a show. She was a real tease. If I hadn't known better, I would have called her a prick tease. She fetched a broom and slid up and down it. She wrapped her long thighs around it, embracing the wooden stick as tenderly as you would a lover. Then she straddled it hard, pretending to be orgasmic, acting the part. She pretended to kiss the head, she made licking gestures. She touched her nose with her long snake-tongue, the broom dangling, like a third man, between her legs.

'Can I demonstrate my piercing on you?' Trent asked Lily, as I knew he would.

She looked questioningly at me. I nodded gleefully. Happy days were here again.

'If he wants to . . .'

'I see,' she said. We grinned conspiratorially. 'First, let's tie him up.'

Trent's face was a picture. We bound him to the bed with a fishing line, his arms behind his head, and we attached his legs to the bed frame. (At the sight of him like that, I was struck with green jealousy. Oh God, to have someone take care of me, I mean really take care of me again . . .)

'I want to lick you,' he repeated.

Lily's skirt slid to the floor. She was wearing knickers and a bra. Unless you examined closely, there was still no sign of anything else. There was just the thin lace between her and Trent's nemesis. He didn't realise immediately. He was still going on with his catch phrase, when she lowered her panties.

'I want to lick you . . . Wha?'

The incomplete word reverberated around the room.

Lily was smoothly sliding down her panties, down her toned thighs, yielding them over those fine knees, down the calves, to rest at her trim ankles. From the top of her legs the core of what she was, was exposed and extended.

'Oh no, no,' Trent stuttered.

'Lick me,' she said. And her penis was big, hard and erect. It was a dream penis.

'Fuck.'

Trent was backing up against the wall like a frightened animal, but he couldn't move far; he was too restrained. Poor baby, there was no escape. But giving away secrets and forcing people to take drugs deserves punishment Trent. Besides he was another one who talked about travel broadening your mind. Well, sex can too, if you let it.

'Fucking hell. What is it?' He yelped incomprehensibly. He was like a puppy that had just been kicked up the backside.

Lily looked tremendous. Her breasts were ripe and upright and her cock was proud and generous.

Trent looked at me pleadingly. 'Honey, I mean Abby, what's going on? Who is this? I'm not gay, you know I'm not.'

'I know you're not,' I said consolingly. There, there, honey. 'She only wants a little lick-icky.'

How could Trent turn his nose up at her, when his

236

little man, his todger, was turning up its vast nose with anticipatory glee?

'Come on, work it, baby,' said Lily. She towered over Trent; she had removed everything except for those knife-like stilettos. Trent kept his mouth closed, even as she pressed her cock against him, but Lily was so cool. She was like a dentist with a mischievous child. She just inserted her nails and levered his lips apart and then her prick was jammed in his reluctant mouth. Slowly, he gave in. He started tonguing her cock. His strokes were hesitant, but helpful. You could tell he hadn't sucked dick before, but if you've done one, you can do the other. One's in, one's out, that's the only difference, and if I had learned both . . .

'That's a good boy, that's good,' Lily cooed.

'Do you like his tongue piercing?' I asked her. She had one hand perched on his shoulder, with the other she was twiddling her hair, or should I say, wig? Round and round her finger went.

'To be honest, I can't feel it,' Lily said.

Trent came up for air, his face blotchy and bewildered, 'What? You can't feel it?' he asked incredulously.

'I can't feel it,' she repeated. Galvanised he dove down and started working, sucking and cajoling Lily's penis with the prodigal piercing. He licked under the balls, those unexpected testicles, working her competently.

'No, I still can't feel it.'

Even I looked at her amazed. Trent was making whirling patterns on the side, suckling her dick, storing it in his mouth, popping it in and out. He was showering it with his eager saliva and the piercing must have added to the fun.

'You can't?'

Trent's piercing was his pièce de résistance. Without it he was just a double glazing salesman.

I looked up and realised that she was lying. Her hair was askew tumbling down her narrow frame and her expression gave her away.

'No, I definitely can't feel it.'

This galvanised Trent even further. He tried to persuade her otherwise. He made these incredible suction noises.

She knew how to work men. I didn't want to let go, but I couldn't help myself, I waited, massaging myself between my legs. A dopey smile of wonder all over my face. Oh yes, they looked fantastic, my live sex show.

'Do you like it?' Trent's need for triumph outweighed his sexual preferences. He let go for one minute to speak, but she held him back.

'It's not bad,' she breathed. But I could see from her broadening smile, that it was more than not bad. Her beautiful mouth was contorted and her cheeks seemed to be spasming.

'Not bad,' she repeated, and then gave out a low groan. It was fascinating to watch her face; it felt right, not strange, but right as rain, normal. She gave a low grumble and then a yelp like a little dog. Her nails were tight in his hair. And then it all came out. The penis was twitching, jerking and expanding, and then Trent was gulping, gulping the arrival for dear life.

His tongue was wrapped around her stalk, like a bee buzzing around the honey, but it was his face that held me, his face. I never saw such a look of ecstasy on any face as I did then.

Of course we wouldn't stop there, how could we? We had to plunge the extremes of pleasure and pain, love and hate. Trent was big and hard. His cock was anxious for entertainment even if its owner didn't know it.

His face was ashen. How he whimpered and protested and begged for mercy. We kept his arms tied.

'No,' he tried bargaining, 'I'll do it to you, not you me. Let me lick you Abby.'

'You already have,' I pointed out quite reasonably.

His penis was twitching like a puppet on a string. I squirmed down underneath him, so that he was tied over me. I opened my legs. I was already wet. I didn't need any touch; mind control flicked the switch. Trent looked thrilled at the prospect of a lighter sentence and his dick leaped forwards volunteering.

Trent delivered his cock inside me, growing even harder there. Then he started moving up and down me, attempting to fuck me like the clappers, trying to get it over with. What a darling.

'Stop, stop,' I slowed him down, well-disciplined, 'Wait.'

I gripped him by his nipple piercings, and he knew better than to struggle then. Each time he pulled back, I wrenched him forward, 'til tears sprung to his eyes. He knew we meant business. Lily was coming up at him from behind. Cautiously, feeling her way around his buttocks. His prick was hardening like wet socks in the sun. Blood was rushing to his head.

'Open wide.'

'No!' he bellowed.

'I'm just going to spread your lovely buttocks.'

'Please . . . no.'

'But look Trent, feel how turned on you are. That's a glorious erection you've got there. I can feel it tight inside me. Two women, don't you remember?'

'Please . . . no,' but his fat erect dick was pleading, yes! Who were we to listen to? Surely not the mind with its caveats and its hypocrisy, surely we should go straight to the horse's mouth to hear what it had to say. His dick surged again most impressively. It was darling. It was thickly wriggling around in my womb.

'Go Lily, go Lily,' I said, like they say to the hosts on those wild chat shows.

Lily didn't need reminding. She yanked apart his buttocks, just like I drew back the curtains, and she found her space. Home run. She pushed her cock forward into the tiny cavity that was Trent's spoilt little arsehole.

Trent howled. I could see the headlines: Raging Bull Ravishes Man. Thousands turn out to support home team. There was no way Selma and José could have missed it. Even if they were on the other beach they would have heard it. But even though he howled and sobbed, his penis stayed strong and true. And while he pleaded and moaned, his penis tripled in size. I knew because it was bang inside me. We were a glorious, celebration; a fabulous viscous circle. Trent, bless him, was being torn apart by the thickest and most unexpected prick in the world. He was out of control. His face about to explode, and his body, well his body was already exploding. I fed off his naked frenzy. The more he struggled, both with his conscience and his cock, the more he screwed himself tighter and firmer into a hole.

'Abby,' he groaned, like a dying man, 'Fuck me now, now, now!'

But it was Lily who was doing the fucking. She was in charge of screwing us senseless and she charged on, gripping his hips tightly. He had nowhere to run, nowhere to hide, except to push deeper and deeper into me. A beacon of hope in a Dark Age. Payback time.

Project Trent had been accomplished. We were both well and truly shafted.

Chapter Thirty

I could cope without Roger, more than cope. My heart did not give out. I gradually realised that even if Angela hadn't become pregnant, our relationship would have ended sooner or later. Once we were apart, once out of each other's knickers, what I had once thought was love, had quickly become a chore.

I have been touched and yet, I have not been touched. Just because people have seen and heard me fuck, does not mean they know me. Just because they have fingered me, licked or penetrated my hottest place, does not mean that they have had me.

I have grown harder. Who was that woman on the plane, so shy, so ashamed? Who was the girl who believed everything they told her? Yes, but I have grown softer too.

The rainy season was on its way. Soon every day would be like that night, that stormy night when I found out the truth about my lover. There were only a few people left on the island. Prem, me, some masseuses, some fleshy white men with pretty Thai girls. I even saw the men who I'd spent the night with. They didn't recognise me of course. I thought it would be funny to sidle up to them, 'Hey, you've got the mole on your prick, still got that premature ejaculation problem?' But I didn't. Occasionally there were newcomers though, out-of-season backpackers. I liked the sight of them with their polished clothes and styled hair. I had been here longer than they had; I knew my way around. They surveyed the area so wide-eyed, while we long-termers had narrow lids, fond, like the way a granddad watches his grand-children.

I walked serenely between bungalow, café and beach. I enjoyed eating dinner on my own. I savoured each bite without interruption or small talk. I hadn't seen Lily or Trent for a few days and Selma and José had both left the island. I saw them off and we kissed and fondled under the palm trees and promised to meet again. I felt very calm and happy.

One day, Prem asked if I would like to drive out to see the waterfall. He said he would pick me up early and that I didn't need to bring anything. Don't get your hopes up, Abigail. I warned myself. What could possibly come of it? The moment for romance had passed its sell-by date. Ours had grown into a friendship.

We rode to the spot, parked up and then lay down in the long grass together letting the morning sun sweep over our bodies. I wanted to touch him but I couldn't betray him. Prem didn't want that. He didn't want me. All the same, when our arms brushed together, I could feel all my tiny hairs rush up to meet him. He absorbed me totally. You know the way water runs down the plug-hole? That was how I felt about him.

'I wanted a different kind of life,' he said abruptly. 'Running Sunita Complex is quite difficult for me sometimes.'

'So, you have to continue here, even though you don't really want to?' I asked.

Prem studied his nails, and then looked at me long and hard. 'I don't have to do anything. It is not a burden. When you love someone the way I love my family, duty ceases to be duty.'

I wonder if that was why Roger and I hadn't worked out.

I looked up at the sky. The clouds seemed to be galloping across while here on earth everything was moving in slow motion. I wondered if I would ever love anyone again. Maybe I just didn't deserve to be loved.

Prem jumped up and pulled off his shirt raggedly. He lifted his T-shirt over his head. Then he pulled down his shorts. He was so beautiful he took my breath away.

'Prem?' I said uncertainly.

'Take off your clothes.'

This was not how I imagined it. Certainly not.

'Take everything off,' he repeated. He was undoing his shoes.

'Is it, is it safe here?' I asked still hesitant.

'No one is here, we're totally alone.'

That sent a shiver through me. I stripped off slowly and put my clothes in an uncharacteristically neat pile. When eventually I turned around he had disappeared into the undergrowth.

'Prem? Where are you?'

'This way,' he yelled. I anxiously followed his voice. There, through the bamboo trees, was a huge waterfall. Prem grabbed my hand and before I could register anything about the terrific depth, or the velocity of the water, we had jumped. We sloshed down, down, down, sliding and knocking into each other. It was like a giant chute. I didn't know when it would end, and then we were underwater, my lungs were exploding, and I don't know how, because I didn't make an effort, but I popped up gasping for air. Prem was right by me. We were in the most beautiful cove in the world, brimming over with wet-water plants, and flowers.

It was a secret, secret garden. The waterfall rained down on us. We splashed each other furiously, slamming our hands on the water surface, creating our own microstorms and laughing like lunatics.

You know in the movies the moment where the

laugher stops and the passion moves in? The crunch point, when finally, after all that waiting, the couple move in on each other? Well, that didn't happen. Prem didn't let the window of romance open for one second. I wanted it to. Oh, I yearned for it so much that I was physically aching for him and his touch. My nipples were constantly alert, my pussy was contracting. All rational boundaries, all prosperity ratios were blurred. So what if he didn't like foreign tourists? I wasn't exploiting him. I needed him. Was that so bad?

After a while, Prem led me back to the bike. I was naked but he didn't look back. We quickly put on our clothes. I cast sneaky peeps at his brown body as he fiddled into his clothes, but he didn't look at me once until when we walked back to the motorbike. Then he stopped, looked deeply at me, and drew in to pick a leaf out of my hair. I hardly dared breathe for fear of disturbing the moment. I felt the rise and fall of his breath on me.

'There!' He picked out the intruder and dropped it to the ground.

'In England, we say that is lucky.'

'In Thailand, the head is the highest part of the body and the foot is the lowest.'

I looked up into his eyes, but he turned away. He wasn't having any of it. I remembered how stupid I had felt that time I had kissed him and he had turned me down. Yet I wanted him so much. While he was this close to me it seemed unnatural not to kiss.

Oh, the moment had passed again. There must be a law against this. Against exciting someone and failing to deliver. Surely, it was contrary to advertising standards. Oh, Prem, why won't you touch me?

On the bike, I squeezed myself against him, my nipples drilling two holes into his mahogany back. The bike seat was hard against my bottom, and the movements sent sweet sensations across the top of my thighs. The bike was a finely-tuned machine. I liked those words. They

244

reminded me of sexy calendars of finely-tuned men: firemen, builders and cheeky men in safety harnesses. Calendars to die for, calendars to masturbate over. Stare at them over your computer and be transported to a world where the men are big and tough but gentle and cheeky and grinning. Imagine escaping with a calendar man. It would have to be dramatic. The fireman, rescuing you, giving you a fireman's lift, and then eating your fanny. The juice would squirt out like a hose. A builder, making him tea, a quickie while the hubby's negotiating with the others about a price.

I was living my fantasy now. Only my calendar man was stuck on last year. Didn't Prem know, didn't he notice how tightly I held him? Or was he so contemptuous of tourists that he couldn't recognise one who was hot for him.

Fuck him and my ludicrous fantasies. So what if Selma had got a ticket and I hadn't? He wanted me stuck on the island; not so he could fill me up with his juices, but just so he could tease and taunt me.

I had misjudged the situation.

We returned by a different route on an unmade road of hairpin bends. Prem drove fast, and I leaned against him, sniffing his jacket like a horny dog. Faster and faster we cruised down the dirt tracks. We skidded. The wheels tried to get a grip and failed. We slammed hard on the rocky surface. I remembered seeing a dog skating on ice, and how bewildered he was, as he dug his claws in trying to get a grip. And I remembered Trent saying 'Motorcycle accidents are the main cause of death on the island,' and I recalled the lecherous way he looked at me and touched me. And then it went blurry; the ground was swimming before my eyes.

My body tumbled to the stones, the bike smashed on top of me, and I felt like I had been smashed by a house, like the wicked witch of the East, only I was a wicked over-privileged cow from the West.

I must have blacked out.

The next thing I knew Prem was up and barking at me. I was lying some yards away from the bike.

'Abby, are you OK? Abby?' Prem shook me so hard I thought my brains would fall out and it was almost worse than actually falling off the bike. Blinking, winking, up at him. His beautiful face was grey with fear. Everything I saw was shaky, like bad camera action, and my eyelids were too heavy to keep open. I knew I would be OK though. My legs were in agony but at least I could feel them.

'How's the bike?'

He sat me up, and stared at me in, I think, amazement but I was not sure of anything yet. Maybe I just died and this is heaven. It could be.

'The bike?' I repeated.

He bounded back towards the machine, he hauled it upright, and came back concerned and crazy.

My legs were bleeding. I tried to stand up and then crumpled. He put his shoulder under my arm and pulled me towards the bike. My legs scraped against the ground. Then he picked me up tenderly and placed me on the back of the bike, sidesaddle like graceful women in cowboy movies. Only I was not graceful, I was pathetic. My body was creasing up like a paper flower; the tears were coming to my eyes. It was a miracle we weren't badly hurt.

Prem examined my knee gravely. He dropped down in front of me, and touched my leg uncertainly. He traced the line of my damaged leg, a slow waltz from ankle to knee. I watched the progress of his dancing finger. He brushed off the dirt. Then he bowed his head to lick off the remainder. He sucked the stones out of the creases. He spat small bits of gravel on the ground. Taking them out of me.

'Keep it clean,' he said.

'Mmm,' I hummed. All I could feel was his hot wet mouth on my hot skin.

He touched my thigh with his index finger. He touched

246

my thigh! He whispered 'sorry', and even before he said it, I knew it was for more than the accident. His mouth stayed pressed at my knee. Shivers of excitement rocked me. I felt better. I felt his breath on my leg, his saliva, and his warmth. The pain had gone. He raised his head and he was eye level, we were face to face, eye to eye, and then before the second was out, I leaned forward and gave him a kiss. It was just a tentative kiss, more a breath even than a kiss. I waited; I couldn't move away. Oh, I wanted, craved to ravish him, devour him, to eat him, but I couldn't make that move. I waited for Prem to decide. But he wouldn't.

So I kissed him again. Just dusted my lips like fine powder, like a butterfly flapping its wings, like a leaf blowing on the ground.

'I can't.'

'Yes, you can,' I whispered into his mouth.

And he gave out this sigh and to me, it was like hearing the agreement of a starting gun.

We kissed again for longer and longer. I was sizzling, bacon in the pan. He allowed me to linger. He didn't push me off. I was trampling over his property, but he liked it.

'Sorry,' he groaned again. This time, when we kissed, I opened my mouth as wide as I could. I wanted to swallow him whole, and I was pressing my tongue into him. He relented, responded and I could feel my fanny oozing, I wanted some of that too! How we kissed, deeper and deeper, until we were almost inside each other's mouths and I was scared my teeth would grate his skin.

'I'm a bad boy,' he murmured. Oh please be bad. Be very bad. Finally, complete surrender. He moved down, he raised my vest and sank his face into my breasts. I pushed them up to him. My tits for his lips. I held him around the waist. A narrow line of hairs emerged from his shorts, like a dark pillar of smoke from the chimney. The twin sacks thumped at me, like they wanted to get

247

closer. And I wouldn't let him take his mouth from my breasts, not for a minute. My nipples were red and hot for him.

I made him lie horizontal on his bike. His arms were down by his sides, his legs keeping balance, and I got on top and started to ride. My hands were on the handlebars, and my legs were slung either side. He protested that maybe I was sick, delirious perhaps. I should see a doctor, but I wasn't going to let him escape again.

I lowered myself onto his wondrous shaft. I couldn't wait. I couldn't hold back what I was feeling for him. His cock was up me, and I was sawing in and out, up and down. I had never felt this good, I had never felt so fucking good.

The sun beat a celebration on my back, and my hair dangled down tickling us both. Prem tendered my nipples with his fingertips, just lightly, but each stroke was sending waves of pleasure through my body. I remember I was shouting, 'Yes' and I think I was also shouting his name, but they were the only sounds I could make, they were the only words I knew. And I must have been shouting them awfully loudly because afterwards, my voice was hoarse, and Prem said that he had temporarily lost all sense in his left ear, which was where my mouth had been. I don't remember much though. All I knew was that we were taken over by this incredible force, a wonderfully benevolent power. My head was swinging wildly. My body was loose and free. I was abandoned, frenzied, and as I came I thought that Eros must have shot an arrow and for once he had hit a bulls-eye. It pierced my heart and soul.

Chapter Thirty-One

She cannot choose when he comes to visit, and some nights (most nights) she wishes, no, prays, that he would come more than once.

The King and she are the perfect fit. Each time he dives, she flips. Now that he has shaken off the tyranny of his duty, the King is a happy man.

The King comes to her later and later in the evening; he doesn't want an audience any more. He dismisses the court, and they move off sulkily, seeking out other entertainments. Later, she hears that the Queen herself has volunteered for the dark room game, and that the hammock game is already fascinating the lower quarters.

She fears that the King is growing sentimental and that she is too. Sometimes he wants her to read poetry, love verses about wandering clouds and fields of golden corn.

He reads to her, and then he kisses, nibbles even, her face. Then he may test her moistness down there, quantifying her readiness.

But one night, when they fuck, she jerks and pulses too far, too strongly, so that her hands are ripped free.

'Governess . . .' he gasps, mortified.

'Goodness,' she says, gathering the strings around her protectively. 'I seem to have come undone.'

The King shakes at the ties around her ankles and her knees. He checks the strange contraption that ensures that her pussy is open, and her arse unimpeded and he finds that that too has been meddled with. Nothing is tied, her hands are not bound.

'Governess!' he repeats, he appears to be tongue-tied (or is it, tongue-thai'd?) 'What, what can this mean?'

'It means that I am your willing servant.'

'But, you have been free to go for how long now?'

'For a long time, my lord, since three months ago.'

'Why didn't you say?'

'I gave myself to you voluntarily. I come to you, not because you forced me, or even out of duty, or loyalty, I stayed with you because I love you.'

The King pauses. He wants to think about it for a while. His world has been upturned by the events of the past few months, everything he had held to be true is untrue, all that he feared he now loves.

'Governess, I have something to ask you?' the King says breaking free from his reveries.

'Yes, my lord.'

'How about you tie me up for a change?'

And, as in all the best fairy tales, the King and she lived happily ever after.

Nothing beats being woken up from a sexy dream with a stiff hard penis inside you. I was asleep, dreaming strange whirling pictures, dazzling non-stop jigsaw pieces. I was awake half dreaming, clutching Prem's hair, Prem was inside me, Prem was in me, strange words, strange things penetrating me thoroughly, the weight of him imprisoned me. My legs opened around him, welcoming his prick, anxious for his touch. He was in me, filling me, fulfilling me, and stuffing me with joy.

Last night, when we got back to his room, after our 'ride', I was abrasive, awkward. What must he have thought of me? The way I behaved! Did I disgust him?

Another foreigner here for what she could get. Another slapper.

But he was gentle and concerned. Got me a cold flannel for my forehead, just in case, and shuffled me into bed.

Each time he touched me I shivered. I trembled even at his fingertips. My skin grew so hot; I wanted to peel it off.

'Abby, what's wrong?' he asked. 'Is it the accident?'

'No.'

'Look at me, Abby.'

I wouldn't meet his eyes, how could I?

'I'm so embarrassed,' I sniffed.

He must have thought I was really crazy. Did he know I slept with his best friend? Or that at the party, I slept with everyone?

'Punish me?' I whispered.

'What for?'

'For being a bad girl.'

'You're not a bad girl.'

'I am.'

'I don't care what you did.'

Perhaps I still looked sceptical.

'You are gorgeous.'

'Thank you, darling,' I said relieved. He didn't know! Hurray, hurray. My shoulders relaxed.

'I don't give a damn about your past, I want you now,' he added for good measure.

'Yes,' I gurgled. Feel how wet I am. I was an ocean on legs.

'But I am still going to punish you . . .' he grinned, his fingers pressing on my thighs.

'Yes please.'

Flat out, all yours. I was his slave. He possessed my body, every little bit of it, even the white moons in my nails, the silver fillings in my teeth, from the creases in my belly button to the blue-veined rivers behind my knees. All that I gave to him. His tongue explored the

251

dimples in my thighs, the swell of my calves, the tender-
ness of my nipple, the fleshiness of my earlobe.

I was crying out for his prick, but he gave me his
mouth. I felt like mother earth being fucked by big
business. His tongue flickered in my slit, and my out of
control body was wracked with orgasm.

'Now,' he said business-like, putting my hand on his
erection. 'Don't you think it's time we had some nooky?'

'Who told you that word?' I said grinning despite
myself.

'No one,' he lied. But I knew, he knew. And he didn't
mind.

I groaned again that morning as I felt him feel open
my cunt, slip into place, bang into me, the perfect fit, as I
struggled to regain sanity.

'Mmmm,' he breathed heavily in my ear. He was the
most perfect alarm clock in the entire universe.

'What time is it?'

He opened the curtain behind me. Prem could tell the
time from the moon.

'Four.'

'Four a.m. Are you mad?'

He didn't answer. Instead he started moving, rocking
me, swinging me. I felt his penis surge against my secret
tunnel and my clitoris was quivering gently awake. He
put his fingers to my re-growing bush, and under, and
under. He pampered me there until I couldn't stand it
any more; I had to have release. He said he loved my
face, the slope of my nose, and the fullness of my lips.
He said he always thought of me as anxious, 'You have
the expression of worry,' he said, about the first time
when he saw me and I had just cut my hand.

'On a bit of paper,' he said incredulously, 'You must
be very delicate.' And I agreed. I knew I wasn't anymore,
but I didn't have to spoil his illusions.

He woke me again at six, with butterfly kisses on my
lips and on my nose.

'Wanna go catch some fish?'

Prem struggled getting the boat out. His knees hurt. He said it was from our accident, but I suspected it was from our endless congresses. We rode around the bay. The water was smooth and the sky blue. It was a heavenly day in paradise.

Prem worked hard, the fish jerked on the line.

'This fish,' he said 'mates for life.'

'So where is its partner?'

'Out there,' he said, and pointed out to the endless turquoise sea. We were in the slip tide and the boat was tugged in all directions.

When I asked him about sharks, Prem said that it was rubbish, there were no man-eating ones about.

'Only me,' I laughed.

As he worked, he made little grunting noises. Just the sound of him turned me on. I loved the sound of sex, if I could record myself and play it again and again. Lily's shrieking, Selma's fast groaning, the driver's steady chorus of moans, and José's athletic grunting.

I sat opposite him and opened my legs distracting him from his task.

'You naughty woman,' he said 'Abby, what are you doing?'

'I just want to show you something.'

'What . . . do you want to show me?'

'My cunt.'

'Oh.'

I took the rod and fish, while he parted my thighs, running his hands up and down my flesh. I leaned back luxuriously and he fished around in my bikini bottoms.

'Well, what does it look like?'

'It looks like,' he paused. '. . . Very hungry.'

'I think you mean delicious.'

'No, I think it looks hungry. It wants feeding.'

He followed the line from my belly button down to my wakening pussy, covered in wetness, wet as the sea.

I shuddered. I couldn't help myself. We were sitting opposite each other, looking at each other deeply, and three of his fingers were up my hole. He was fisting me. Oh God, you wouldn't believe how wide open I could go, how much could fit in there.

'Look at me.'

I still couldn't. I was too embarrassed to meet his eyes. I was too close to jerking like a fish on his line. Prem, how could you do this to me? Water cascading from my hollow, water all around us. I wondered if I could insure my pussy, the way stars insure various parts of their body: their legs, their eyes, their whatever. Oh boy, my pussy was my most important part, worth millions.

I looked up and saw that Prem was hard and ready, thank God. He slid to the bottom of the boat, to the bottom of me. He pressed his tongue against me, brushed his face against my fanny.

I heard a voice, somewhere out at sea. It was Trent. Trent; the sailor in a rubber dinghy. And he was with someone who had his or her back towards us. I couldn't tell if it was a he or she.

'Abbs, are you on your own?' he shouted. Prem was prostrate beneath me.

'Yes,' I said weakly, 'in a way.'

'Come and join us.'

I was going to come but not join them.

'Ha,' I said incoherently.

Prem's face was fixed, plundering me for gold.

'Phew, smells like fish.'

'You rude sod.'

I slapped him gently. I liked smacking him. His body quivered and I could see the full effect of my handiwork.

Lily was waving at me, precariously from their shaky raft. I could see she was wearing her make-up, even a set of false eyelashes decorated her lids. Trent supported her; his hands were under her outstretched arms.

'Trent and I are engaged,' she screeched. Her unusual accent reverberated around the bay – En-Gay-jud.

'No!' I started laughing. 'Where's the ring?'

She stuck out her tongue at me.

'Wha-at?'

A shiny stud was perched on the end of the red plain.

I was straddling him, my unseen man. And they didn't know that as we were speaking I was fucking him; I was fucking the biggest prick in the country, and his fingers were rubbing me, thunderously. I knew his game, I knew his cheeky ploy, he wanted me to come in front of an audience. I let him move me up and down, glad of the love handles that enabled him to steer me on and off his cock.

'Where are you going now?' shouted Lily.

'Oh God, umm, yes, nowhere really.'

My words rushed out. That excited Prem. His hands were too hard, too ready; I knew what he was going to do.

'Don't touch me,' I hissed. 'Prem, stop it now.'

But I was still holding the rod with one hand and the other was on the side of the boat, he had a free run, and he knew it. Sexy bastard. Too late, his finger was squirming, searching for the tiny hole between my cheeks, the tiny hole where he was going to be made so welcome, whatever the proprietor might think. I felt my whole body bow in subservience to my sexual organs.

Trent yelled out.

'You look real pretty, honey.'

Prem was whispering obscenities. He learned his English quick.

'Oh you're so horny, you're so fucking wet, I want you, do it, do it now. Come for me baby.'

I should have left England years ago. There was a world out there, a world, and there was a corner for me. I had thought that to find love, I had to be still and make a nest, when all I had to do was show courage.

Prem's finger tunnelled in, up my arsehole. Tight and contained, every orifice covered, stamped with his approval. I was bounding up and down, pushing his fingers further in me, possessing me, possessing him. Yet, at the same time, I was afraid. They didn't know what I was enduring, what I was enjoying. I had to pretend my world wasn't spinning.

I heard Lily's concerned voice from across the waves.

'Abby, are you OK?'

I could distinctly hear Trent whispering, 'Is she ill? What's the matter with her?'

I heard their voices, but I couldn't hear anything anymore. I was up and down on him, like a hammer and tongs. I couldn't stop, I really couldn't stop, don't ask me to stop. His fingers were fluttering in my arse, pressing on my pleasure zones, forcing me to this embarrassing conclusion.

'Let's take the boat nearer.' Anxious talk. 'Abby love, are you OK? Don't worry we're coming now . . .'

'Yes,' I screeched, 'Oh God, Oh God, fuck, fuck, fuck.'

My knees were raw with my exertion, I slammed harder and harder, impaling myself on his prick, on his fingers, my clitoris was rubbing against him. I was rubbing against him. I threw myself up and down, the boat rocked furiously and everything disappeared. Everything except for the terrible motion of cock in my cunt, and the hands chopping at my resistance, exploring where no hands should be, and I was coming, coming, coming. And I was screaming.

'Yes, yes, YES.'

The boat capsized and we were thrown into the warm foamy sea.

That evening, Prem said it was going to rain. The airport was going to be flooded.

'You have to stay longer,' he said. 'One more week?'

'OK, one more week,' I agreed.

I wrote my last letter to Roger while Prem cooked. Roger was in the hospital. I had called his wife (as a concerned co-worker naturally), and she told me the address. She also said there was no lasting damage, but that his face wouldn't look the same. Still at least his passport photo was nice. In the letter, I laughed about his leaving present and said not to worry; pleasure and pain are the same thing. I said that I shouldn't have settled for his half-hearted love, but naturally, I wished him the best of (indifferent) luck in the future.

Prem didn't ask who I was writing to, but I think he guessed. When the food was sizzling in great big iron pans, he put his arms around me, squeezing me tight, and he planted smoochy kisses on my cheek and neck. He was grilling freshly caught fish.

'With mushrooms,' he added, eyeing me salaciously. I wolfed them all down, and even pulled off the little black bits left in the frying pan so that I could enjoy every last bit of them.

Chapter Thirty-Two

I would rub the pilots raw. I would go in the cabin at take-off time, plump myself on the pilot's knee. Watch him, mouth-watering, fly the plane, control the machine, our lives in his hands. I would slowly slip off my jacket, unbutton my shirt. He would lunge towards me, towards my breasts encased in a lacy bra.

'No, you fly the plane,' I would say, 'I'm in control here.'

I would swivel over him; straddle him. Flying the pilot. All this time, the co-pilot would stare, his eyes huge, his fear massive, and his cock as big as a Boeing 747. What a miracle, this great big piece of equipment was, suspended mid-air.

The pilot would switch on the speaker.

'Ladies and gentlemen.'

I would have my hands in his pants, wandering all over his lower belly, his balls, and his dick.

Maybe, one of the stewardesses, one of the girls who never liked me: one who has always secretly lusted after the pilot, would come in laughing. She would catch us flying en flagrante.

'I'm so sorry to disturb you.'

'No problem,' the captain would groan. His cap would be askew.

Maybe I would duck down to feed off him, and then the co-pilot would take me from behind. He would say that he loved my demonstrations – how well I explained the life jackets, he would say he wished he were that fucking life jacket, he wished every time he saw it, every single time, that he were wrapped around my breasts, saving my life.

The co-pilot would open up the crease between my two moons. I would shudder and sigh for more, fly me, fly me. That's what I would do if I were a stewardess.

My neighbours on the flight were a pompous business-man and a whiskered old woman. The woman spilled over her seat onto me. I regretted that I hadn't staked my claim for the armrests more forcefully. I read the in-flight magazine and prepared for the video.

'Meat or fish?'

The stewardess dully moved towards me. I noticed how heavily made up her face was, how unattractive she was, compared to how attractive she believed herself to be. She thought ageing was her enemy. Yes, ageing would exasperate the misery lines, the poppy eyes, but her mean expression was the problem. The tray was plonked undignified on my table.

'Don'tcha have nothing else?' There was a disgruntled voice behind me. I peeped between the seats and the first thing I saw was a shirt of swirling colours. Looking up, I glimpsed a square jaw, a proud nose. A moustache flapped over soft lips and I noticed small teeth in a glorious straight line. A few minutes later, I watched him swagger down the aisle, like an amateur actor playing a cowboy.

I had been jealous of Selma, jealous of her spontaneity, her passion. There was no need to be jealous of things I already possessed. I walked down the aisle, blushing like a bride. I knocked faintly on the toilet door. I hoped I had not made a mistake. I hoped that he was ensconced in there, not the family of a hundred from Dubai.

259

'Who is it?'

His voice was like a growl.

I pressed my face against the door in a retarded effort at discretion. 'Let me in.'

The unlucky sods that had been placed next to the toilet scowled at me.

I slid in. There was no space to spin a cat, and he was such a groovy cat, with his tight jeans and psychedelic shirt. At first, he looked startled and then pleased. Swept my hair off my face holding my cheeks too tight. And then he kissed me roughly, ugly bloody maniac kissing, all over me, gagging for more. Sweeping his wet tongue over the contours of my face. I kissed him, darting my tongue in his mouth and that made him all frenzied, tugging at my clothes even though he didn't know me. Gripping fingers, clutching tight, struggling to breathe. We were pulling and squeezing, a confined, frenzied fuck. He hoisted me over the sink, panties down on my knees, spread wide, plunged into my black box. 'Jesus,' we both hissed and then working my legs, working my cunt. Fast, fast, no time to think, no time for distraction, pure orgasm-chasing. He was vibrating inside me, buttocks working like crazy, and I was praying, 'please God' for more fucking turbulence.

The stewardess was, if not hammering, then knocking very firmly on the door. A queue had formed outside. The specky eleven-year-old had his legs clenched together. I went back to my seat. A girl, quiet and bookish, in the aisle opposite looked up at me and smiled. Her teeth were yellow, but she was pretty.

She asked my name and I told her and then gesturing the fellow on the seat behind she said, 'So what's your boyfriend's name?'

'Him? Oh, I don't know. We've only just met.'

You would have loved the look on her face.

BLACK LACE NEW BOOKS

Published in October

LURED BY LUST
Tania Picarda
£5.99

Clara Fox works at an exclusive art gallery. One day she gets an email from someone calling himself Mr X, and very soon she's exploring the dark side of her sexuality with this enigmatic stranger. The attraction of bondage, fetish clothes and SM is becoming stronger with each communication, and Clara is encouraged to act out adventurous sex games. But can she juggle her secret involvement with Mr X along with her other, increasingly intense, relationships?

ISBN 0 352 33533 5

ON THE EDGE
Laura Hamilton
£5.99

Julie Gibson lands a job as a crime reporter for a newspaper. The English seaside town to which she's been assigned has seen better days, but she finds plenty of action hanging out with the macho cops at the local police station. She starts dating a detective inspector, but cannot resist the rough charms of biker Jonny Drew when she's asked to investigate the murder of his friend. Trying to juggle hot sex action with two very different but dominant men means things get wild and dangerous.

ISBN 0 352 33534 3

Published in November

LEARNING TO LOVE IT
Alison Tyler
£5.99

Art historian Lissa and doctor Colin meet at the Frankfurt Book Fair, where they are both promoting their latest books. At the fair, and then through Europe, the two lovers embark on an exploration of their sexual fantasies, playing dirty games of bondage and dressing up. Lissa loves humiliation, and Colin is just the man to provide her with the pleasure she craves. Unbeknown to Lissa, their meeting was not accidental, but planned ahead by a mysterious patron of the erotic arts.

ISBN 0 352 33535 1

THE HOTTEST PLACE
Tabitha Flyte
£5.99

Abigail is having a great time relaxing on a hot and steamy tropical island in Thailand. She tries to stay faithful to her boyfriend back in England, but it isn't easy when a variety of attractive, fun-loving young people want to get into her pants. When Abby's boyfriend, Roger, finds out what's going on, he's on the first plane over there, determined to dish out some punishment.

And that's when the fun really starts hotting up.

ISBN 0 352 33536 X

To be published in December

EARTHY DELIGHTS
Tesni Morgan
£5.99

Rosemary Maddox is TV's most popular gardening presenter. Her career and business are going brilliantly but her sex life is unpredictable. Someone is making dirty phonecalls and sending her strange objects in the post, including a doll that resembles her dressed in kinky clothes. And when she's sent on an assignment to a bizarre English country house, things get even stranger.

ISBN 0 352 33548 3

WILD KINGDOM
Deanna Ashford
£5.99

War is raging in the mythical kingdom of Kabra. Prince Tarn is struggling to drive out the invading army while the beautiful Rianna has fled the fighting with a mysterious baroness. The baroness is a fearsome and depraved woman, and once they're out of the danger zone she takes Rianna prisoner. Her plan is to present her as a plaything to her warlord half-brother, Ragnor. In order to rescue his sweetheart, Prince Tarn needs to join forces with his old enemy, Sarin. A rollicking adventure of sword 'n' sorcery with lashings of kinky sex from the author of *Savage Surrender*.

ISBN 0 352 33549 1

THE NINETY DAYS OF GENEVIEVE
Lucinda Carrington
£5.99

A ninety-day sex contract isn't exactly what Genevieve Loften has in mind when she begins business negotiations with James Sinclair. She finds herself being transformed into the star performer in his increasingly kinky fantasies. Thrown into a game of sexual challenges, Genevieve learns how to dress for sex, and balance her high-pressure career with the twilight world of fetishism and debauchery.
This is a Black Lace special reprint.

ISBN 0 352 33070 8

If you would like a complete list of plot summaries of Black Lace titles, or would like to receive information on other publications available, please send a stamped addressed envelope to:

Black Lace, Thames Wharf Studios,
Rainville Road, London W6 9HA

BLACK LACE BOOKLIST

Information is correct at time of printing. To check availability go to www.blacklace-books.co.uk

All books are priced £5.99 unless another price is given.

Black Lace books with a contemporary setting

DARK OBSESSION £7.99	Fredrica Alleyn ISBN 0 352 33281 6	☐
THE TOP OF HER GAME	Emma Holly ISBN 0 352 33337 5	☐
LIKE MOTHER, LIKE DAUGHTER	Georgina Brown ISBN 0 352 33422 3	☐
THE TIES THAT BIND	Tesni Morgan ISBN 0 352 33438 X	☐
VELVET GLOVE	Emma Holly ISBN 0 352 33448 7	☐
DOCTOR'S ORDERS	Deanna Ashford ISBN 0 352 33453 3	☐
SHAMELESS	Stella Black ISBN 0 352 33485 1	☐
TONGUE IN CHEEK	Tabitha Flyte ISBN 0 352 33484 3	☐
FIRE AND ICE	Laura Hamilton ISBN 0 352 33486 X	☐
SAUCE FOR THE GOOSE	Mary Rose Maxwell ISBN 0 352 33492 4	☐
HARD CORPS	Claire Thompson ISBN 0 352 33491 6	☐
INTENSE BLUE	Lyn Wood ISBN 0 352 33496 7	☐
THE NAKED TRUTH	Natasha Rostova ISBN 0 352 33497 5	☐
A SPORTING CHANCE	Susie Raymond ISBN 0 352 33501 7	☐
A SCANDALOUS AFFAIR	Holly Graham ISBN 0 352 33523 8	☐
THE NAKED FLAME	Crystalle Valentino ISBN 0 352 33528 9	☐

------------✂------------------------------

Please send me the books I have ticked above.

Name   ....

Address   ....

              ....

              ....

              .... Post Code ....

Send to: Cash Sales, Black Lace Books, Thames Wharf Studios, Rainville Road, London W6 9HA.

US customers: for prices and details of how to order books for delivery by mail, call 1-800-805-1083.

Please enclose a cheque or postal order, made payable to **Virgin Publishing Ltd**, to the value of the books you have ordered plus postage and packing costs as follows:
    UK and BFPO – £1.00 for the first book, 50p for each subsequent book.
    Overseas (including Republic of Ireland) – £2.00 for the first book, £1.00 for each subsequent book.

If you would prefer to pay by VISA, ACCESS/MASTER-CARD, DINERS CLUB, AMEX or SWITCH, please write your card number and expiry date here:

....

Please allow up to 28 days for delivery.

Signature ....

------------✂------------------------------